Nicholas Blincoe

Nicholas Blincoe is the author of four previous novels including the award-winning *Manchester Slingback* and the acclaimed *The Dope Priest*. Born in Rochdale, he attended art college before going to Warwick University, where he completed a PhD in contemporary European philosophy. He is also a screenwriter and a founder member of the New Puritans Movement.

ALSO BY NICHOLAS BLINCOE

Acid Casuals

Jello Salad

Manchester Slingback

The Dope Priest

All Hail the New Puritans
(co-edited with Matt Thorne)

NICHOLAS BLINCOE

White Mice

SCEPTRE

Typeset in Sabon by Palimpsest Book Production Limited,
Polmont, Stirlingshire
Printed and bound in Great Britain by Clays Ltd, St Ives plc

Hodder and Stoughton
A division of Hodder Headline
338 Euston Road
London NW1 3BH

In memory of David Eyre

1

I don't sleep at all on the night of my twentieth birthday but still, somehow, wake lying next to Jodie Kidd. I recognise her arm. The hotel sheets are swirled around her body, leaving me naked. If I did not know it was her, I could never tell from the shape beneath the heavy covers. But that one arm is enough: from the fractured tip of her middle nail to the Wu-Tang tattoo covering her TB scar. I put the tattoo there myself, damping a square of her skin with the tip of my tongue so the transfer would take. My tongue was numb from a shot of frozen vodka but I remember being surprised by the fine grain of her skin, like warm sandpaper. Now, as I press my cheek to the soft burr, I try to imagine how it would feel to be in love with Jodie Kidd. The sound of our names together: Jamie and Jodie. She wouldn't have to call herself Jodie Greenhalgh. I could call myself Mr Kidd.

I try to run through the events that brought me here but hang up almost immediately. All I am getting are flashbacks – nothing that is at all coherent. If I ever get quoted, I know how feeble I am going to sound. *Oh yeah, it was like a Versace fashion party but it was also my birthday.* I slide my feet to the floor and start looking for my notebook when I hear the ringing of Stan's Nokia.

Stan is dyslexic, which isn't unusual at art college. He

never reads instruction manuals and no one has taught him how to reprogramme the ring tone. It still has the default setting, that extra-annoying Nokia melody. I chase the tune around the room until I find the phone in the pocket of a man's coat, hanging on the back of a chair. I know that it isn't Stan's coat, it couldn't be. There is no one but me and Jodie in the room. But it isn't my coat either. I press the answer button on the cellphone and my sister barks at me.

'What happened to you, spaz boy?'

'I don't know.' I look around. 'It's like a hotel room but it has Jodie Kidd in it.'

I pause, long enough for her to finish laughing but not long enough for her to slip back with a question. I don't want to answer the kind of questions she would ask: *So how was Jodie? Did she perform?*

'How did you know to call this number, Louise?'

'It's the same number I called you on last night. Duh!'

She is right, she did telephone. I was sitting in an Arab café close to the youth hostel in the Bastille, drinking the warm milk and brandy that Stan had insisted on ordering. He said it was an Arabic drink. I had my doubts but, because I speak French and he doesn't, I was the one who had to ask for it. The waiter brought the milk and brandy in separate glasses and we mixed them ourselves, careful not to disturb the flecks of pistachio that lay on top of the milk foam. As I drank, I tried to measure the flow of nuts with my lips. The ringing of Stan's Nokia cut through my concentration, clashing with the ballads that drifted from the tape deck behind the bar. Stan was in the toilet. I choked back a shard of pistachio and answered the call, too embarrassed to leave the ringing any longer. I never expected to hear Louise's voice. She was supposed to be in New York until the twenty-fourth, the day after my birthday. She had invited me to Paris for the couture shows as an apology. She called it a day-after-birthday treat, promising me seats at any show I wanted.

Now that Louise has rung the cellphone twice, I ask her, 'Yeah, but how did you get Stan's number?'

'You asked me the same thing last night. I didn't get it. Fred got it for me.'

The name means nothing to me but I don't ask for an explanation. The way my sister speaks, she always barks. Louise has this deep voice that makes her sound like a dog. Like a sexy dog, especially when her brain is working too fast for her mouth and the words don't come out right. She is speaking slowly now, snapping at me. But when she called last night, she was running so fast, telling me to get this *add*-ress. Her accent was American: she had been in New York since New Year's Eve, almost a month ago. She was like: 'You got a pen? Okay, the *add*-ress.'

That was my invitation to the Versace party. Louise promised to put my name on the door and, when I told her that I had brought Stan with me, she promised to make it *plus one*. Suddenly I remember how we lost Stan. The last time that I saw him, he was fighting with a woman outside the party. He was actually rolling across the pavement with his fingers dug deep into her wig. The woman was ripping at his face with her nails.

I tell Louise, 'You didn't even put my name on the door last night, did you?'

'What are you talking about?'

3

'Last night, you invited me to the Versace party, you didn't even put my name on the door.'

'I didn't *even* invite you to that party, Jamie. I told you, Osano scheduled his own party for the same night so I had to go to that. And I never said it was a Versace party, all I said was that Donatella might show.'

I don't want to argue. I have found my notebook now, inside the same pocket in the coat as Stan's cellphone. I am sure I have the details: the *add*-ress of the party just the way Louise gave it to me.

'Come up to my room, Jamie.'

'I can't. Jodie's still asleep. I want to wait to say goodbye.'

'Leave a fucking note. Come up to my room.'

I look back across at Jodie, sleeping in our bed. I can see her face from this angle, her features silhouetted against the pillowcase. She has something between her lips but I cannot tell what it is. It is still so dark in the room . . . I don't even know at *what* time in the morning.

Louise says, 'Room four one six. Got it?'

She disconnects before I can ask if she knows the time. It could be anywhere between 7 a.m. and noon, and even if I pulled back the curtains I imagine that I wouldn't be able to tell: just a dark winter night washing into a grey January day. I think the reason that they hold the fashion shows from January through February is because no one in the industry can stand the light.

I still cannot tell what Jodie has between her lips.

The curtains are like tapestries, so heavy that I feel I could dislocate a shoulder as I pull them apart. I wonder if there will be a landmark outside the window, something definitive like Notre Dame or the Eiffel Tower, to

4

tell me where I am. But the window faces inward, into a courtyard, and all I can see are marble-topped tables, glistening with rainwater, and the windows of the rooms opposite. The rain has left the windows streaked with dirt, which I realise is probably lucky because I am still naked. I drop the curtain and look around for my clothes. Whenever my sister calls, I end up running.

There's no sign of my clothes on the backs of the chairs or even the floor, so I wander towards the bathroom. The décor is kind of imperial, very nineteenth-century France, but when I snap on the light it breaks into a feisty white glare. I end up sitting on the edge of the cast-iron bath and rustling through the last pages of my notebook. I write everything in the book, so I cannot understand why there is nothing that looks like directions to a Versace party address. I only realise why when I catch sight of myself in the bathroom mirror. The address is written down my arm in thick black marker pen. That was Stan's idea. I mimed *Biro* at him as Louise barked out the details. Stan pulled a fat marker out of his pocket. I nodded down at the notebook that was lying on the café table, but Stan ignored me. He grabbed my arm and scrawled the address from my shoulder to my wrist as I repeated it to him.

I have to stand and twist my arm into a hammerlock to read Stan's scrawl. Every letter is about three inches high. His marker is so fat, a piece of graffiti hardware. The words I can make out are *QEENS* and *VERCASE*. I knew I was right – Louise had told me that it was a Versace party. I remember Stan's excitement as he asked me whether it was the real Versace – *the dead guy's sister*.

I start thinking about my old comic books. A few

years ago I wrapped them in cellophane, and only my mother reads them now. She likes the Teenage Mutant Ninja Turtles best because, she says, at six years old I spoke mutant turtle better than English. There is one day that she talks about in particular, soon after we moved to Cornwall. She had walked up the hill to collect us from the community school and found me in the older kids' playground, surrounded by girls from Louise's class. Mum says I was shouting *tubular* and *cowabunga* and doing karate moves while these ten-year-old girls stood around saying *aah* and telling Louise that her little brother was dead cute. In those days, Louise was always carrying me over to her yard. We were new to the town and Louise wanted to be noticed. Together, we seemed like the prettiest kids in the school. We had white blond hair and blue eyes and, whatever you think of that, it looks startling on very little kids.

So as I remember Stan getting excited about the Versace party, the first image that comes to mind is a mutant turtle that only gradually blurs and refocuses into a photograph of Donatella Versace – actually a photograph that I had seen in last month's *Harper's Bazaar*. There is no subtext there. I like the way that Donatella looks. If I was asked about Leonardo di Caprio, I would still see a turtle first.

The second thing I think of is a smell: Blonde, the Versace perfume. It's like a night-sweat of sticky, sweet flowers, spiked with citrus. Donatella is said to have helped create the scent, as a tribute to herself.

I cannot find a robe in the bathroom. I return to the bedroom and look down at Jodie, wondering whether I could return to bed and postpone seeing my sister for longer. The bathroom light is strong enough for me to see what Jodie has between her lips: a cigarette, burnt to the filter, the ash in a perfect curve from the cork-effect paper to the sheet beneath her chin. I cannot believe that she could sleep so peacefully, that her cigarette would burn so evenly, the ash preserved all night. It could not happen. I need a camera to record it but all I have is a notebook.

One of the requirements on the foundation course at Falmouth Art College is that I keep a notebook. I should sketch ideas but I mostly fill the book with directions, telephone numbers, lists of things I have to do. I hold an open page up to the light in the bathroom. Anything that I wrote last night is in a much worse scrawl than usual. But I see the words *coke slut* and *Angelina Jolie*, written right next to each other. I am open mouthed for a second, wondering how I managed to pick up skank on Angelina Jolie. Then I remember what happened: Stan was bouncing on the platform of the Métro, talking about the party and what he would find there. His mind running, going *coke coke coke*. He was actually saying it, banging in my ear as we waited for the train to arrive. *There's going to be a sugar mountain of cocaine. It's going to be like 1812, a Russian winter of cocaine.*

Stan has a shameless position on freeloading: he wants to be there, deep inside the zone. When I told him that we were invited to a real fashion party, he began to imagine himself surrounded by slow-moving models, beckoning him to join them at the piles of free drugs. As he ranted away on the Métro platform, a tension headache sneaked out of nowhere and began to crack open my skull. I put my hand over my eyes and, as I looked up through my fingers, saw part of Angelina Jolie's face on a film poster. The memory that I was trying to fix inside my notebook was Angelina's face but Stan's words. Angelina's sore lips, framed between my ring and index finger, and Stan's fat mouth, laughing away.

Stan was too excited to sit on the train. He spent the whole journey swinging on the pole, whipping backwards and forwards. Although Stan is already at college in London, we are the same age. I finished my A-levels and even started a French degree at Exeter before I took time out to think. Instead of travelling or, even, working somewhere, I joined Stan on the art foundation course at Falmouth. But because I had begun so late, I couldn't apply for a degree course. It didn't matter to me, I still couldn't decide what I really wanted to do. Exeter has offered to keep my place open but I am mostly decided, I want to study fashion. I will apply to St Martin's when the forms are due in next month. The only reason that I haven't told Stan is because he would think I had switched from painting because of my sister.

When I tried to write about my memory of Angelina's poster, I was in the same position that I am now: hovering in the light outside a bathroom door. The difference is the location. Last night I was standing close to the toilet doors in the VIP area of a nightclub, listening to the people giggling and snorting inside the cubicles. Stan was right about the cocaine and it was beginning to upset me. I am not straight-edge exactly, I smoke cigarettes sometimes, but I hardly drink at all and take drugs even less. I definitely did not want to come over as another teen coke slut. But I could see myself tagging on to the end of a queue out of nervousness, because I wanted an excuse to join a conversation. I could see myself as Stan: hovering at someone's shoulder while they snorted a line off a cistern top. And these are people who would send back a glass that had a stranger's lipstick around the edge. But it isn't just the hygiene aspect. I hate that moment in an evening when all dignity just evaporates. I really do want a career in fashion, but it is something that I want to do with dignity.

Stan would have pushed hard for the cocaine. But I had lost him before I even reached the party. The only other legible thing in my notebook, *NO GUESTLIST*.

We arrived at a private club called Le Queen, the name Stan tried to write on my arm. As we stood at the doorway, we could feel the heat of a party inside. Perhaps it even was a Versace party. Something makes me doubt it, but I don't know for sure. We were stopped by a tall transvestite before we made it past the first set of doors. There is a phrase that people use, 'door-bitch', and I guess the transvestite was a professional in her world, but I could tell that her heart wasn't in it that night. She didn't seem to care who got in and who got excluded. There was no art in her decision, she just went off the list provided.

I told her that I was a guest of Louise Greenhalgh. And she ran a heavily lacquered and finished nail down her list.

'*Ma soeur. Elle est une modèle.*'

'*Okay, chéri. Quelle agence?*'

I realised that the model agencies must have phoned in their guest lists. The last I knew, Louise was with the Ford agency, but I held back a moment, something stopping me from saying it. Maybe a premonition. I didn't say anything.

'*Si tu ne connais pas l'agence . . .*' The transvestite was flipping her nail across the edge of the papers that made up the guest list, showing me how thick a document she had to work with. It was the size of a magazine.

Stan was pushing at my back. He was so hungry to get through the door, I could feel the salivation. He was saying, 'Don't give me this *liste* shit. This guy here is Louise Greenhalgh's kid brother and Louise is a top model.'

'I never hear of her.'

'You never *hear* of her? You never *hear* of her?' Stan's voice was rising, his Cornish accent coming out. He was going for it. 'You don't let us in, this will be the last fucking door you fill, you butch fucking freak.'

He had gone too far, calling her *butch*, but he was too wired to even see it. Her body twisted, a shrink-wrapped package of cables, and she fixed Stan with a look that scared me, even though I only caught the blunt edge. She placed a hand on his left shoulder and pushed him away, saying, 'Step back, my friend.' Stan handed me his phone as he told her, 'Get your hairy hands off me, you fucking tart.'

Stan slapped her hand away. She raised it again, he slapped it down again. Suddenly, they were throwing rabbit punches, actually boxing in the street outside the club. The punches weren't connecting, just scrabbling hands that left their bodies untouched. At that moment it could have gone either way, someone might have been able to calm them down and end it. But there was no one around, just me. As Stan leaped on to the transvestite, he plunged his hands into her wig. She couldn't shake him off. He was snarling into her face, she was clawing at his body, teetering on her heels with his weight.

A hand fell on my shoulder. I turned and felt the nap

of a linen suit against my cheeks as someone said, 'Let's get the fuck out of here.'

I was released into a limousine, the hand moving to the crown of my head and guiding me into the interior the way that policemen do in films. Louise was inside the car, shouting at the driver to move it, they were late.

I said, 'Hello.'

Louise didn't even look at me. The other people in the car at least did that much, even if they didn't speak. There was the designer Gianni Osano, looking fatter and redder than his photographs in the magazines, opening and closing a damp mouth either to catch breath or to wish me *Ciao*. At the other end of the car was a woman, actually a girl, bony and thin, white as her cigarette and just as stiff and fragile. The fourth person was the man who had guided me into the car. He scooped me into a forward-facing seat before he took his own place, next to the smoking girl in the far, faraway seat.

He said, 'Okay. Let's go.'

We swept past Stan and the transvestite, rolling from the pavement into the road.

'Do we have room for Stan, please?'

I spoke to the man who had put me in the car, choosing him because he seemed to be so much more together than anyone else. The only person together. His suit was made out of very black linen. I don't know how anyone could have got it so black.

He said, 'Does it look like we've got room?' He had an American accent.

I continued looking around the limousine, wondering whether he could be telling the truth. The car seemed enormous, bigger than the inside of an aircraft. The more I looked, the bigger it became. I began to think there was a vortex at the limo's centre, that it was the spinning of the vortex that was causing the space inside the car to expand so rapidly. I was trying to tell myself: in accordance with the laws of physics, don't worry about it. I clutched at my seat and tried to focus on one spot. I found myself staring at the thin girl riding next to Louise. She had straw-blond hair, heavier and longer than my sister's. There was something I wanted to know.

'Are you Jodie Kidd?'

'You kidding? She's like eons older than me.' She shook her head as she blew out the bookmatch she had used to light a fresh cigarette. I never saw what she did with her last cigarette.

Louise was shouting to the car as a whole: shouting but not so loudly. Her voice is so deep it doesn't seem able to raise itself ever.

'Who's going to give me a fucking cigarette?'

I asked the other girl, the one who was smoking, 'You really aren't Jodie Kidd?'

'No.'

One last thing in my notebook: a drawing that looks like a fifties textile design. It is a swirl of irregular shapes, in a spiral pattern. I think at first that it must have been inspired by the spinning movement inside the limousine. Then I remember the bits of pistachio floating on my milk in the Arab café. There was more than just pistachio, though. I didn't know at the time, only later when I was on the Métro with Stan. He started giggling before he told me that he had mixed the remains of last year's magic mushrooms into the drink, sprinkling a few crumbs on top as a garnish.

He said, 'Happy birthday, James, my man. Enjoy the trip.'

The week before Stan left for London, I went along on a farewell mushroom expedition. There were five of us and soon I would be the only one left behind in Fowey. I didn't know that Stan had saved any of his mushrooms. I know that I threw mine away the moment I got home.

I am seriously beginning to doubt whether the woman in the bed is Jodie Kidd. She is definitely beautiful, pale as the ash arcing from the cigarette between her sleeping lips. With just my gaze brushing against her, I could be in danger of disturbing the ash.

Someone begins banging at the door. The woman in the bed wakes. The ash of her cigarette cascades across the bed-sheets.

I say, 'You're not really Jodie Kidd, are you?'

'It was what I was telling you, all last night,' she said. 'Is your sister right: you've really got Asperger's syndrome?'

I want to say, *No*. I could explain about Stan and his mushrooms but the banging at the door is getting louder, it sounds as though someone is ready to batter their way into the room.

I grab the strange coat off the chair and swing it on to my shoulders. The coat is much heavier than I expected, the one unexplored pocket banging against my hip. As I turn the catch on the door, it opens with so much force I stagger back. Gianni Osano is standing there, panting and even redder faced than last night.

'What do you want?'

'Shut up, Louise. Where's Amanda?'

'I'm not Louise,' I say.

Osano stares at me with bloodshot eyes, the whites a nicotine cream. I think, if everyone believes that I am autistic, what do they say about Osano when he can no longer distinguish between men and women? But as he squints at me, I realise that he is very short sighted.

He says, 'The kid brother, yeah? Tell me, is everyone in your family a faggot? Is that how it is with you?'

Osano's gaze has moved on to the woman in the bed. She is sat on the edge, naked and nearly completely flat chested. I realise that Osano thinks she is a boy and has now assumed that I am queer. I don't know what to say. I don't see why I should deny it: not to any stranger who asks, not to Italian madmen who storm hotel bedrooms. And it's a moment before I connect what he has said back to my sister. I don't know whether it is true that she is gay. I can believe that she is trying that out now.

Osano might have been able to work out his mistake if he had stared at not-Jodie for long enough. But she turns her back to him, showing the bones in her naked bottom as she bends towards the bedside table and searches for another cigarette. The only pack there is empty. Cigarette stubs fill its lid and cascade on to the table. We could not find an ashtray when we came to the room last night, although I have a clear idea I will find one if I look in the drawer below the writing pad on the desk.

Osano is shouting at her, 'Hey, you, fag. Where's Amanda?'

She says, 'Put your glasses on, Gianni. I'm Bibi and I have no idea where Amanda is.'

He fumbles inside his jacket and produces a pair of spectacles. Once he has twisted them on to his face, he looks at the girl. 'Bibi, you are looking beautiful.'

Then he turns to me.

'Why are you pointing a gun at me?'

I am holding a heavy, silver-plated pistol in my hand.

It was in the other pocket of the coat; I pulled it out without thinking. I don't know how many times I have imagined holding a gun, although I never expected one to weigh so much.

2

Osano looks at me, looking at my hand. I see a tremor
pass through him, but he swallows it down. He is barely
even shouting when he says: 'It's not your coat?'

I shake my head.

'It belongs to Fred,' says Bibi.

It's the name of the man who gave Louise the number
of Stan's cellphone. I wonder whether I have stolen the
coat: not that it sounds my kind of behaviour, but last
night I kind of wasn't me.

A sequence breaks through. I remember the drifting
rain as we left Osano's party, filling the fifty feet between
the doors of the brasserie we were leaving and the
waiting limousine. Bibi had both her arms around my
waist as we hovered at the door. The rain had coloured
patches of the wind in blue-greys, filling the air with
Manga dragons. A man put the coat on my shoulders,
covering Bibi at the same time.

If it was Fred's coat, then it was Fred who draped it
over us.

I am still holding the gun. 'What should I do with
this?'

'Give it back to Fred,' Bibi says. 'You got a cigarette,
Gianni?'

She sounds so calm. I cannot tell whether she has an
easy American attitude towards firearms or whether
she is using a non-threatening tone she has learnt from

therapy or self-help programmes. Perhaps she just puts cigarettes higher on her agenda than life-threatening situations.

I tell her that I don't know Fred.

'Sure you do,' she says. 'You think you could put the gun away *now*?'

I nod. Inside the bathroom, I take the smallest towel and wrap the gun up into a parcel. I noticed a sliding catch on the side of the pistol, which must be the safety, but I didn't want to touch it. Once it is all wrapped up, I hope that it cannot be fired accidentally.

My clothes are tucked under the far side of the bath, hidden by the lion's-claw feet. By the time I have finished my shower and returned, almost dressed, Bibi and Osano are comfortably smoking. I pick up the bedside telephone. Osano looks my way to say, 'Tell your sister I need to talk to her.'

Once I am through to reception I ask a sweet-sounding woman to connect me to Louise Greenhalgh. She understands my French but asks me to repeat the surname; I try Green'akh, with a soft, Maghrebian cough. After the click to transfer the call, I wait through six ring tones. It seems a long time to wait when no one is ever more than three beats from the telephone in a hotel room. I am so close to hanging up that when a woman answers I have the receiver balanced a millimetre above the cradle.

The woman has a non-specific north European voice. I know how fast my sister absorbs accents but it is only thirty minutes since we last spoke. I ask for Louise.

'Louise is coming, yeah?'

I assume that I am supposed to wait. I hold the receiver, two into three minutes, teasing my bare feet on the silky woollen carpet. I am wearing pretty much my own clothes, plus the strange Fred coat with my notebook tucked into one pocket, Stan's cellphone in the other. A nickel-plated semi-automatic wrapped inside a towel and tucked under my right arm. No shoes, though. I don't know where they are.

Bibi is on the bed, now sitting hugging a pillow, either for warmth or to cover herself. Osano sits the wrong way round on the desk chair. He stopped shouting a while ago. Maybe Bibi was trying to calm Osano rather than me with her flat, therapy voice. Maybe she dampened him down with her cigarette smoke. As I was dressing, I listened to them talk through the open bathroom door. Osano had asked Bibi for the latest from New York: about American designers and especially those bringing couture collections to Paris. Bibi kept to oblique, non-confrontational phrases. She said: 'Tom seems really together, I hear some of his clothes are cute' or 'Marc is Marc, you know, he's got a real eye.'

Listening to Osano, both then and now, it seems that his main problem with other designers is that they are younger than him. Although he nods in agreement as Bibi speaks, he manages to work in phrases like 'You think about his age and already he's ploughing the same furrow,' or he turns one of her neutral phrases into something more negative. When she suggests that someone is new to the scene, he says: 'Yeah, they are *immature*.' He learns that Puff Daddy's Sean John collection will be broadcast live on television and his voice becomes tense, but all he says is, 'Let's hope he's not in prison.' I get the feeling that he could have said a lot more if he wanted. The only explicit moment of bitchiness I hear is when he describes another designer as 'a failed rent boy, too ugly to sell his ass'.

Osano began when he was quite young, only a few years older than I am now. When Louise did her first show for him two years ago, I trawled the design books in college and looked at photographs of his collections from the 1970s. They had an overheated libidinous quality that Osano later seemed to lose. He used African patterns, exotic furs and feathers, and dressed his models in rasta and black power wigs. For spring-summer, there were any number of bikini tops and headscarves in tropical flowers prints. For autumn-winter, he designed tribal robes with huge turbans or silky robes with slits to the thighs and zebra-skin underwear. His models looked like Bianca Jagger, Diana Ross or Donna Summer, his idea of couture, prêt-à-porter and diffusion. The mix of influences was beyond eclectic, but the collections were packed full of feeling, even if they were just the feelings of a horny Italian twenty-five-year-old obsessed by black women.

His current collections no longer seem like the work of the same man. Perhaps Osano's libido finally failed him, perhaps he lost interest. He doesn't seem bothered that he can barely distinguish men from women. But there would be no way back to his designs of the seventies: his gingham slave dresses were a definite mistake.

Louise springs barking on to the line. 'You're taking your fucking time, Jamie. What's your problem?'

'I forgot your room number.'

'Four one six.' Then I hear the voice of the woman I spoke to earlier. I do not know whether Osano was serious when he said that Louise had turned queer. But my sister was talking about a model named Amanda Van Hemstra the last time she called home, and now I remember that Osano was looking for an Amanda when he stormed into our room.

Louise croaks, 'Get off me, you cunt.' She isn't talking to me. In fact, she has stopped talking to me. There is a dim clatter then I am cut off.

I run out of the room, skidding barefoot on the wooden intervals between carpets in the corridor. I hear my sister as I come off the stairs on the fourth floor, growling: 'I'm not interested, don't bring me along on your needy fucking degradation trip.'

I push the door open. Louise is wearing an old-style dressing gown that could have been torn from a 1930s film still. She is the mobster's girlfriend; the scalloped neckline of the gown plunges to expose the stretch of bone between her breasts. The look is completed by the mascara that streaks her face in tear stains. If I unwrapped the pistol from the towel, I would fit right into the scene. I could fold my upper lip into my gum-line the way Humphrey Bogart does. But all I do is stand in the doorway as Louise continues to harangue the other woman, really harangue.

I would have expected the other woman to be annihilated but she barely seems to care. She is not even looking at my sister; she has her back turned as she sits on the dressing-table stool, taking baby sips of champagne from the top of a bottle. Louise breaks off and looks towards the door, staring through me before she focuses. Then she clutches the top of her gown, hauling the material clear of her ankles, and runs for the bathroom.

I was right: the woman scanning me via the mirror on the dressing table is Amanda Van Hemstra, the Belgian model who featured so heavily in the coverage of last October's spring-summer collections that even people who never follow fashion are beginning to know who she is. Even if I had never seen her in the magazines, if I had never even seen a model before, Amanda would be my idea of one. She is so full-on, with a beauty that is so much about bone structure it is indestructible. It doesn't even matter that her hair is sparse and lifeless, like the hair of the women that queue outside post offices with their pushchairs before the doors are even open.

Amanda sways towards me. She doesn't seem either drunk or strung out. She just walks in a way that puts all her body into movement. She speaks with the accent that I heard on the telephone, which I know now is Flemish.

'Hey, little brother. What a welcome, huh?'

She leans in to kiss me on both cheeks. I get a faint taste of dark tobacco and a warm smell of soap that comes from the base notes of her perfume rather than anything to do with cleanliness. Then she leaves. I turn and sit on the bed and look around the room. It is scattered with hotel debris: sushi speared with cigarette stubs and bottles on the floor.

When I look up, Louise is standing there, her eyes turned to the door that Amanda has closed behind herself.

'She's rehab ready.'

'Are you okay, Lou?'

'I'm fine. It's that bitch who's got problems.'

Our eyes lock, the first time that she has looked at me since I arrived in Paris. I cannot tell whether she and Amanda are lovers, whether I have stepped into the ruins of an affair. I do believe that Louise has not been happy for a long while.

All I say is, 'I recognise her.'

'You know why? Because she's working her way through every booker and photographer in Europe. That's the way to get press. She works it, baby.' Louise flips the bottom of her robe from side to side, waggling her hips for emphasis.

In the past two years, Louise has done minimal photo sessions. Her work is mostly the shows. She flew in from her holiday in New York yesterday and when the couture shows are over here, then she will do the whole tour of fashion weeks, returning to New York, then London and Milan and back to Paris for the ready-to-wear collections. That's a heavy couple of months, but it leaves another ten months when she does practically nothing. She gave up on university years ago and I doubt that she will ever get back into education, she just freaks out with her friends in London. I cannot even remember the last time she saw our mother. And she makes no money. If she didn't do occasional work for Gianni Osano, modelling at his salon in Milan or his New York shop, she would not be an international model. She would never leave England.

Louise started in teenage magazines like *Just Seventeen* and *19*, mostly every issue. Her big blue eyes, almost pop-eyes, looked as though they were embossed on the covers. But three years ago she moved to the Ford agency and was told that she needed a different strategy. She needed editorial work in the style magazines and she had to ration herself. Louise thought that she would be taking work off Kate Moss inside six months but it has not happened. I have the same premonition that I had when the transvestite at Le Queen showed me the guest list: that Louise has split with her agency. That she is in trouble.

She steps towards me. I stand up and we hug. She asks, 'What was up with you last night?'

'I was just in my own head a bit.'

I don't want to explain what Stan did to me. I don't want to talk about drugs at all. Every time I looked over to Louise she was kneeling at the drinks tables, grinding along cocaine lines. She has real stamina for anything like that, she can take so much abuse. I don't understand. I look fairly weak beside her.

'You were the party zombie,' she says. 'You still pulled, though.'

I nod. I must have pulled, I woke with the girl and the flashbacks. My brain is grinding out so many flashbacks, I guess some of them must be reliable. I always like to kiss and I have an impression of the taste of Bibi's mouth, even if I cannot time and date every position. In retrospect, it is possible that the mushrooms helped me though the night. Maybe I only coped with Osano's party because I was the corner introvert, playing with my fingers. Bibi must have found something interesting about me.

Louise says, 'So what's Jodie Kidd going to think? You didn't stick around for breakfast, you bastard.'

'She's not Jodie Kidd, she's called Bibi.'

'I know that,' Louise says. 'Duh!'

Of course she does. She is teasing me now, but her tone has changed so rapidly, from tragic to tough, that I don't know whether I should swing with it or try to discover what upset her so much. Louise has always claimed that I am autistic, but how am I supposed to act when I am so dazed by her mood shifts?

So I say, 'I'm not having breakfast with Bibi because you told me to come here.' I want to put the blame on to her but I immediately admit that, once Osano arrived, I wanted to leave.

'He was raving. He thought I was you, then he thought Bibi was a boy and started ranting about faggots.'

'He thinks you're a fag?'

'Until I pulled a gun on him.'

Louise laughs. She doesn't know that it is true.

'Osano's got a thing for homos,' she says. 'He thinks he's the only straight designer, the fags have got it sewn up. *Joke*. No, Osano's kind of scared, really.'

Louise is sifting through the cigarette packets on the bedside table, looking for one that still has cigarettes inside. I don't want to justify Osano's prejudices, but I also wonder about the number of queer designers. I am not likely to wake up gay any time soon and I do wonder whether they have an advantage. That, freed from desire, they bring a strange perspective to women. Rather than putting them on pedestals or inside go-go cages, they help them find fresher ways to look.

Louise has found a Marlboro in a crumpled packet. She straightens it out until it is smokable. But she doesn't have a light. I see a book of matches on a sushi tray so I pick them up and walk over.

Louise is saying, 'Yeah, fairly fucking scared. And if Osano goes down, what's going to happen to me?'

I rip off a match, stiffen it with my thumb and manage to strike it. As I lift it to her cigarette, I say, 'Are you having problems with your agency?'

'Don't even start me.' She is drawing on the cigarette as she speaks. 'They fired my ass, honey. I can see the disclaimer coming up: *No animals were harmed in the fucking-over of this model*.'

'Oh Christ, Louise. How are you feeling?'

'I'm pissed off.' She puts the cigarette out. It is mostly unsmoked. Maybe smoking is just a film gesture for her now, the swift nicotine kick and the anxious stub-out, as she wears her 1930s gown. Louise carries it off. She asks, 'Can you stick around today?'

'Sure. I mean, I need to meet Stan but we can swing back later.'

'No. I want you to stay all day.'

So then I have to stay. That's it, and maybe in the course of the day I'll find out what's happening in Louise's life. But I still need to get hold of Stan. I know I should be angry with him for the mushrooms, but instead I feel guilty about the way we abandoned him. I have no idea how he is coping with Paris. He cannot speak French and he is too dyslexic even to read a Métro map. Another problem, for me; Stan has the key to the locker at the Gare du Nord where we stored our bags.

I tell Louise, 'Okay, I'll stay.' She goes back to the bathroom. I shout after her, 'But I still need to speak to Stan.'

From inside, she says, 'Fred left his number on the pad by the telephone.'

I need to ask everyone not to mention Fred's name, at least until I have given him his gun back. It is either his name or my comedown daze, because I pick up the bedside phone and dial Stan's number.

The cellphone in my pocket begins ringing. I snap it off, feeling stupid, and shout back to Louise.

'How can I get the number of the youth hostel?'

Her voice does not carry above the noise of the water. I hear the delay of the faucet as it switches from tap to shower, and then the slap of her feet as she steps inside.

Anyway, the hotel reception will give me any number I need, all I have to do is call down. So instead of asking Louise about Stan, I shout, 'Who is Fred?'

She answers from inside the shower.

I put my head around the door. 'What?'

'Fred. You know.'

'I don't. It's why I'm asking.'

'So what's the story with his coat?'

Oh, yeah. I was enjoying the coat. It is fairly long with a slight waist that makes the quilt lining feel warm and close. But then it has a swing to it as it drops away, accentuated by a fur trim that give the coat overall weight. Louise's shower is filling the bathroom with steam but I close the door to look at myself in the full-length mirror on the reverse. I know without looking at the label that the coat is by Dries Van Noten.

I have a clear image of Fred now, although it is from earlier in the evening, as our limousine cruised past Stan. It was Fred who told me there was no room in the car. It was obvious then that he was the fixer type. I do not know how he got hold of Stan's number, though. I ask Louise.

She sticks her head round the shower curtain. 'What?'

'Stan's number. How did Fred get the number for you?'

'I don't know. I was upset.'

It is too hot in the bathroom. I return to the bedroom and dial reception for the number of our youth hostel.

I am just ending my message to Stan when Louise walks back into the bedroom, a towel wrapped around her body and another around her head. She crosses to the window, drops the head towel and stands rubbing her hair with her hands, drying it in the weak January sunlight.

'Do you have a cigarette, Lou?'

'Empty.' She nods at the bent-up Marlboro packet on the bedside cabinet. I look down, then see her bag in the space between the bed and the cabinet.

'Do you have a fresh pack?'

'Maybe. Look.'

There is a dried condom draped over the bag's clasp. I assume it means that Louise and Amanda are not lesbians, unless there are things about lesbians that I do not understand. I brush the condom under the valance and lift the bag on to my knee.

I bought Louise the bag for her birthday. It wasn't expensive, but it is a good puritan design. The address book is a whole other thing, bound with a lizard skin, like crocodile. I wonder how Louise could have afforded something that must have cost hundreds of pounds. As I flick through it, I notice that the top few names on each page have been crossed out. It's only when I reach '*QR*' that I realise Louise has stolen the book and scored through the names of the old owner's friends.

Before I can ask about the book, the cellphone starts ringing. It can only be Stan.

'Jamie, the fuck happened to you, you bastard?'

I expected him to freak on me, but he is mostly hurt.

'Are you okay, Stan?'

Louise lifts her head up, sweeping the hair back as she drawls, 'Who is it?' I don't know why she is asking. She heard me say Stan's name. But I cover the mouthpiece and answer her. By the time I tune back to Stan, he is listing his injuries.

'And you don't want to see the bruises. I think that

bitch left her nails in my ribs. I tell you, I have to walk like a geisha.'

'What does he want?' Louise has no time for my friends, or anyone from Cornwall.

'Don't blame me, Stan. You slipped me those mushrooms. I only started coming up on them when you started fighting.'

'What's that about mushrooms?'

I cannot do three-way conversations. I cover the mouthpiece and shake my head at Louise.

'You were on mushrooms? Jesus, Jamie.' She is standing staring at me, bugging me out. Then she turns and slips into the bathroom, saying over her shoulder: 'Did the mushrooms make him want to pick fights with trannies?'

It takes a moment before I realise that she saw Stan get into the fight. She did nothing to stop the limousine. I scramble after her, pushing at the toilet door.

Louise is sitting naked on the toilet seat, rubbing Canesten cream between her legs. I step back fast.

Stan is saying, 'You know the problems I've had phoning you? The phones don't take coins, do they? It took me three hours to suss that I needed a card and then another hour to find someone to sell me one. Do you know the French for telephone card?'

'Télécarte.'

'Well, yeah, you know it. But where the fuck were you?'

'Hold on, Stan.' I shout to Louise, 'What's the name of this hotel?'

'Hôtel Costes.'

I had no idea that I was staying in the Hôtel Costes. I recognised the quality of the hotel from the sheets and the carpets and the floor tiles in the bathroom, but it never crossed my mind that I would be staying here, in a hotel that I only knew from the fashion show reports in magazines. As it is, the experience has mostly passed me by, thanks to Stan's drug experiments.

Louise is still talking. 'Don't have Stan come here. Fred's about to pick us up.'

I cannot believe Louise, she is not even dressed. And I am getting more and more annoyed about last night. She knew I was with Stan and I am sure now that it was her idea to ditch him.

I cover the mouthpiece of the cellphone as I hiss through the bathroom, 'You left Stan deliberately.'

Louise appears in the doorway. 'Fuck you, Jamie. Do you know what I went through in New York? Now I'm asking for some support, you're only interested in ligging with your hick friends.'

We are standing so close that Stan can hear us. He shouts, 'Hey, who's a fucking hick? What's happening there?'

I turn slightly and say, 'Sorry, Stan. Call back in an hour.' I try to cut him off but he gets in quickly.

'Wait. Wait. You know you owe me, don't you? Make sure we get invites for Osano's after-show party.'

For someone who can barely read, Stan has a better idea of the schedule than I do. And Louise is right that he is only here to lig as many big parties as he can. Louise heard what he said. She fixes me with a look before slamming the bathroom door in my face. After a pause, I hear a crash that sounds as though she has pulled an entire medicine cabinet off the wall.

'I've got to go, Stan. Give me an hour.' I click off and knock on the bathroom door.

The door opens. Louise is wearing her gown once more.

I wave the Nokia at her. 'I'm off the phone.'

She just nods. I look around the bathroom, I can't even see any damage. But then I look towards the bathtub. It's splattered with green slime and glass shards, a giant jar of Borghese mud smashed there.

'What happened in New York? Why did your agency chuck you?'

She shakes her head. 'Later.' She looks down. 'What happened to your shoes?'

There is a courtesy car – a black Citroën – to take us to the venue for Osano's show. I am now wearing shoes. I found them outside the bedroom door. I didn't see who left them but I know that Louise put in a call to Fred. I still have no idea why Louise is so keen for me to stay with her, nor what happened to make her fall out with her agency. There were those moments when she seemed so upset and erratic that I became scared, but by the time we pull into traffic on the rue St Honoré, her mood has gone through an entire one-eighty. Well, maybe a ninety. I sit between her and Bibi with the hotel towel on my lap, the gun inside. We share the Citroën with a make-up woman, a French girl originally from the South. Bibi smokes all the way but she doesn't say much. Aside from the long kiss she gave me as we got into the car, she only looks at me once, flashing me a big-eyed wink. She is as quiet as Louise and as tired looking, but less wired, I would say.

The make-up woman fills the space with all the gossip. She wonders why Osano came to Paris and then chose to have a private viewing only. Other designers are staging

31

their shows in bigger venues, the Rodin Museum, hotel ballrooms and palaces, she mentions buildings I have never heard of before. I don't even know what a private view means exactly: whether it is the press or the buyers that are to be excluded.

As we cross the Seine, I ask, 'How long will the rehearsals last?'

'Take a guess. They are scheduled to start at two, so that means four if we are lucky,' she says. 'I know these types Osano hired to organise everything and I do not trust them. They are club night promoters, only. Perhaps they told Osano he would have the best music if he hired them.'

I would have thought Osano would want to organise his own music but the make-up woman shakes her head.

'What kind of music do you think he likes? Me, I think Elton John.'

Bibi says, 'All designers like Elton John.'

I am left on my own once we reach the venue: the Institut du Monde Arabe on the Left Bank by a university. I want to go and look at Osano's collection in close-up but it hasn't yet arrived. There are roadies and contractors carrying pieces of scaffolding, masonite, speakers and lighting rigs. Osano is showing his collection on the roof terrace and all this equipment has to be brought up to the roof and assembled. Louise and Bibi make their way to the back of the terrace restaurant, which is to become the backstage area. I remain outside, looking across to the river and west towards the Ile de la Cité. Once the workmen begin to erect a marquee over the terrace, I worry that I will be in someone's way. I am in someone's way wherever I stand, and though I ask around, no one has seen Fred or can tell me when he might arrive. I return to the elevator lobby and ride the ornate, jewel-box-like elevators down to the square in front of the building, hugging the towel to my chest as I go.

I want to watch the skaters. The paving stones have a rough finish which makes the wheels clack like a train on rails. I always find myself looking around when I hear it, looking for the skateboarder. I scuff the soles of my new shoes across the surface of the square. They are two-tone Old Sail sneakers, fine shoes with a sole similar to that of a football boot, except that they have fewer and broader studs. The sneakers don't suit Fred's coat but they sit well with my Silas skate pants. The studs are no good for skating, though. I scuff the soles, not trying to wear them down, only trying to imagine how I would skate the square, looking at the street furniture and the kerbs and ledges the way only skateboarders do. I picture myself riding the edge of the square, letting a back wheel slip over the kerbstone and grinding my trucks. Around the corner, on the main road, there are steps leading up to the yard of the local university. I could ride the wall around the yard and see how far I could olly the gap. Living in Fowey, there isn't so much scope: you either skate the carpark by the Bodinnick ferry or you skate downhill. Not that I am skating at the moment. I've got a blue knee and my skate is back home. Even so, I continue looking at the steps by the sign, 'Université Paris VII', and imagine myself trying to clear them. The distance is ridiculous, far too big for me ever to make.

It's not that I'm a good skater – I rarely clear a metre. And I don't live for skating; I keep my decks long after they've lost their snap and I've got only six videos in total in my collection. But there is a secret to being a skater: it gives you the power to see the world in a new way. I can be in the same space as everyone else, the people hurrying along the high street, the old women waiting on the quay for the ferry home, and I know that I read the space completely differently. The way that I imagine using the street transforms it, turning it into a space of movement and possibilities.

My sister has her own ways of transforming her world. It is always possible to say that she is gorgeous or that she is a nightmare, without ever getting at the thing that is most interesting about her. It is the way that she alters her environment, making it scarier, or more lurid, exciting or deeper or just full of erupting drama. She was ten years old when the three of us moved to Cornwall. It was my mother's idea and Louise didn't like it. So for the eight years she lived there, she kept on creating escape routes.

The way that I feel about my sister comes back to me when I read fashion magazines. There is always a certain amount of text, all about the inner life of women and what they hope for, or where they place their expectations. If they were replaced with an A-level set text by Henry James, they couldn't be more claustrophobic. But then there are the photo spreads, and the magazines suddenly open out. I don't understand the focus on the internal; the idea of inner peace or beauty. There is no beauty or peace or drama or anything else on the inside: it only exists out there, in the ways that we approach the world and each other. With Louise, you have no choice – you either flow with the changes or you become an earthquake victim.

If I was skating the Université Paris VII, I would pick up speed as I came along the wall, approaching the steps from my right, backside to the edge. As I reached the steps, my leading foot would turn inward and begin to slip against the grip tape, sliding towards the nose of my deck. Then my left leg would bend slightly, the ball of my foot poised on the tail. At the moment of take-off, my back foot would snap at the kicktail. It is the impact of the kicktail hitting a hard surface that makes the board olly. The board would leap forward as I moved with it, into the air and across the gap. If I snapped too hard, I wouldn't be able to bring the board back under control. I would leave it too late, wondering whether I ever had a hope of clearing the whole gap. The weight of my body falling back as my feet continue upward, pursuing my deck. My head meeting the concrete of the steps with a crack.

I could so easily be a fuck-up, I know. I have no idea why I want to move into fashion. I sometimes believe that I could be good. It's just that I don't yet know how I would be good. I have no idea how I will do it.

I end up walking all the way round the block, watching the students mill about, some of them sitting on the wall listening to French hip-hop on their radios. I feel Stan's cellphone flap against my thigh and wonder why he hasn't called yet – it's been more than three hours since I spoke to him. It is getting late, the light is already fading. As I return to the Institut du Monde Arabe, I look up at the steel shutters on the windows. They are supposed to widen like a camera aperture to let more of the available light into the building, but I think they are already as open as they ever get.

At least Osano's collection has arrived. A large truck

is parked outside the Institut and racks of clothes are being wheeled through the elevator lobby. There are not so many of them: this will be a couture collection. But there are still more than I expected, zipped into bulky grey plastic coveralls. As I follow them inside, I see Osano ahead of me. He is talking to a man about my size, with dark long hair and looking about twenty-eight years old. The man is obviously a photographer, he has a light meter hung around his neck. As I approach, Osano abruptly pushes the other man in the chest and calls him a *cocksucker* and a whole lot of Italian words. The man doesn't retaliate, he just straightens and recovers. He has a smile that is close to a leer.

He says, 'This is bullshit, Gianni.'

He has a French accent.

Osano says, 'You fuck around with Amanda, you end up fucking with my whole organisation. That's not going to happen.'

The photographer says, 'I already fucked her. Her and Louise together. I was beautiful, man.'

3

Now that I have seen the Frenchman, I guess I can put a penis to the condom I found under Louise's bed. If what he said is true, I might have found a whole nest down there, beneath the valance. I hate the idea that I touched it. I would chew my hand off, except that I wouldn't want to bring my fingers anywhere near my lips.

Osano and the Frenchman are locked together: two Mediterranean types staring each other down. I know that they are counting; I count along with them. Their hairstyles are so similar, dark hair swept back past their collars, though the Frenchman does not have a collar. He is wearing a white string vest. I guess he knows what he is doing: string vests are going to reappear this season, although they are summer wear and it's now the end of January. His chest is shaven or waxed but it needs attention; the V-shaped outline of a stubble shadow is beginning to appear under the string mesh. And suddenly I have forgotten to count, although I am sure that neither of them has. When Osano turns, he does it on a beat, punctuating it with a *Fuck you*.

A PR woman with a clipboard hovers between Osano and the Institut doors, but he pushes past her. The light catches a bald spot beneath the thin sheen of his hair as he leaves. The Frenchman stands still, preening himself, then he turns and heads for the elevators. I feel the weight of my towel parcel and imagine unwrapping Fred's pistol right there and holding it at the Frenchman's back, making a new hole in the string mesh of his vest.

I look back at the PR woman. She doesn't seem sure of what she has seen, whether it is a problem that needs her attention. I have my own request.

'*Excusez-moi. Avez-vous une enveloppe?*'

She snaps to, recognising me as someone that she has seen upstairs, and asks what size. I mime an A4 envelope and tell her, '*Comme ça.*'

'*Suivez-moi.*'

She leads me to an office by the side of the information desk and points to a pack of envelopes on the corner of the desk. I begin to look for one that is big enough and strong enough to hold Fred's pistol. The longer I keep it wrapped in the towel, the more self-conscious I will become.

There was a time when I would mime using guns. I did it when I was alone, in the most everyday situations, whether I was walking between my bedroom and the kitchen in the morning or sitting on the lavatory. I knew the sounds different guns made as they were loaded from watching films: though I realise now that the sound effects were over-dubbed to make them crisper. I would flick my wrist and hear the slamming sound that a revolver makes as the drum snaps back into place. Or hear the pump of a pump-action shotgun as I moved a cupped hand up and down in space. I would even make the noises as I mimed the action, krr-krr from the side of my mouth as I primed it. You would think that it would be easy to grow out of that kind of childish habit, but I actually had to concentrate hard before I could stop.

I unwrap Fred's pistol, looking over my shoulder to make sure that the PR woman has gone. She has. I hold the pistol in my hand: it is one of those with a ratchet across the top. I make the sound as I pull the sliding piece of metal rapidly backwards and forwards, and this time the gun makes a sound back. I hear the first round click into the chamber.

Jesus.

My palms are suddenly flooded with sweat. The gun has become something live and I have no idea how to make it safe. I hold it at arm's length, scrabbling for an envelope with my other hand. I ease the gun inside. Then I rip the backing tape off the gum strip and seal it up. It still doesn't feel safe.

An hour later, I am sitting by the terrace doors inside the restaurant, the envelope on my lap. There is still no sign of Fred, and now Osano has disappeared too. I catch sight of a watch on the wrist of one of the contractors and realise that time is going to be an issue. I feel panic sweeping through everyone, even as they bustle around. Their panic mixed with mine. I still have a sick feeling in my stomach – the venom I built up for the French photographer and the fear of the pistol on my knee. Even if I could calm down, the general anxiety would continue to seep through. It actually has a taste, like a thin yellow breath that infects everything. Not so much the workmen contracted to put on the show. They probably aren't even aware there is a problem. But Osano's own organisation and the PR company he has hired, they need Osano to be here. He isn't anywhere.

When Bibi comes to sit next to me, she trails a hand across my shoulder to warn me. I look up into her smile, beautiful white teeth, small and evenly spaced rather than big and American. She asks if I would like a smoke. I nod and ask whether there is any sign of Osano yet.

She shrugs, *No*.

Bibi is wearing a T-shirt and pants . . . underpants, in schoolgirl white. The men carrying the lighting rigs and the speakers cannot take their eyes off her but Bibi does not seem to notice. She just rustles inside her rucksack and takes out a bottle of Evian and a bong. She fills the reservoir with the water and lights the oily resin that she has prepacked into the bowl. I shake my head when she passes it over. When she asked if I wanted to smoke, I had assumed that she was offering me a cigarette. I wonder whether she is smoking because everyone else is so on edge. Though she doesn't seem to care at all, and she probably hasn't been working as a model long enough to know if the situation is serious. She just likes smoking.

I ask her, 'Is there a Freud-type theory about oral gratification?'

'For sure. It was written for me.' A cloud of smoke hangs in suspension like a ball in her mouth. She holds it there for a moment the way that old reggae stars do in photo portraits. As she swallows she croaks: 'I feel sorry for those guys.'

She is pointing to a PR woman.

'The line they're selling, Osano is a Grand Old Man of fashion. But Yves Saint Laurent is in town, stoking a feud with Tom Ford. And now there's all the gossip about McQueen's show for Givenchy, why it was private-only and what that means about him signing with Gucci. So who cares about Osano? For sure, he's been around for ever, but so has Luxembourg and no one's getting excited about that either.'

I say, 'They can't sell anyone anything unless Osano turns up.'

'Fred is out chasing Osano and Osano is supposed to be chasing Amanda, making sure that she does the show tonight . . .' She takes another hit. Another pause while she waits to inhale. '. . . phew-wee.'

I wish that I had paid more attention to Amanda Van Hemstra when I saw her in the morning. I guess I was distracted by Louise. I tell Bibi that I saw Osano earlier, attacking the French photographer, and I tell her their argument was all about Amanda.

'Jesus. Etienne,' Bibi says. 'It's not so bad he absolutely has to fuck every model he comes across, but he makes such a deal out of it.'

I tell Bibi the rest of the story, what is really on my mind. 'Etienne says he did Amanda in a threesome, her and my sister.'

'I guess he'd call that a baguette.'

'Have you slept with him?'

'No-o.' Bibi doesn't sound so sure. But she says, 'To be fair, he does have a good reputation. He is a good fuck.' She stands up. 'Okay. Break over.'

I stay sitting, I just nod goodbye.

'You want to come backstage, Jamie?'

'Won't I get in the way?'

'Like there's any kind of organisation there. Come on.'

It is the moment I see Fred. He appears out of the elevators, heading for the terrace. He is bigger than I remember and also a little younger; perhaps only thirty or thirty-two. He stops on the terrace, seeming to shiver with fury, a suit bag in one hand and the other hand clenched. Two lines of concentration flare above the broad plateau of his nose. The PR people, the contractors, everyone is looking his way, but his eyes move across them. As he scans towards me he slows and pauses. The blood in my neck freezes, leaving a pulse beat stranded. I start to rise, holding the envelope out towards him. But his gaze passes on. He has fixed on the French photographer, Etienne, dopily wandering out of the models' dressing area.

Fred beckons to him by raising a couple of fingers, holding his black-gloved hand the way that Catholics do as they make the sign of the Cross. I want to get rid of my package but now doesn't seem the time. When Bibi pushes at my shoulder, I move with her, disappearing into the backstage area.

It is still chaos back there. The dressers are carrying clothes around, trying to organise individual racks for each of the six or so models. It must be impossible without Osano here to tell people what he wants. A model stamps her feet, the first time I have ever seen anyone do that outside of a cartoon. She doesn't like what she is seeing on the rails.

We keep moving. Rails continue to be organised and reorganised, pushed around the dressing area by worried-looking assistants. It could be a piece of choreography, two ingenues moving through so much action. It's a long strange moment before I realise that Bibi has slipped her hand into mine and we are walking together. She swings her arm high, and when I pick up the rhythm she laughs, breaking the tension that I wasn't fully aware I was feeling. Then a space opens between the rails and I see the make-up desks with the lights around them lit. Louise is there in a little crowd around a TV set, drinking champagne. She is laughing too. She sees me and whoops, 'Oh, baby.'

As I walk over, she catches me around the waist, separating me from Bibi as she introduces me as *her Jamie*.

'What do you think? He's my brother, he's got to be a fox.'

Right away, it is like being back at school with her.

'Sorry about this morning, babes, I got stranded in the bitch zone.' She pours me a mug of champagne.

The make-up woman is the same one who shared our car on the ride to the Institut. She asks, 'How is it going out there?'

I shrug. I don't know what it is supposed to be like. I say, 'Fred's arrived.'

A tall blonde girl asks, 'Is Gianni with him?' Her accent is a blend of French and something more foreign, I mean eastern European.

Louise says, 'If he was there, you'd know it. He's such a drama queen.'

'Not a queen, I think.' The blonde girl again, very seriously.

'No. He thinks he's Caesar,' says Louise. She pulls at the broad white sash of the dress she is wearing. 'And this is going to be the world's most expensive toga party.'

The dress is heavy pleated silk, an evening gown with a single band of material running from her left shoulder across her breasts. It does look a little like a makeshift toga, but still . . . it never takes Louise long to find her way back to the bitch zone.

But abruptly Louise is through sniping. I realise why when she stands. Fred has appeared round the racks of clothes. He beckons to Louise using that same gesture, the two fingers of his right hand. As she moves towards him, I try to delay her with a touch. I want her to take the envelope and return it to Fred, but she drifts through my fingers.

They stand and talk a little way from the make-up table. I try to listen but it is difficult over the sound of the portable TV on the make-up bench. Some-one turns the volume up, which makes it even harder. The girls are watching a daytime repeat of *Murder She Wrote*, dubbed into French, and that provokes a rumour about Angela Lansbury. It is the make-up woman who tells the story. Bibi seems to be the only one who has never heard it before. She is saying, *No way, not Angela Lansbury!* I smile at her but keep one eye on Fred and Louise. I cannot read Louise's face.

'A *hermaphrodite!*?'

I move a little closer to Louise and Fred. Their heads are so close; they speak softly but I can almost hear them. Then the mobile rings.

I snap it open. 'Stan?'

'Where are you?'

'Hi. Yes.' I am garbling, one finger poked in my ear as I turn my back on Louise and Fred. 'I'm at the Institut du Monde Arabe.'

'The what doo what?'

I repeat it more slowly but he still cannot get it, saying: 'Am I supposed to write this down?'

Over my shoulder, Louise and Fred are still talking. 'Can you call back in a bit, Stan?'

'I'm hungry.'

'Get something to eat.'

'I don't know what to have.'

He sounds so plaintive, perhaps it's hunger. I tell him to ask for *omelette frites*, assuring him that he'll find it anywhere. He practises the phrase before asking, 'What's the French for vegetarian?'

'Take a wild guess, Stan,' I say. Louise is walking towards me now. 'I've got to go.'

I break off with Stan, over-breathing a little as I turn to Louise and ask if there is a problem.

'Fred wants to talk to you, now.'

'Me?'

'Are you going to keep him waiting?'

Fred is talking to a PR man. When I walk up, he puts out his hand. The leather gloves could be intimidating but the handshake is warm. He asks how the shoes fit, speaking English with an American twist.

'Oh. Thanks for that.' I almost say *Fred* but pull back. I ended up doing the *Mister er . . .* thing, letting the blank hang there, ready to be filled in. The envelope offered in an outstretched hand. He doesn't take it.

'Call me Fred, Jamie.' His Italian accent is so slight he must have lived in the States for years.

'I really like the shoes, Fred. The coat, too,' I say. 'I'm not keen on this, though.'

This time he takes the package and rips it open. After a glance down, he smiles back at me; the dimples that appear in his cheek are so deep they look black. 'Oh, yeah. It must have been a surprise.'

I don't know what I'm supposed to say. I had been wondering what kind of man carries a gun, only to forget about it. Maybe Fred reads my mind. He folds over the top of the envelope and begins to slip the package into his pocket.

I have to stop him. 'I think I loaded it. I think I put a round in the chamber.'

He gives me another amused look, kind of sidelong,

and reopens the envelope. In three seconds he has tipped the gun into his hand, removed the magazine and ejected the bullet in the chamber. Both me and the PR guy are open-mouthed.

'Safe now,' he says. He turns to the PR guy. 'Some crazy in the club last night. I didn't want to make a scene. I just took the gun off him.' He shrugs and smiles again, turning back to me. 'That's why we left the first place in such a hurry. Sorry we didn't have time to pick up your pal. But I was worried it was going to get all ugly and Puff Daddy in there.'

Turning from one to the other, he gets in his introduction. 'Jamie, have you met Benoît?'

The PR man leans in, his hand out to shake, reintroducing himself as *Ben* in a strong French accent. He asks, 'You are the brother of Louise, right?'

'Yes.'

'You want to model.'

'No.'

Fred says, 'Not as a career. We mean, are you prepared to help us out of a situation. We need someone for this press bullshit.'

'Oh, right.' I am surprised. The request has come out of nowhere; it is not as though I want it. 'I'd be pretty lame. I mean, why not get a professional?'

I am thinking, at least someone who has modelled before. The only time a photograph of me ever appeared in a magazine, I was skateboarding. I was caught bailing out of a lip plant. Not a glorious moment.

Ben says, 'It's the brother and sister angle, it's a gimmick for the morning papers.'

'Right.'

'We are telling them you are twins, okay?'

Even this far into the sale, I am incredibly slow. 'We're not twins. Lou is three years older than me.'

'You look the same age. You look a lot alike.'

Fred says, 'Gianni even mistook you for your sister, isn't that right?'

It was. I nod. But I had just thought of a reason for not doing it. 'They'll soon find out we're not twins. What happens then?'

Fred says, 'We don't care. We'll be back in Milan by tomorrow night.'

'It's not a problem.' This is Ben. '"Models Not Twins."' He says it in a voice that puts it into inverted commas. 'Does that sound like a news story to you?'

'No.'

Fred says, 'Go join your sister over there. And you want a guest list place for your friend Stan, it's done. He gets a seat here and a place at the party afterwards.'

It is mostly just strange being up in front of the cameras. Although we are standing on the completed catwalk, photographed against the dark of the terrace awning with spotlights behind us, it isn't like a fashion shoot. It's not even like the shoots that I've done at college, trying to put a portfolio together before I apply to St Martin's. These are press photographers and TV cameramen and they don't care about constructing the shots, or checking the flesh tones by clicking off light meters. It is just a battery of flashes, motors whirring. If they say anything, it is just to shout encouragement. They have to shout because the DJs have started their sound check, playing French house music and snatches of Cuban and Creole hip-hop. The three-man TV crew weave around the pack as they try to make a story out of the photo session. Posing with Louise, I don't know what to do, but she subtly prods me, as though we are ballroom dancers. She leads, I fall into step. The music gives Louise cover as she whispers instructions to me, if I ever miss her move.

We do look similar, more so even than usual. A stylist has cut Louise's hair so it is closer to my length, while mine has been shaped to curl around the bottom of my ears, the way that Louise wears hers. I also have foundation on, making me paler because I have a lot more tan than Louise. The make-up woman even put shading along my cheekbones because Louise has a thinner face. We are both wearing mascara so that our eyes stand out, bulging in the same shape and colour. And we both wear long white shirts: more of what Louise called Osano's togas. They are well finished, appliqué dragonflies fluttering across the breasts in that kind of kitsch eighties way that was popular last year, except that the embroidery is white on white. But they are also pretty shapeless, which is why I took them in. I'm not a fantastic tailor, but anyone can use a sewing machine. I just hammered the stitches in, trying to get the material tight enough to give Louise her figure back without breaking the casual shirt feel. I am fairly lean so I took in my shirt to give a slim silhouette. It was nothing, but I still got a couple of Louise's friends hovering around me, and Bibi leaning over my shoulder and embarrassing me. I tried to tell them that I was just killing time until it was my turn with the hair stylist.

Etienne the photographer wanders over. He edges into the side of the pack of photographers, making sure that there is a distance between him and them. He is smoking a slim cigar as he takes in the scene. I would say that he is throwing more deliberate poses than either me or Louise. He shifts his weight from foot to foot and moves his head around, as though he is so dedicated to his art he cannot stop working even when he isn't working.

I say to Louise, 'You see him there, that guy Etienne, what do you reckon he's on?'

'What's he on? A narcissism kick.'

We have our arms around each other's waists and our noses touching, emphasising the similarities in our profiles.

I say, 'He was bragging about making it with you and Amanda.'

'Amanda, yeah. I got stuck in the voyeur role – and it was my fucking bedroom.'

Etienne is getting tired of standing there. He wants more attention. He shouts, 'You're looking fine, baby, you really got it.'

He is calling out to Louise, pitching his voice so that it carries over the music. Louise moves me into a different pose, our backs to the camera but our faces still turned to profile.

Etienne cannot keep quiet. 'Hey, baby, keep it cooking.'

He catches a lull in the music, his voice coming out louder than he expects. I turn and say, '*Merci, chéri.* I'm keeping it warm for you.' I slap my arse and blow him a kiss.

Etienne catches on slowly. More slowly than all the photographers, who have turned to see who I am shouting at. Their motorised cameras are so sensitive at least two of them are still shooting off film, and they catch Etienne's changing expression. The sequence begins with the sleazy insouciant look he used on Louise, then a faltering moment as he works out what I am saying, to

49

surprise, to a freaked-out blush. I wiggle my bum at him and pout, trying to speed him through the brain work.

Etienne says, 'I'm not talking to you.'

'That's our problem. We never talk, baby.' I put my hands on my hips, doing the outraged valium-wife thing. I drawl the words out in a camp whine.

Etienne practically screams: 'Fuck you, pansy cunt.' He turns and walks away. The cameras follow him for a few more seconds before turning back to me and Louise.

After our shoot, I never stop to think how quickly the TV news editors need to turn around the product. We finished around 4.30 and the early evening Paris news goes out at 5.35. Louise and I appear as the last item. The newsreader continues to sell the line that we are twins, and we absolutely look the part. You cannot tell the age difference, which for some reason is a surprise to me. Louise could pass as seventeen when she was only thirteen years old, and twenty by the time she was sixteen. I was a little kid still when I was thirteen, not very much different to the way I had been at ten. But at twenty-three, Louise now looks about eighteen years old, like my age or even younger.

I have just finished giving Stan directions to the Institut when the news begins. We watch it on the portable set standing by the long stretch of make-up tables. The electric cable connects to an extension that runs thirty metres across the restaurant floor. It is a lot of cable for a twelve-inch screen. There is no other TV, so it is surrounded by about twenty people, models and stylists and seamstresses. Everyone except Bibi, who I haven't seen since the photo shoot. When the item about me and Louise begins, Osano's people are stoked. These are the only visuals connected with the evening's couture shows. And when there are so many big names bringing their rivalries into town, it is a real coup for Osano to steal the heat. Though the fact that it is only an end fun piece on the local news mutes the effect.

The item looks as though it will end on a freeze: Louise and me caught in an Eskimo kiss. But then the reporter's voice-over switches register, losing its authoritative edge as it detours into snide, saying: '*Mais, il ne règne pas une harmonie totale dans le camp d'Osano.*' And then we see me blowing my kiss at Etienne and him sulking off, mouthing, '*Pédé con,*' like a sulking husband. He is nailed, righteously. Everyone around me begins clapping, telling me that I have set him up perfectly.

Then I feel a hand on my shoulder and an American-Italian voice saying, 'Very cute.'

I know that it is Fred but I cannot work out from his voice whether he is annoyed by the spin I'd given to the broadcast, or whether he is relaxed about it. I don't want to follow him when he says, 'Can I have a word?' But I follow him anyway.

We walk out through the restaurant kitchen. I didn't realise that the kitchen was working, but there are a handful of chefs around, building hors d'oeuvres on patterned salvers. Fred moves easily through the steel-topped workbenches. I follow him and see Osano standing at the end of the kitchen, his back to us as he waits at a service elevator. Only now I realise that this was the elevator used to bring all the equipment up to the roof. It makes sense – the public elevators are so small and so ornate, the last thing anyone would want in them is a contractor with a length of scaffolding.

Osano holds the elevator and greets me as we step

inside. I don't know whether he has even seen the TV news, but when he tells me I have 'done well' I assume that he is talking about our twins act. He says, 'It was a nice piece: fun. It proves Osano still has vivacity.'

It seems a generous interpretation, but maybe he is right. He has been around a long time. The images were good, so the PR people are betting that the same story will probably appear in tomorrow's newspapers. Maybe even the national French TV news, later tonight.

Osano presses the elevator buttons and we begin to descend. 'That gag with Etienne, it was astute. I think he's a serious closet case, probably.'

I don't know. Actually, I don't think so. Not everyone who has problems with gay men is a repressed gay. You can be straight and still be jealous of them, like Osano.

Fred says, 'You know what? We already need another favour.'

The elevator doors open. I am not even sure what floor we are on; I am looking at Fred, who is simply nodding comfortably at me. Osano sets off down the corridor and Fred turns and follows him. I do the same.

Osano speaks as he strides along, not even looking back. 'I saw what you did with those clothes. It was you who did the alterations, right?'

I keep walking. It is Osano's collection, a couture collection, and I was banging in stitches with a sewing machine. I wonder what kind of favour they want from me. I begin to think it may be a euphemism: the favour is that Fred is going to work me over for messing with the maestro's clothes.

Fred said, 'It's here – in the dressing room.'

We are standing outside a partially open door. Inside I see part of a shower stall and a fitted dressing table.

The dressing table has a vase of white lilies on it.

'A medical emergency,' he says. 'I know you and Bibi are close.'

The truth is, I am still trying to remember how well I know Bibi. But Fred has me worried.

'Is Bibi ill?'

'She'll be fine. We just need someone to sit with her while we get hold of a friendly doctor.'

I look from Fred back to Osano to see how he is reacting to this medical emergency. If she is in this room on her own, why isn't he dealing with her? I only just notice now how edgy he is, or at least he seems edgy now.

I push the door fully open. There is a sofa against what had been the hidden wall. I see a head of lank hair and recognise Amanda Van Hemstra. She is sitting, bent over a curled-up figure. It is Bibi, trembling like a scrap of white paper.

I say, 'It's an overdose?'

Fred says, 'No. A panic attack. She was smoking the stuff, I don't know if she's done it much before.'

I take in more of the room all the time I speak. There is burnt tinfoil on the dressing table, so I guess they have been chasing heroin. Amanda looks up. Her eyes are pin sized. She holds Bibi's hand and says, 'Hey, Jamie.' Bibi says nothing.

Fred says, 'Come on, Amanda. Jamie will take care of her now. You go and work.'

4

The doctor gives Bibi a shot to bring down her heartbeat, dropping the syringe into his open Adidas bag when he is finished. Bibi asks for a cigarette immediately she is able to speak. The doctor laughs as he lights his own, telling her to take it easy. I follow him out to the corridor, where he confirms that this was something different to, and worse than, a panic attack. He also confirms that it was probably heroin induced. Fred was careful to tidy the evidence from the dressing table before the doctor arrived; the squares of smoke-stained tinfoil. I watch the doctor waddle off down the corridor to the elevator. I wonder what sort of doctor he is.

Bibi's voice has become see-through: flat, calm as it always is, but with no weight behind it. She tells me that she needs to use the bathroom. As the shower stall is inside the room, I assume that she means the lavatory. The cubicle door stands next to the shower. I help her off the sofa and, seeing her shiver inside her sweat-soaked T-shirt, pull a robe off the back of the dressing-room door. The material wraps twice around her body. As I help her towards the lavatory I am mostly carrying her, but she has to manage alone once she is inside. I sit on the Bibi-shaped damp patch on the sofa and find myself thinking about Fred and the gun again. I asked Louise whether she remembered an incident in Le Queen, before Stan and I showed up. She asked what kind of incident.

When I told her that Fred had disarmed a man with a gun she laughed and said that she could believe it. She hadn't seen anything herself, though.

Maybe the whole medical drama thing has left me dazed. I am perfectly calm, then suddenly spooked, wondering why Bibi is not out of the bathroom yet. I run across the room to bang on the door. Bibi shrieks. That scares me. She is always so dry; I didn't think her voice did high pitch.

I start apologising rapidly. 'But you're taking so long . . . I don't know, maybe you'd passed out.'

'I'm okay. I'm just leaning against the tiles. They're quite cold.'

'What are you doing?' I realise that this is not a good question. I hurriedly change it: 'I mean, are you just sitting?'

'I'm sitting but I might be doing . . . I haven't made my mind up, Jamie.' She pauses, either because she is thinking or because she is pretending to think as a joke. Her voice is becoming more opaque all the time. Finally, she says, 'I'm going to be one more minute. So talk to me.'

'What about?'

'Anything. Tell me about your family.'

Now I have to think. I press my hand against the wood of the toilet door. 'Okay. My mother is small, dark and pretty.'

'She's small? How small?'

'Five foot. We call her Mini-mum.'

'So you guys take after your father?'

'We don't have a father.'

'Oh. You don't remember him, even?'

'No, we really don't have one. We never have had. Do you?'

'I've got a father, yeah. A mother, too. Both extant, both normal height.' There is movement behind the door. 'I'm coming out, Jamie.'

She emerges, smoking a cigarette. I guess my work as a chaperone is done.

As she offers me the packet, I ask, 'Was that a close call?'

'I don't know.' She shrugs. 'It was a first for me.'

'You don't need to try rehab or something?'

'For sure. I'll try rehab.'

'What now?' I wonder whether I should telephone somebody or call the doctor back.

'Not now.' She drops back to the sofa and exhales. 'I'll check in once the shows are over.'

We sit smoking together, my arm around Bibi, one of her legs crossed over my lap. Soon we are kissing, little deep kisses. The wet strands of her hair plaster themselves to my cheek, sticking like spider webs as she pulls away to take drags on her cigarette.

'Do you like being a model?' I ask.

'It's hard to think of it as something you do,' she says. 'It's not like a job. Not that I've ever had a job. I travel abroad, ignore the locals, spend my free time getting wasted. Like being a soldier without the soldiering bit. And you get better bed-linen.' She stares out, as though she needs to look over what she has said before she can reflect on it, and her words are standing there, on an invisible plain, lined up in rows just as she placed them. 'It's better than being a regular tourist because there's no pressure to look at a castle or a big pillar or a museum. I just get to stay in different cities, any place that publishes an edition of *Vogue*.'

Bibi is still weak after her near-coma experience. But

another pull of her cigarette gives her some energy. She says, 'I guess I like European cities, they have centres instead of downtowns, it makes a difference. In America, the downtown is just the place people abandoned to go and live somewhere else, out by the new mall. Have you been to the States?'

'No.'

'Where would you go, if you could go anywhere?'

'Miami?'

'You mean South Beach, and it's okay but it's like four blocks. Any Spanish city is livelier, more beautiful and the food's better. Where else?'

I get the idea. I wonder if I had said San Francisco or New Orleans, could Bibi really think of a superior European version? Or what she could compare New York to except London, and I know that they are very different. But I also think of Antwerp or Edinburgh or Bilbao, and wonder whether I would really love Houston or Charlotte or Des Moines as much as I love them. But what really interests me about America is the part that she had dismissed so quickly: the suburbs where everyone has gone to live, because they don't want to live in a city.

I say, 'The place I was born, they were big new houses with wide front lawns that stretched down to a tree-lined road where we would ride bikes. And the back gardens were huge and had climbing frames and swimming pools, at least a lot of them.'

'You were born in an American sitcom?'

'Or the *Virgin Suicides*, or a teen horror movie. I've probably filled out my memories with bits of videos and TV programmes, but I was six when we moved away. Louise remembers it better than me.'

'This was England, right? Are you sure about the swimming pools?'

'That part's accurate. The pools were under plastic tents, so you could swim all year round. And maybe one week in summer, the tents would be taken down and we would run from pool to pool, climbing over the fences between the gardens.'

'Why did you leave?'

We left because of my mother. But I don't really know why she decided to go. Maybe it was to do with money, or maybe she had always wanted to move to a small Cornish town where she could be blown around on cliff tops and cry into the wind on her own. I say, 'We moved to the seaside.'

We are kissing again when someone drums on the dressing-room door. The handle turns and my sister walks in.

'Poor baby. I just heard.' She drops on to the arm of the sofa, above Bibi. 'How are you feeling, darling?'

Bibi lets herself be drawn into a hug. Louise is big enough to just fold her up. I realise that Bibi is a little younger than me, maybe eighteen or nineteen, so Louise could be her older sister, too.

'It's a bit full-on, isn't it? Heroin overdoses the first day of the shows.'

'It wasn't an overdose. And I'm feeling okay, LouLou.'

'What happened to the smack?'

'Fred got rid of it, I think.'

Louise looks around. 'Pity.'

I cannot tell whether she is joking. She is my sister, I ought to know her better than anyone else. But the deadpan style even throws me.

Bibi asks, 'How's it going out there?'

'Oh. Yeah. The rehearsals are a joke. I don't think Amanda even knows what planet she's on. The way she's clumping down the catwalk, we might as well dress a sack of potatoes and throw it at the audience. Gianni started blaming the choreographer, then he tried to show her how it should be done. The problem is he can't follow the music. Every time the DJ drops something new, Gianni's stranded.'

'Should I be out there?'

'You won't do worse than Amanda.' Louise looks around the dressing room. 'Nice flowers. I heard they'd given Amanda a private room.'

The show is scheduled for 6.30 and it is after five now. Louise's best guess is that it will be 8 p.m. before the curtain goes up. She thinks Bibi should stay where she is, just chill and recuperate. The show is relatively small anyway. I am not sure how many outfits but Louise thinks that it is less than twenty; the models will wear three or four each. She tells us that the real difference will be Milan because Osano is saving his biggest collection for there. *Home-town gig, ooh-ooh*. I know that Osano is treated with more respect in Italy, I see it when I look through Italian magazines.

Bibi wants to move, though. She claims she is getting prickly rushes and needs to distract herself. She is mostly steady on her feet, but Louise and I are so busy watching her that we forget the way to the service elevator and soon we are lost in the corridors. When we find someone to ask, we are directed to the front of the building, where we catch the public elevator. The invited guests are already arriving and we ride up to the terrace with two smartly dressed Japanese women, both wearing sunglasses. I take a guess that they are buyers from Tokyo stores. As we file on to the terrace, I realise that Osano's show might be small but it has cost him a fortune. Now that it is lit, I begin to appreciate the care put into the details. Out on the terrace, the marquee's ceiling is canopied with clouds of soft gauze, bathed by warm dim lights in different shades of cream. And there is the catwalk, running down the terrace, freshly painted and studded with tiny light bulbs set into its surface. We move through to the restaurant, where all these elegant women stand among flower-decked pedestals while waiters weave through with trays of mezze-style canapés. I really cannot imagine the cost. Osano has been in the business for ever, but I wouldn't be surprised if he is still under fifty years old: only a year or two older than, say, Jean-Paul Gaultier, and younger than Gianni Versace if he were still alive. And where other designers long ago struck deals with bigger houses or even multinationals, like Prada or Domenico de Sole's Gucci group or Bernard Arnault's LVMH, Osano remains simply Osano Srl. A one-man limited company. I can't begin to work out the sales he would need to generate to justify his shows. The idea that Osano will do a couture show in Paris, followed by New York Fashion Week because he owns a store there, then Milan and possibly Paris again, with different collections and an entourage of models, dressers, make-up people and different PR companies, not to mention the parties. It would be as easy to tour a musical or put a stadium rock act on the road.

The show begins long before the models even hit the stage. Champagne is served alongside the mezze in what remains of the restaurant, after half has been turned into a dressing area. There are very few photographers, because the show is closed to the press, but they are already in position on a raised gantry at the end of the catwalk, some of them standing on their flight cases. The buyers are shown through to the restaurant, along with a few selected private customers. I don't know about celebrities. I try and think how many French celebrities I could recognise: Vincent Cassel and Vanessa Paradis and a few others. Catherine Deneuve. None of them are here. But a few people being treated with a special deference by Osano's PR team, perhaps they are the famous ones. Louise whispers that Osano has spent a chunk of the past two days sending desperate messages to Sting and begging him to watch the show. He has even sent airplane tickets by Fed-Ex to Sting's home. Two seats lie waiting, front row towards the centre of the catwalk for Sting and his wife, Trudi. I get the feeling that Louise expects me to laugh at Osano's Sting fixation. But it was Louise who told me that, outside the UK, Sting is treated as a modern great, and all the New York restaurants have his songs on a permanent loop. I know that Osano needs to attract big stars to his shows and that it will look good in France and Italy if he has photographs of Sting ringside. One Sting counts as a George Michael *and* a Jon Bon Jovi.

Osano is nowhere around. When I ask Louise, she tells me that he is backstage checking the clothes. And as we slip through into the dressing area, I see him. His entire concentration is on the clothes; there is none of the frantic switching of attention that Louise had described as Osano fretted over the lighting, the music, or tried to personally reinvent the choreography.

Although Fred has given me an access-all-areas pass,

I am scared to abuse it. I want to be backstage for the atmosphere, imagining how I would cope if it was my collection. Not better than Osano, I'm sure. I also want to stick close to Bibi; I don't know how I feel about her going ahead with the show. At the same time, I don't want to be in the way. After a while, I begin skirting the edges of the dressing space. I see Amanda, naked except for a thong, talking to one of Osano's people. It is a technical discussion; she is pointing at a dress hanging third on the rail. I cannot lip-read from this distance but she has a problem and everyone seems anxious to sort it out. It is becoming clear that Amanda is the star of the show. I creep on. Most of the other models are at the stylists' benches, working on their hair and make-up schedules. I have never seen a Paris show before, but even at the smaller ones, the college shows or last year's London shows with Louise, the make-up tables were always the most impressive part of the action. Doing quick changes with clothes is not so difficult. But when you see how quick the make-up has to be, you begin to appreciate the make-up artists and what it takes to be a good one. Bibi is sitting at the edge of the row of benches, still wearing the robe that I found for her in Amanda's dressing room. The make-up woman talks constantly but Bibi looks blank. Maybe she understands the instructions.

Louise crosses in front of me to pick up a bottle of champagne. She is naked. She looks so comfortable, though, with the bottle and the flute glass.

I turn and stand, goofy footed on the floor tiles. I am feeling kind of helpless; there is no reason for me to be here. I wonder whether I should go and check whether Stan has arrived, whether he is bothering anyone or fighting with the waiters. I am on my way out, but my backward glance catches Bibi's eye and she waves me over. Her hair is rolled into a tight pin curl at the back, the bangs at the front lacquered so they stick out straight like asymmetrical bat wings. Her eye make-up is also scary.

She sees the way I look at her and says, 'You want to try it from this side.'

'How are you feeling?'

'Can you get me a glass of iced water?'

I tell her, *sure*. I head for the kitchen doors to snare a waiter, just missing one as he swings out. I decide to go into the kitchen myself. There seem to be no chefs around: the food has been prepared and only needs the waiters to dish it out. Then I see a chef at the sink and walk over to him, asking for a glass of water. He shrugs and walks off.

There are tall glasses on a silver tray, filled with a peach-coloured liquid. I don't see any clean glasses so I take one of the peach drinks, empty it out and rinse the glass. All I need is ice. The bank of refrigerators stands at the back of the kitchen, towards the service elevator. It is only when I get down there that I see the security man.

'*Où vas-tu?*'

He is definitely security. He has a strange accent, the 'v' sounding almost like a 'b'. I guess that he isn't originally French, although I would not know where he is from. He is just a classic security guy, assembled in the alien factory where they put these guys together. His black bomber jacket keeps him in the shadows and his huge grey-brown face looms towards me like something from a 3D film. He weighs ninety or a hundred kilos and his nose has been broken, maybe more than once.

I show him my pass.

He just shakes his head and says *non*. It is no good out here.

I do not want to argue. I mostly want to get away from him and do it in one piece. Behind him, the service elevator opens and more men like him step out; maybe the alien factory is in the basement. I know that it's necessary to have security at a place like this. But it seems strange that they are all back here. If they were out front guarding Sting, it would make more sense.

Before I turn, one of the new men takes a look at my face and asks who I am. *Am I a model?*

'*Pas de problème. C'est authentique.*' I am talking about my pass. '*Je cherche Fred.*'

I don't know why I say that, except that I believe Fred would be comfortable among these men. I wonder whether they know who he is. Neither of the two men who have spoken to me so far says anything else. I guess they are mostly silent types.

'*Savez-vous où est Fred?*'

'*Il n'est pas ici.*'

I realise that I actually have a reason to look for Fred. I want to make a last check that Stan's name will be on the guest list. I try to look through the men, as though Fred might be standing with them. The first security guy puts his hand on my chest and tells me again that this section of the kitchen is off limits.

I tell them that I've come from out there, and wave a hand towards the restaurant doors. I am allowed to be here.

This time he speaks semi-English: 'Fuck off, *bébé*.'

I could have been on my skate, I move so fast. I almost forget to fill the glass. I slosh tap water into it and apologise to Bibi when I hand it to her. She is looking almost as dazed as she did earlier.

She says, 'Whatever that doctor gave me . . .' She doesn't finish the sentence, just gulps the water.

I can see drops of sweat on her forehead. The make-up artist sees them at the same time and dabs at the forehead with a paper towel.

Bibi says, 'And my ass is sore.'

The injection went in her bum. I tell her, 'I've got another Wu Tang tattoo. Do you want me to put it over the needle hole?'

At least she laughs.

The show is about to start. Louise is waiting in the wings, a dresser fussing at the back of her white gown. Louise seems to be doing an exercise, she blinks her eyes and then opens them wide, pulls her mouth into a tight grin and then relaxes. As the dresser progresses around the hem of the gown, I catch a glimpse of bare flesh from Louise's shoulders to the base of her back. I do not understand how the gown stays in place but as she turns, ready to step out, I realise there is a whole cat's-cradle of drawstrings across her body. It isn't bad technically. I don't know about state-of-the-art; I saw something similar at a London show a few years ago. Osano has found a way to make it more distinctive, but also much less practical and fussier.

Louise steps out. As she disappears, the entrance to the catwalk blazes with camera flashes; they burst so white, it is like a door thrown open on to a white-hot world. Behind her, Amanda steps into line, another dresser doing last-minute adjustments. I creep up behind them, hoping to see Louise on the catwalk.

She is poised facing the photographers above her on their gantry. The flashes blaze again, making a searing white wall. As the flashes die, she turns and begins to sashay back, her face the expressionless mask she has had in her repertoire since she was at school. At the mid-point she crosses with Amanda in another white, backless gown and the flashes open up again, even brighter and blazing for longer. Before Amanda turns into the glare, I notice that the cat's-cradling is more visible on her gown. The drawstrings swoop to her neck to make a kind of halter neck. Her breasts are heavier than most of the other models', which I guess is the reason she was chosen for this particular dress.

Louise pushes past me in the wings, making a *grrr* noise. For some reason I think that she is mad at Amanda, that she feels she has been upstaged, but then I realise that the problem is her shoes: they are a size too small. She kicks them off before she is three steps into the wings. I watch her head back to her clothes rail. Next out is Bibi, and her dresser has to push her because she is about to miss her cue. Bibi is also wearing a gown that ends with a web of crossed strings, though this time they go far below the level of her bum. I guess that is a less fussy effect, having your backside on show. The gown is cut so low I cannot understand at first how it stays so close to her body. Then I realise that Osano must have a whole cobweb of drawstrings sewn into the material and pulled tight. It is clever, so long as you don't ever need to use the bathroom.

As Amanda emerges from the wings, Fred appears beside me. I hear him say, 'Where's that fucking singer?'

and follow his eyes to seats at the edge of the catwalk. Sting's chair is empty.

'Let's hope we get some bodies in Milan.'

Fred is not in an amenable mood, but if I do not ask now about Stan I do not know when I will get the chance.

'He's on the list. And what are you standing around for anyway? You're supposed to be looking after that junkie Bibi.'

'I didn't know what to do. I couldn't stop her from doing the show.'

'You're not supposed to stop her. You're supposed to get her through it. Look at her out there.'

I blink at Fred. Then I look out to the catwalk. Bibi is trying but she doesn't have Amanda's hip-swinging strut. Her feet fall flat and heavy on the boards. And as she returns, she begins shivering. I turn to look at her rail and see that she has to wear a trouser suit next.

Fred says, 'Look at the state she's in. She needs a dresser all to herself and we don't have the personnel. Sort her out.'

As I start work on the back of Bibi's dress, trying to get the secret cords undone, Fred waves a nervous Italian woman in my direction with a few rapid instructions in Italian. She hands me a sheet of paper labelled with Bibi's name. I have to follow a schedule and get Bibi on stage, in the right clothes, at the right time. She has to be back on the catwalk soon and I don't know whether I have a minute or thirty seconds to get her out of this dress and into the trouser suit. I almost rip the dress off her and move her into position in the wings, passing other people doing the same job. Osano is in a frenzy, trying to keep on top of everyone's work. He points at me without speaking, guiding me like a traffic cop. I follow his directions and put Bibi third in line for the catwalk.

She is beautiful but glazed, make-up like clear-dried glue or even sperm across her face. The effect clouded from the smoke of the cigarette she has snatched off the model higher up the line. I allow her one drag before taking the cigarette off her and crushing it under my heel. I have her step into the trousers and, once they are belted, I begin to arrange the jacket on her shoulders. There is something wrong; her breasts are almost falling out, which is an achievement when she is all but flat chested. I put a hand under her elbow, guiding her around as I try to assess what needs to be done. The seam down the back of the jacket is off, badly tailored. I run a hand up the inside, between the cloth and the cold sweat on Bibi's back. There is a loose flap of material. I realise that someone has already made a quick alteration, taking it in to fit Bibi's body. She must have been slumped over when it was done. It may not matter that the line of stitches is so twisted, perhaps no one in the audience will see. I pull up the back of the jacket to double-check the trousers and find someone has used a safety pin to attempt to pull them tight. Again, it may not show, hidden by the length of the jacket. Bibi is not wearing shoes but I check the list I was given; there is no mention of shoes. Bibi's feet are long and slim, the raised bones like talons. I look again because something catches my eye. There is bruising around the toes, even a rust stain of blood. I wonder what kind of shoes she has been wearing.

She is limp at the edge of the stage. I smooth a finger down her spine, saying, 'Backbone.'

I feel like one of those ballet mistresses, the stern type you read about in girls' books.

Bibi says, 'I need a cigarette.'

'I'll have one lit and waiting for you by the time you get back.' I nudge her forward.

She sways into the corner between the stage and the catwalk, crossing with a black model in another formal suit. As Bibi finds the central line on the catwalk, her focus seems to improve. Perhaps she is picking an arbitrary point ahead of her and using it to navigate, perhaps she is focused on one particular photographer as the flashbulbs blaze up. Anyway, something works. She seems better this time, as tall and proud as the black model before her.

I bum a cigarette off one of the dressers and light it for her. I hold it to her mouth as she comes off the stage. She seems to take a breath and the cigarette leaps between her lips and fastens there.

For the next ten minutes, I work like a dog. Not a dog, maybe. But not a couturier either. The trousers of my skate pants fill with cotton reels and boxes of pins; I have ready-threaded needles stuck in the hem of my T-shirt where I can pull them out quickly to work on Bibi's clothes. There are only two more outfits, but they were never made for Bibi and she missed the earlier fitting and rehearsals. Yet she is pliable; it is like working with a passive child. A size six, English, even though she is almost six foot tall. I slip her inside a sheer dress, trying to work out the geometry behind Osano's clothes, what his intentions might be. He seems to want to show flesh, and I begin to wonder whether Bibi's flesh should be paraded so openly. She is mostly bone. But the next time she hits the catwalk, she seems to be even more together. And she can do flesh: at least the idea of it, even when there is so little of it on her.

Her last costume is an evening dress. The design is a return to the classical white gowns of the beginning of the show. I wonder whether I can stitch Bibi into her gown; I cannot decipher the lacing that should hold her in place. I would need to have seen some-one wear it before to give me a clue to the design. I take Bibi to the wings partially dressed, hoping to find one of Osano's Italians to help me. I find Osano himself there.

He grabs a handful of the laces, pulling the bib-style front tight to Bibi's flat chest. 'Fix it like that.'

I could have guessed that much. I wasn't thinking of sending her out tits showing and string trailing behind.

'Yeah. How?'

Osano says, 'I didn't design this. I don't know.'

'Who does?'

I am surprised that he is not the designer. It is normal for designers to take a step back from the diffusion and ready-to-wear collections, perhaps setting the theme, even designing the key pieces. For the rest, there are always anonymous people fresh out of school and des-perate to work their way up. Even Donatella designed for Versace long before anyone knew who she was. But I thought the couture line was supposed to demand the entire attention of the name designer.

Osano takes another look at the webbing of strings at Bibi's back. He yanks them again, tossing Bibi around as though she is a marionette. Then he pushes Bibi back into my hands.

He says to me, 'I'm fucked. How do I look?'

I shake my head. 'How do *you* look?' I don't under-stand how he flipped the conversation from Bibi to himself.

'I got to take my bow, asshole. How do I look, do I look fucked?'

He is an out-of-shape man in middle age. He could look better. But Alexander McQueen used to take his bows in a pair of old denims slipping off his beer belly.

I look at him while I work away at the back of Bibi's dress. 'Your suit is pretty wrecked. It looks like you slept in it. Have you got another one?'

'At the hotel. And that slut Louise threw up on it in New York.'

I have Bibi's lacing figured out. Now I almost let it slip. Osano is so wrapped up in his own drama he doesn't even see that I am hurt. Then he apologises, kind of.

'Your sister, yeah. She got sick. I didn't get time to clean it yet.'

I let Osano's words and apology go. I am still caught up in the panic of putting the show together. Bibi is laced. Now Osano needs a suit.

'I saw Fred bring a suit bag with him earlier. He might have brought a change of clothes for the party tonight.'

'Fucking Fred.' Osano thinks for a moment. 'Okay. Ask him.'

Fred is not in the dressing area. I scan the room and then look into the kitchen. The security guys are still there, standing in a semicircle between the refrigerators and the elevator doors. Fred appears out of their centre, striding out to meet me halfway.

'What's up?'

'Osano needs to take a bow. I wondered if I could borrow a suit for him.'

He chews the side of his face. 'You figure you can keep him from sweating?'

'I can't do that.'

'Okay. It's hanging in the gents' toilets. You'll probably see it.'

The security guys watch me, five of them in their bomber jackets. I nod and set off back through the restaurant and into the gents' toilets. This must be the quietest place in the building; it is within the models' dressing area and, apart from myself, Osano and Fred, there are no men involved with the show. But there is someone inside, a woman in an evening dress sitting on the washbasin unit. She is bent forward, her back to me. It is a cream dress with a sash running diagonally from the shoulder. I think to myself, that is a toga. And then I recognise Louise. She is wiping the space between two toes with a cotton wool bud.

There is something wrong with the scene, but before I can piece it together I find myself saying, 'You're supposed to be taking your bow.'

'It looks like I'm missing it.'

She breathes out, her head back, her mouth opening and closing around a deep sigh. The hypodermic syringe that was hidden in her hand clatters to the melamine surface of the unit.

I don't know what I say. I must say something because Louise turns to look at me, slowly focuses and says, 'Shut up, Jamie.'

I don't even want to be around her. I pull Fred's suit off the hook where it is hanging and slam the door as I leave. Osano is waiting for me in the wings to the catwalk, standing in his shirt and underpants.

5

As Bibi leaves the catwalk, I am waiting with Fred's overcoat, ready to wrap her up and take her back to the Hôtel Costes. We find a courtesy car in the square below, and Bibi huddles against me on the back seat, both my arms around her. She is in no shape to go to the after-show party and I won't risk seeing Louise again. But at four in the morning, once Bibi is asleep, I am sitting in the corridor outside Louise's room, mostly quiet but knocking every ten minutes.

I have been there for almost two hours when Osano clatters out of the elevator, his elbows at right angles to protect himself from the automatic closing doors. I watch him sway towards me. His head is down, frowning at the carpet as though he blames the elaborate oriental design for throwing him off balance. When he reaches my chair he stops, shimmering in a haze of alcohol and sweat like a heavy mirage. He has basically ruined Fred's suit.

He squints to focus. 'Is that Jamie?'

'Yes.'

'What's the matter? She sick again?'

I don't want to tell him why I am worried about my sister.

Osano rubs the side of his face. 'If she won't come to the door, maybe she's taken another overdose.'

I assume that he is confused: he must think I am sitting

outside Bibi's room. But when I suggest it, he shakes his head.

'No. Bibi this afternoon,' he says. 'Louise last week in New York.'

I scramble to my feet. I don't even know why I am not yelling at the man, he is so calm.

'What?'

'You don't know? She almost bought it, four or five days ago.'

'Where can I get the room key?'

'Reception's got a key. I don't. I'm the designer, I'm not the chaperone.'

Reception is too far away. I take a step back and kick at the lock as hard as I can. There is a little give. The second kick brings splinters and the third gets me inside. Osano follows me, looking dumbly around the empty bedroom. The bed is made. Louise has not even been here.

I stand there panting. After a while, Osano says, 'Why did you do that? She's probably still at the party.'

He is right. She probably is.

Osano sticks his head inside Louise's minibar. 'Anyway, the party should be over. She'll be back soon. Open this, will you, kid.'

He is holding a bottle of champagne in his outstretched hand. I take it. Osano wanders off as I begin flicking at the wire tab with my nail, trying to prise it free of the foil wrapper. I am not even thinking.

Osano shouts from the bathroom. 'This is no good. I can't drink champagne out of tooth mugs.'

There are champagne flutes in the same cupboard as the minibar. I take a glass for him, putting it down on the desk while I finish working on the wire cork trap.

As I twist the bottle free of the cork, Osano is back at my side. He takes over, filling the flute to the brim and handing it to me. He drinks from the bottle.

'Were you at the party?' he asks.

I shake my head. 'I was mad with Louise. I didn't want to face her.'

'Yeah? I thought you looked upset.' He takes another swig and starts dabbling through the cosmetics scattered over Louise's dressing table. 'Oh, thanks for getting this suit. Armani is probably going to thank you too, once he sees the photograph of me.' Osano cannot be too bothered, he hasn't taken it off. Unless he is continuing to wear it as revenge on Fred. I cannot believe that I managed to collect the suit and bring it to Osano after what I had seen of Louise in the toilets.

I ask Osano, 'Are all your models taking heroin?'

If Osano understands that I am attacking him, he doesn't rise to it or even get defensive. All he says is, 'I read somewhere that they take it to keep their weight down. You think I need to get myself a habit?' And he slaps his stomach.

'What happened to Louise in New York?'

'Her agency held this grand party. Louise decided it was a good night to overdose. What do you think that was: a cry for help or attention-seeking?'

Osano wanders around the room, pawing at anything he finds along the way: the clothes that the chambermaid has folded on to the back of the chair, Louise's hairdryer on the bedside table by her exotic-skinned address book. But once he has made a full circuit, he comes back, close to me. He is Italian, so maybe it isn't strange that he rests a hand on my shoulder as he talks. But then he pulls me forward one step and stares into my face. 'You think I don't care? I only care about my clothes?'

I don't know what to say: it is definitely what I think.

'You know it was Fred who found her a doctor? She was lucky we were even there.' He shakes his head in emphasis. 'I was in New York to raise money. Suppose I had given up the fight and stayed home, hey?'

Then he lets go, as though he has made his point. Losing interest in me, just as he lost interest in everything that he picked up around the room. He rubs at his temples and begins complaining instead.

'My eyesight is so bad. I always forget my spectacles. Maybe I should wear them around my neck like Lagerfeld.'

'Why not get a fan, too.' I remember an Annie Leibovitz photograph I saw in *Vogue* a couple of years ago: a picture of Karl Lagerfeld talking to Gaultier after a show. Lagerfeld is holding a black lace fan that covers his mouth as he speaks, as though he is scared what might slip out. Gaultier is leaning in towards him, so Lagerfeld must be speaking very quietly. I wondered at the time what he might be saying. Whether he was really being as indiscreet as he seemed, or whether it was an act.

Osano says, 'You know how much I hate that fan? I'd like to grab it and smack him around the face.' He slings the champagne bottle into a bin. I hadn't even noticed him finish it. 'Do you think he knows what it says about him?'

'What does it say?'

'What does it say? It's Freudian, kid.' Osano has dropped on to the edge of the bed. He lies on his back, talking at the ceiling. 'You got to imagine Karl as a little boy, so in love with his mother but already aware that men are supposed to have the real power.' He raises himself up slightly to give me a knowing look, as though I understand what he is saying. 'Well, Karl is a mama's boy but he's got a pee-pee and he knows his mama's got nothing down there. But, you know, he's too frightened of his mother to face reality, so he needs to invent a new story. Then one day, Mama whacks him across the nose with a fan, and he's got it. His twisted mind tells him that if you wave a fan around, it's even better than having balls.'

Osano keeps his knowing look on me, letting it deepen with every word. 'You know what I mean?'

'You mean Karl Lagerfeld has a thing for fans?'

'I mean he's a fucking castrato.' The knowing look seems to slide off his face. He is blank for a moment, waiting for my reaction. It takes me a moment to see that he is joking. Kind of. He laughs, yawns and collapses backward again.

I want to ask him about the show. 'Did you design any of that collection?'

He rumbles something. It sounds like a *uhn-uh*. Then he rolls over and says, 'I could tell you who did but then you would have to sign the same confidentiality clause she did.'

'Oh.' There is no lawyer in the room, but Osano quickly proves that confidentiality counts for nothing in his business.

'It was a woman who used to work for me. I hear she's talking to Arnault now about taking over Donna Karan. I haven't seen her in two months.' Then he asks about Louise. 'She is okay now, isn't she?'

I tell him that I caught her injecting heroin in the lavatories.

'Oh no.' He sounds genuinely sorry. 'She promised, if I brought her to Paris, she'd quit. I hate that.' Osano points at the hotel door that I kicked in. The wood of the door frame has given way and now the jamb hangs a few degrees off on torn nails. 'I wish you hadn't done that. I can't afford to pay for the rooms anyway; if you go vandalising them, I won't even be able to get credit any more.'

I begin to realise how much trouble Osano is in, if it is really true he has no money and has lost his chief designer. His organisation seems to be just himself and Fred.

I ask, 'Where is Fred now? Is he at the party?'

'No. He's still talking to the police. After the show, my entire collection was stolen. You believe that? Who'd want to party after that?'

Osano's collection was stolen from the rear of the Institut du Monde Arabe as it was being loaded into a truck. I take the news back to the room with me, where Bibi is emerging from the bathroom. She sees me and her eyes kind of brighten, though I can tell she's been crying. I realise why when she says, 'I woke up and you weren't here.'

'I'm sorry, Bibi. I was talking to Osano.'

'Oh.' She climbs on to the bed, sitting cross legged with the covers pulled up over her shoulders. 'I was sleeping fine, and then I wasn't.'

I climb up next to her and take her hand.

'Osano's collection was stolen from the venue.' Bibi's final outfit is lying over the back of the chair, a little torn because we had trouble undoing the lacing. 'That's probably the only piece he has left.'

'He's welcome to it,' she says. 'Bummer. Hope he was insured.'

I only nod, because I am looking at Bibi's feet. I remember that I saw bruising and what I thought was blood between her toes. I don't know why I am so slow, but it's the same spot that Louise used to shoot up. I slip down the bed to cradle one of Bibi's feet in my hand, rubbing it as though I am trying to warm her up. But I give it away when I tell her that I caught Louise injecting between her toes.

'Is that what you're looking for?' she asks. 'I've never tried that.'

'Your toes are bruised.'

'Osano's crappy shoes. I had a blood blister, too.' She pulls her foot out of my hands and twists it to her face. 'They're a mess.'

'I'm sorry, Bibi. I was just spooked. I only just heard that Louise overdosed in New York.'

'It was something Etienne had given her. It turned out to be completely pure or something. Maybe it was the same stuff he gave me, unless heroin always has such a horrible effect. I'm never taking it again.'

I think first: Etienne is a dealer. And then I realise that Bibi has never tried heroin before. I guess it makes sense that she tried smoking it first. She is smoking now, a Marlboro Light from the packet on the side of the bed. She waves the packet in my direction but my throat is raw.

'Have you seen Louise since?' Bibi asks.

'No. She's not in her room.'

'Did you try Etienne's?'

I shake my head. I hadn't thought that she would go there. I didn't even know Etienne was staying in the hotel.

'You really think that's where she'll be?' I am beginning to get worried.

'For sure. They've been going out together for months.' Bibi looks at me. 'You didn't know he was her boyfriend?'

I cannot even shake my head. I think my mouth just falls open.

Bibi says, 'He's on the second floor. I think it's two-sixteen.'

I don't remember leaving Bibi's room, or what excuse I used. I think it was just *sorry*, as I ran. I kind of come around in the elevator lobby. I remember that Bibi wasn't sure of the room number so I slow down when I reach the second floor, listening for any sound. A bellboy is dropping the morning newspapers outside the rooms and I think to pick one up, wondering whether the theft of Osano's collection has made the papers. It has. There is a statement from a man named Federico Sossa, who is described as Osano's business manager. I realise this must be Fred's real name. There is also an insurance figure: three quarters of a million US dollars.

Room 216 is quiet. I press my ear to the door but hear nothing. I move up to room 218 and down to 214 before trying the other side of the corridor. I am kind of deflated; I don't know how much sleep I have had in the last three days. Not very much. I feel like a toddler, so tired that I only want to cry. As I press my face to each door in turn, I leave wet smears behind me. I cannot hear anything. Then I notice a streak of blood on the handle of the first room, 216. I try the door. It opens.

I walk in and stare at the remains of the bed. The mattress is torn with criss-crosses that look like knife wounds, opening up its insides. Shreds of white wadding material tangle with burst springs. Standing there, I feel I hate Louise so much. I had thought I could walk into the room and tell her that she can crucify herself with drugs and deranged boyfriends, I don't care any more. All I want to do is go home, finish my course and try to get a place at a good college. But Louise is always fifteen steps ahead of me. The bed is the sign: I know that I am not going anywhere, I cannot escape.

I look around for somewhere to sit and wait, then notice the bundled figure in the corner. It is Louise, crouched down with a sheet wrapped around her and pulled over the top of her head like a cowl. The sheet covers her face.

'Louise?'

She pulls the sheet back and I see a face so sodden with tears it looks like a foam rubber toy left in bath water.

'What happened?'

'I'm finished,' she croaks. 'This is over now.'

'What is?' I hope that she is talking about her affair with Etienne.

'Me. I'm over.'

'Over what? You'll get another agency. Or you'll do something different. It's not over.'

'Fuck off, Jamie.' Even when she says this, there is no emotion. Just the hoarseness of her voice. I still get surprised by that voice. 'I'm not talking about work.'

I look away. Although the bed is slashed to pieces, the room is not touched, except that a chair is overturned and a knife and a mobile telephone are lying on the carpet. The knife is close to Louise's feet. It has a black plastic handle and a serrated edge, like something used in big-game fishing.

'Where's Etienne?' I ask.

'There's nothing for him here, so he left. Clever, eh? Now there's nothing for him to fuck up, I got rid of him. Neat work.'

Now she is scaring me.

'He thought I was going to kill myself but I killed the bed instead. Do you know, whenever someone asks you something, it's what they secretly want from you. Did you know that?'

'No.'

'You didn't know that, Jamie?'

'I didn't, Louise. What did he ask you to do?'

'You're not listening. He asked if I was going to kill myself, which means he *wanted* me to kill myself. Wouldn't that be like a great fucking drama? Once he's tired of saying he's fucked her and her and her, he'll have a dead girlfriend to talk about.' She gives me a meaningful look. I cannot read it. She says, 'I wanted to cut everything out of myself, but I wasn't going to do it for *him*. So I cut up the bed.'

Now I wonder whether she is in shock, whether that is the reason she is so quiet.

She says, 'It's better than suicide, it lasts longer.'

I'm not sure this makes sense. But it's true that the bed is permanently fucked. I pick up the phone.

Louise says, 'What are you doing?'

I don't reply. I just want a doctor to look at her. The receptionist tells me they don't have a doctor on duty, instead she can give me the number of the doctor they use. I am picking up the pencil by the phone when Louise presses down on the phone, cutting me off.

'I think you should see a doctor.'

She stands there in her sheet-shroud. 'For what? Emotional suicide?'

'I want you to see him so that I know what to think. You're frightening me. Have you taken an overdose?'

'Of what?'

'Heroin, I guess.'

'I haven't taken an overdose. I skin-popped a little back at the show because my feet and my back were aching and I was hungry but that's it. I hardly take it.'

'Didn't you have an accident in New York?'

'Because fucking Etienne gave me ninety per cent pure heroin and didn't tell me.'

I am beginning to wonder if Etienne really wants her dead. But instead of saying anything, I just push a hand deep into the bed. 'You really killed it.'

'I was going to hollow it out completely, but I got tired.' She stretches, lifting the sheet. 'I think I've got ME.'

I am so tired I think I could even sleep on the remains of her bed: except that it isn't hers, it is Etienne's. I cannot see any sign that he ever stayed here, though: no clothes or flight cases with his camera equipment. I assume that Louise is right, Etienne really has gone.

'Shall I buy train tickets?' I ask her.

'Why?'

'To go back home.'

'I'm not going home. Osano said I could stay with him in Milan until the New York shows start.'

I cannot believe her. 'Don't do that, Louise. You need to rest.'

'If you're worried, come with me.' She sees the news-paper I brought, lying on the bed. 'Is our photograph in there?'

I need to slow her down, her mood has changed so rapidly. The New York shows are two weeks away and she can't make me responsible for her for all that time.

'I can't come with you, Louise. I need to get back to college soon.' I wonder if a twenty-three-year-old can be made a ward of court, whether there is a mechanism that I can use to have Louise sectioned. I say, 'Louise, please. Come home with me.'

'Don't go back to Cornwall.' She sings it to the tune of 'Don't Go Back To Rockville' by R.E.M. She grabs the newspaper and starts flicking through as she sings. 'Don't go back to Corn-wa-all. Oh-oh, here we are.'

She lets a corner of the paper fall so that I can see the photograph: myself and Louise turned side-ways.

'Don't we look sweet, sweetie-pie?'

'I'm going to phone the doctor.'

She flaps the paper in front of me. 'What's the matter? A touch too manic?'

She flaps the paper again, more vigorously and closer to my face. I swipe it out of the way but I am too late. She is holding the telephone in one hand, the other wrapped around the cable.

I hold out a hand: as though I really believe she would just hand the telephone over to me.

She smiles then jerks the phone violently to the right. The cable remains fixed to the wall. She almost looks mystified. It always works in films. She tries again but the cable still won't give. All that happens is that the sheet falls away now that she is no longer trapping the material with her elbows. While she looks down at herself, I wrench the phone out of her hands.

My finger is on the zero button as she darts sideways. My eyes can't help but follow her, caught by the speed of movement and the blur of naked flesh. Then I remember the knife on the floor.

I drop the telephone and lunge forward. Her fingers are closing around the plastic handle. As I slam against the floor, she whisks it out of the way. I land on my knee, the bruised knee from my skateboard accident. The pain storms through my whole body. My eyes completely fill, I cannot help it. Across the room, Louise is carefully readjusting her sheet. Then she cuts through the telephone cable.

I roll back over. Underneath my chest is the mobile telephone that she has forgotten about.

That she suddenly remembers.

'Give me the phone, Jamie.'

'No.'

I grit my teeth. The pain is beginning to edge back, out of my head and my spine, flowing back to concentrate on my knee once more.

'Give me the phone.' She is standing above me now, the knife in her hand.

'What are you going to do? Stab me?'

I imagine the knife at my back, working its way beneath my shoulder blade. The sensation is mirrored by the hard corner of the mobile phone, digging into my breastbone. I lie still.

She kicks me.

I don't want to move. I can mostly ignore Louise's kicks. She has bare feet, it is not as though she can give me any more pain than my knee. I press myself harder on to the mobile phone.

'Give it me, Jamie.'

I don't even want to speak. I don't have anything to say.

'Fuck you. I'm going to Milan, not Cornwall.' She kicks me another two times before she walks away. 'And you're coming with me.'

I listen to her walking around above me. Then I hear a rustle and the sound of the bed springs. I guess she has retrieved the newspaper to take another look at her photograph. I lift my chest slightly and slip the mobile into my hand, cradling it beneath my body. The light behind the LCD screen has come on. It says there are seventeen missed calls. I stare for another moment before I realise that it is Stan's mobile. I had been doing my best not to think about Stan but I hadn't realised that I had lost his phone. Or that Louise had stolen it.

Behind my back, I hear Louise leap to her feet. 'What about this horrible photograph? We look like tarts. Now I really don't have a career.'

Her feet patter across the carpet and the bathroom door slams. I stay where I am for maybe two minutes, listening for her return. Carefully, I lift myself a little higher and try to scroll through the missed calls on the mobile. All of them are from different numbers: I guess from Stan, trying to get through to me from call-boxes. I didn't see him at the show; I assume he never made it to the party. My bag must still be at the Gare du Nord, with my only clean clothes inside. I have been wearing the same shirt and strides for almost two days and I don't like the feeling at all. I wonder whether Stan might still be close to the last telephone on the list.

I press 'call back'.

'*Centrale.*' It is the French equivalent of a call-centre-style voice. '*Oui?*'

'*Je cherche David Stanley,*' I say. '*Pardon. Qui est là?*'

'*La Préfecture Centrale, monsieur.*' She sounds patient. '*La Police.*'

I disconnect.

Louise is back in the room.

'Have you read this? Osano's collection was stolen last night.' Her fingers flick against the newspaper. 'And an Englishman is helping the police with their enquiries.'

6

I don't know what to do, but I know that I cannot think
with Louise around me. She has no use for poles of right
and wrong in her world, there are only Louise hot and
cold spots. I take a last look at her room as I leave. She
has done more damage to her bed than I did to the door
of the other bedroom, and if Osano cannot afford to pay
for that he definitely won't be able to pay for all Louise's
vandalism. Then I remember that it is Etienne's room;
maybe he will get the bill.

I limp down the corridor. There is a chair in the
elevator lobby so I sit on that, figuring my best bet. I
could probably walk over to the central police station
and ask for Stan. Then I have another idea.

I press 'recall' on the mobile and when a woman
answers I ask for the bureau of the media officer,
guessing at the probable French terms as I speak. The
telephonist must understand me, because I am diverted
to another woman. Unfortunately, all she tells me is
that the bureau will not open until 9.30. 'What is your
query?'

I tell her that I am interested in the incident at Gianni
Osano's couture exhibition last night: 'I am a journal-
ist with *The Times* of London.' I choose *The Times*
because the fashion coverage is pretty good, especially on
background and colour. My first impulse was to claim
that I worked for the *Herald Tribune*. I changed my

mind partly because Suzy Menkes, the paper's fashion editor, is famous in her own right, but mostly because I remember Jean Seberg wearing a *Herald Tribune* T-shirt in *A Bout de Souffle*. I thought my influences might betray me, the police would see through my cover.

'Do you wish to speak to the officer in charge of the investigation?'

I am not sure. I don't have any real reason to connect Stan with the Englishman they are holding in custody. At the same time, I know that it is him. I tell her, *Yes*. That is who I want to speak to. Thank you.

She puts me on hold. Not for long. A policeman comes on the line.

'Inspector Hervé. How can I help, sir?'

'Hallo. Yes.' Again I say that I am calling from *The Times*. 'I understand that you have arrested a man: David Stanley.'

'How do you know that?'

I avoid the question, asking instead: 'Does Stan have an advocate, Inspector Hervé?'

The policeman wises up. 'Who is this?'

I click off again. I wonder whether I should have phoned Stan's parents instead.

The telephone rings back almost immediately. I answer and the same policeman is on the line. 'You're a friend of David Stanley's, is that so?'

'Yes. That's right. Sorry.'

'Fine. And who are you?'

'I'm called Jamie. Stan intended to meet me at the fashion show. We missed each other.'

'Your friend was found close to the Institut du Monde Arabe. He was wearing one of Monsieur Osano's creations on his head.'

'Oh.'

'Do you want to come down to the station and speak for Mr Stanley?' Hervé asks. 'God knows, he cannot do it for himself.'

'Okay. Of course.'

I push both the up and down arrows on the elevator buttons, a sign of indecision: mostly because I cannot decide whether I should speak to Louise. I do not know how long I will be at the police station and I am worried that she will have left the country by the time I return. I am still basically dithering when the down lift arrives. I let it go and press the buttons again.

The next elevator arrives with Fred inside.

He says, 'I hear you're coming to Milan with us.'

'I've been asked to go to the police station.'

Fred smiles. 'I don't think so. Go and help Louise pack. I'll get a new suit for you.'

Bibi arrives in Louise's room thirty minutes later, carrying my new suit. We leave within the hour.

I last wore a new suit at the christening of Stan's daughter, Bonnie. They held the ceremony at the church in Lostwithiel. It was the beginning of winter. Stan was already at Falmouth, on the intermediate course before his foundation year. I was in the sixth form. As far as I know, it was Stan's girlfriend who wanted the baby christened: either her or her family. Stan had no say. They had broken up by then and the only person shooting Stan dirtier looks than Rebecca was her mother. No doubt I was the most cheerful person there, enjoying the feel of my crisp white Helmut Lang suit. Now I sit up straight and tighten the seat belt across the lap of the suit that Fred has given me. He sits behind, switching back and forth from Italian to English until the air stewardess tells him to turn his mobile off. We are about to start taxiing.

I had already bought myself a suit for Bonnie's christening. It came from a charity shop. I was going to make the alterations myself. I really wanted to do it. At the time, I didn't know how a suit was put together and the best way to learn seemed to be to take one apart and put it back together. But then my mother insisted on buying me a new suit. She thought it would come in useful some other time: she meant when I went for my interview at Exeter University. But if she had bought me a suit, it would have come from one of the shops in Truro like Next or Fosters. I remember my mother as very young and fashionable in the eighties; she never had big hair or huge shoulder pads. In her late twenties, she looked like the dark-haired woman in the Human League. But the longer she has lived in Cornwall, the more functional and all-weather her clothes have become. I felt that she wouldn't understand what I would want from a suit, and she would have no idea how much it would cost. So I told her no, I really wanted to do it my own way. Mum must have spoken to Louise, though, because a Helmut Lang suit arrived by courier from New York. The suit was great. I loved the way it strapped me in, pulling me upright out of my slouch. I didn't sit down all morning. I didn't want to damage the fresh-pressed feel of the suit. Maybe if the suit loosened on me, it wouldn't be able to hold me in position.

When Stan saw it, he asked why I was dressed in white: *There ain't going to be no fucking wedding.*

I am ashamed that I abandoned Stan. But I tell myself that I would feel a lot worse if it had been any one of my other friends. I know for certain that it is not the worst situation Stan's ever been in. He is, at least, innocent this time. I could tell from Inspector Hervé's tone that he didn't believe Stan was behind the robbery. If I had gone to the station, I could have helped speed Stan's release. But everything happened so seamlessly: Bibi brought me the suit, she took my arm as we followed Louise to the convoy of cars. And we were whisked to Charles de Gaulle airport.

If I was worried about creasing the suit that I wore to the christening, I have no similar worries today. The suit is linen; it would crease no matter what I did. And we are flying first class: I have so much room to stretch out, I could be flying on an American recliner chair. Bibi sits next to me. Louise is across the aisle next to a Swiss businessman. She has her eyes closed and headphones covering her ears. Osano is one row ahead with people I recognise from last night's show, although I do not know their names. Fred is right behind me, sitting alone with a laptop and a palm top on the seat next to him. Osano's entourage is not huge, just seven in total. There is no sign of Etienne, which is good. I still do not understand why Osano has taken Louise under his wing and me with her. But I know that Bibi is here because of me, she has told me.

The voice on the Tannoy asks us to make sure our mobile phones are switched off. I switched Stan's off more than an hour ago.

Bibi stops a stewardess. 'Can I smoke?'

'The no smoking light is on, madame.'

'Yeah, but am I going to be able to smoke later?'

'This is a no-smoking flight, madame.'

Bibi gives the stewardess a hard look, but turns to

me when she says, 'It's like: ask a simple question, you know?'

The stewardess quits hovering and heads back up the aisle. I agree with Bibi, it was a simple question. I still try to shoot the stewardess a sympathetic look. She doesn't see it, though.

Bibi sighs. 'I always hated flying.'

'I used to love it,' I say. 'I remember the first time, when I was little. We were flying to Greece for a holiday and I got my turn at the window seat just as we reached the island. I remember circling above it, seeing the outline of the beach in the shallow water and the deeper sea all around that.'

'So what happened: you got blasé? If you want the window seat, you've only got to ask.'

I shake my head. 'Thanks. I started liking flying less the taller I got. Mostly it was feeling uncomfortable. I began to feel cramped in the seats and started hating it.'

'You don't have enough legroom now? This isn't Economy.'

'It's fine. Anyway, I began to like flying again.'

The plane has been speeding up for the past few seconds and now the nose is quivering as the front wheels peel off the runway. The last time I was on a plane, this was the part I loved. It is the feeling of total relaxation that comes as the plane tilts upwards. Take-off is the most dangerous time in a flight and there is nothing you can do except go with it. I have been tense for so many years that I unwind with a rush. The tension is sucked out so fast that it feels as though I'm being pulped.

The plane thrusts forward, finding even more speed

as we swing up to a steep forty-five degrees. I close my eyes and imagine a sudden ignition and explosion as a fireball rushes through the cabin against the direction of flight. Ten times as fast as the aeroplane, flame-stripping the cabin bare as it roars back to earth. Turning me into steam. The exhilaration stays with me even when the plane levels off at thirty thousand feet. I look back across to my left towards Louise. There is still no sign she is about to resurrect herself, she is still in emotional suicide mode.

I try to watch the TV screen set into the leather of the seat in front of me. The plane is showing a new Hollywood film starring one of the Baldwin brothers, but Bibi has seen it before and keeps leaning over towards my screen to push a thumb into the Baldwin's face. Her thumb leaves a coloured indentation in the plasma screen, like a bruise that takes a moment to fade.

After a while, Bibi pulls up her T-shirt and nudges me. There are three nicotine patches stuck in a line across her stomach.

'Do you think these things work?'

'They should, I guess. I've never tried.'

Actually, I don't believe they can work. I know nothing about science, but I know that when cosmetic companies claim their moisturising products penetrate through to the subcutaneous levels of the skin it cannot be true because skin is waterproof. Maybe skin is waterproof but not nicotine proof; I don't know.

Bibi says, 'If you fall asleep with a patch, you get freaky dreams.'

'Stay awake, then.'

'Or fall asleep.'

Within a few minutes, she is asleep. Her head rests on my shoulder. I read the newspapers for a while, but then detach myself to go to the toilet. It's an awkward manoeuvre, and as I twist around to slip away there is a moment when I am looking straight into Fred's eyes. Ever since he was prevented from using his mobile, he has been talking on the radio telephone in his handrest. As our eyes lock, he gives me a hooded look, a nod and a smile.

I nod back.

Fred was waiting at the terminal at Charles de Gaulle as we arrived. After pointing the drivers in the direction of the check-in and telling them to wait for him, he walked me swiftly across to a special Swiss Air bureau for first-class passengers. I had to sign for a package delivered in my name. I had told Fred earlier that my passport was in a locker at the Gare du Nord but he had been unconcerned. He told me he would get a spare couriered to the airport in less than an hour.

Inside the airplane lavatory, I take another look at the photograph in the passport Fred supplied. It looks very little like me, except that the man is wide eyed and blond. The name, Carlo Tiatto, sounds implausible. The surname is the same as that of a Premier League footballer.

I clean my teeth using the toothbrush provided in the Swiss Air plastic pouch. My teeth seem to turn to moss every few hours, as though my body is too tired to combat wave after wave of invading bacteria. I know that I won't be able to sleep on the plane, it is such a short flight to Geneva. It is not worth the effort. I didn't ask Fred why we were flying to Switzerland rather than Italy, but Bibi has since told me we are spending a few nights in a villa Osano owns close to the Italian Alps. She said we can squeeze some skiing in before the New York shows start.

I should ask Fred if he can find out the news about Stan. As we disembark at Geneva, I tell myself to get it over with quick, before I lose the blank, chilled feeling that the landing has given me. But Fred sets off abruptly and I am only sauntering so the distance between us keeps increasing.

We are all wearing lightweight clothes that have been borrowed or stolen from sympathetic shops or designers, drawn from the spring-summer collections that are beginning to fill the Paris shops. Even though it is January, the women are wearing cotton party dresses, or sheer silk blouses open to their navels with only camisoles underneath. The passengers in first class who have nothing to do with Osano are dressed in woollen suits, the women in old-style Jaeger twinsets and the men in Hugo Boss and Burberry. Set beside Bibi and Louise, they look like rich and sober aunts and uncles who have stumbled across a teenage party. But then we pass through passport control and there is a moment when I look behind me to find that almost everyone from the first-class cabin is suddenly wearing fur. I do not even know where they got them from; I hadn't seen any coats among the hand luggage. Even Bibi and Louise have fur coats. Osano's is ankle length in a spectacularly lush blue-grey. It seems to rustle through its entire colour range in the soft light coming from the airport windows.

I doubt that Geneva is much colder than Paris. Despite the threads of snow I can see on the ground, the sky is blue. I have rarely seen anyone wearing a fur coat before, and never in Britain. But as I pocket my fake passport and move on, I notice that the few people not wearing fur have padded ski jackets. I might be uncomfortable on the fur issue but the coats are much more beautiful than the nylon skiwear. Bibi and Louise are so startling together, like upright animals as Fred beckons them from the doors to the express gate. Even their eyes are like those of animals: the wide-eyed and startled look that Bibi has had since she woke up on the plane, or the spaced and dull look of my sister, like the psychopathic lions in London Zoo. I have barely spoken to Louise since we left the hotel, although I am only here to look after her.

Fred has collected all our luggage together, piled on to four trolleys. But he sends everyone ahead, through customs, while he and the luggage remain behind.

When he sees me hovering, he asks whether there's a problem. I shake my head and shrug. He seems about to wave me on, but then he reconsiders.

'Hey. What you can do is stand by this stuff a moment.'

He slaps a hand on the nearest trolley. I tell him, *Okay*. I assume that he is going to find a porter. He walks off towards a wide screen door that separates the coolly tiled airport concourse from the industrial space beyond, an architectural barrier marking different planes of reality. An electric airport vehicle is rumbling out of this grey concrete space, its wheels suddenly silenced as they make the transition to the concourse. It tows its own wagon train of luggage, three carriages long. And then I see Fred signal to it, waving it over as he walks backward, back towards me.

'Thanks, Jamie. I'll take it from here.'

I look at the luggage he has collected, the original four trolleys and now these three new wagonloads.

'Don't you need help?'

He shakes his head and points to the sign above the red channel. 'It's only going to be a hassle.'

There are porters arriving now. I ask again whether he is sure.

'You imagine what kind of shit the girls have inside their suitcases?' He is smiling. 'You don't need the hassle. Take the green channel. I'll see you on the other side.'

I nod and finally move on, trying to walk in a way that seems appropriate to my new suit. Good clothes are like a wake-up call, you can't help but behave differently. By the time I turn the corner into the green channel, I am striding along. If the customs officials even look at me, none of them raises a finger to stop me. I wonder what kind of power Fred uses: whether he can actually tell a customs officer not to search his luggage.

Osano and everyone else are waiting on the other side, looking like people who could not organise a trip to the bathroom without guidance. Fred arrives after another ten minutes and points at the line of cars that has been waiting beside us. They are ours.

As the porters load the luggage into the cars, he takes me to one side.

'I've got to spend a few hours in Geneva. Try and make sure that everyone behaves themselves, all right? I'll see you at Osano's villa.'

I wait for Louise to choose a car and then deliberately take another one, guiding Bibi in the same direction. It's a Range Rover, belatedly pulling up at the end of the queue. It turns out to be Osano's own car, driven by a square-headed Italian man. As we leave the airport, the snow becomes more obvious. The edges of the road are swept into high drifts and, above us, the mountains are covered. The sky is still blue, though. The road to the Italian border is not exactly beautiful but it is breathtaking. The motorway climbs until it turns into a flyover, stepping across an industrial landscape on giant stilts as it runs the length of a mountainside.

I am sitting in the front seat with the driver. His eyes look straight ahead and I have to gaze past him to see into the valley, on to the tops of the smokestacks. I guess they must be chemical plants; the galvanised steel chimneys have red bands painted around them. Switzerland is known for chemicals: the names on the sides of pill bottles are always Swiss. I imagine a country of pharmacists and bankers. Leaning back in my seat, I angle to see in the rear-view mirror whether Bibi or Osano is interested in the scenery. Osano grabbed the back seat as though it belonged to him. I guess it does. He sits rubbing his face and snuffling and I realise that he is very drunk.

He shouts forward, 'What did you think of your first Paris show, kid?'

I tell him that I don't know. 'I don't have anything to compare it with.'

When Louise invited me to Paris, she promised I would have my pick of shows, including the menswear shows that were running parallel to the couture collections. The Italian men's shows received strong reviews in last week's *Herald Tribune*, but there was no way I could afford to go to Italy. The trip to Paris was a birthday present – Louise was supposed to plan the treats, my mother paid my train fare. Now it's all happening without me. I began by running around after Louise, and ended by running away with her to Milan. I have already missed Tom Ford, who was coming to Paris with his Yves Saint Laurent collection after his rave show for Gucci last week. The real Yves Saint Laurent carefully snubbed him by attending the rival Dior show. I might have seen Saint Laurent there; instead, all I heard were the stories, flying backwards and forwards. Now I was missing Dries Van Noten, though Louise had promised me tickets. And there was Gaultier, who was returning to Paris after a few seasons in Milan, as well as Yamomoto, Raf Simons and even Paul Smith. The closest I would get to them was reading the reviews, except that I would be doing it in Italy rather than Cornwall. Of the couture collections I was missing, I wanted to see Galliano's. I heard that Cate Blanchett would be modelling for him. The rumour that the Givenchy show was closed to everyone except customers turned out to be true, though no one knew whether it was because McQueen had quit Givenchy or whether it was somehow intertwined with Saint Laurent's feud with Tom Ford.

Osano says, 'You'll see how it compares. Wait for New York. That can't fail to be a complete disaster.'

Behind me, Bibi says, 'There you go, Gianni, you found the up-side.'

It is the first suggestion that I might also be going to New York. I suddenly have so many questions, but Osano shouts at me, 'You think your sister can get that bitch Amanda to do the New York show for me?'

So that's the deal. I don't know what to say.

'Anyway, she better. She practically promised to do it.' Osano grunts and rearranges himself on the seat. 'You keep Louise sweet, she keeps Amanda sweet.'

I try to sound calm. 'Louise is supposed to be here for a rest. She's not well.'

'Yeah? Try and keep her away. She's so ambitious, it's not true.' Osano leans into the gap between the front seats to say: 'No offence.' His breath smells of brandy.

I turn back to face the road, feeling the skin of my forehead tighten and throb. Behind me, Bibi says, 'Shut up, Gianni.'

'Hey. It's the way she is.' He snuffles again.

Bibi says, 'It's going to take more than Amanda to save the New York show. You need to find someone to replace Gina.'

'To hell with Gina. Isn't that right, Jamie?'

I shake my head without looking. 'I don't know any Gina.'

Osano says, 'I told you about her. She was my assistant, until she walked out on me.'

Bibi says, 'She wasn't your assistant, she was your partner.'

'Well, that was the problem. I had a partner when what I needed was an assistant. Jamie could do the job.'

Osano's hand falls on my shoulder. He ignores Bibi when she says, 'Jamie doesn't have the experience.' He just shakes my shoulder and asks me again.

'How about it? You scratch my back, I scratch yours. You look after Louise, Louise can look after Amanda and I'll look after you. How does that sound?'

'I can't be your assistant. I don't know anything.'

'You did fine in Paris. Anyway, I'll train you.'

I turn around, 'I can't make Louise do anything. I think she should quit and come back home.'

'But she isn't gonna, is she?'

I shake my head, 'No.'

Osano says, 'All you've got to do is work out what is happening between Louise and Amanda and that cunt Etienne.'

I don't want to figure it out. I want someone else to figure it out for me. And then make it go away. I want to sleep.

The car heads into the tunnel through Mont Blanc; the sudden rush of air makes it impossible for me to hear Osano or Bibi any more. I try and empty my mind by focusing on the orange strip lights along the roof of the tunnel. Soon, the lights bleed into a series of dashes that flash across my eyes. And then they bleed away as I start crying, too softly for anyone to hear. It feels like a kind of release to let the tears flow; they pour out so fast that my whole face is soon wet. I press down on the window switch down and the glass slides down a couple of centimetres. I let my face wind-dry.

Osano's villa is only a few miles beyond Mont Blanc, close to the Italian border. But it is dusk when we arrive. The night comes down so quickly. We are only about a quarter mile off the main highway, but the villa is surrounded by pine trees which make it seem even darker.

The drivers dump the luggage on the marble floor of the foyer. A maid peers at them over a gallery rail but doesn't move. Osano wanders in shouting out a woman's name: *Maria, Maria*.

No one comes.

There are five of us besides Osano. He looks around – four women in fur coats and me, either leaning against the door or sitting perched on a settee under a large gilt mirror. He says, 'Vincente will take your bags up when he's parked the Range Rover.'

Finally, the maid appears and Osano shouts a phrase in quick Italian. Then he turns back to us and says, 'And now my cook has disappeared. Looks like we eat out tonight.'

He shouts at Maria again. And the name Vincente keeps cropping up.

I speak up. 'I need to sleep. Can I go up now?'

Osano says, 'Okay,' and then shouts at the maid again before saying: 'Follow her.'

The room is on the first floor. A double bed in a room that is almost bare except for a settee and a carved wooden wardrobe that might have come from Sri Lanka or another exotic place. I still have my plastic Swiss Air pouch, but when I look in the bathroom I see a new toothbrush still in its box sitting on a fluffed white towel. There is also floss and toothpaste. I can barely get the brush out of the box, I am so tired.

I dream about our first house, in a road full of swimming pools. Louise is younger, although not young enough. She should really be only eight or nine years old and she is closer to fifteen. She is sitting in an inflatable ring in the middle of the pool, lit by the orange glow of the sun through the pool's winter cover. At the same time, my mother is watching television. I cannot see what she is watching, but her face changes from manic to depressed as she watches, the changes coming in long, slow cycles. I realise that she is probably watching Louise, who is on the television as well as in the swimming pool. As I stare at my mother, I am reminded by how slowly her moods change, even more slowly than this. She can be manic for years and then depressed for years.

I am half awake, staring at a room I cannot recognise. I am even sorry to be awake because I know what the dream is about. My mother told me, when she showed me the video of *Baron Münchhausen*, that she found Louise in the sea, in a pearl. There is an image of Uma Thurman in the film, taken directly from Sandro Botticelli's *Birth of Venus*. My mother stole the story to explain Louise's existence. And when I asked where I came from, she said she went back to the same beach and, because she was patient, another pearl washed up over the waves. I was in the second pearl.

Bibi is next to me, on all fours on the bed.

'Jesus, the sheets are soaking.'

The dream was so vivid, but because I know it was a dream I realise that I must be running a temperature. At the same time, I still feel I was on the verge of an insight that is completely lost now. Just because an idea comes out of fever, it doesn't mean it is wrong. A feeling of annoyance comes over me and I cannot shake it.

'You are dripping, Jamie. My God.'

I realise that she is right. I am lying in a pool of cooling sweat.

'Get out of bed.'

'No.' The more Bibi talks, the grumpier I get.

'We need to change the sheet.'

I really don't know whether we do. Could I have sweated that much? I swing my legs off the bed and sit naked on the side. The room seems very cold all of a sudden.

I say, 'Are we sharing a room?'

'You don't want to?'

'No. I do.' I finally seem to wake up. When I look at Bibi properly, I smile.

'Jesus. Now you're shivering.'

She heads for the bathroom and returns with the towel.

'Wrap this around yourself. I'm going to have to do the bed myself. You think Gianni has any staff left working for him? What is it that makes him inspire such loyalty?'

7

The worst part of the day is always the few minutes after waking. But I find it easier with every morning I wake to Bibi. She is one long, smooth limb twisted inside the camisole she wears to sleep, an arm with its own arms, wrapped around me. I wait for my eyes to focus, and for her to slowly emerge from the white pillowcases. I put my nose to the indentation inside her elbow and breathe another person. Day by day, I watch the Wu Tang transfer on her shoulder crack and fade as it surrenders to the soap substitute she uses. I can lie like that for minutes, pretending that I have no memory because all this is new to me.

Bibi told me that I hadn't missed much on that first night. While I ran a fever, they went into the local town, a ski resort called Courmeyer, where Osano insisted on ordering for everyone. He had left his glasses in the car and couldn't read the menu so he improvised, dredging up memories of meals that he had eaten before. It worked until his memory began to fail, soon after the wine arrived. I was better off at the villa, alone, because once my fever was gone, I was left feeling almost revitalised.

I am the first out of bed each morning.

The first morning, Bibi woke only as I dropped to the floor. She asked what was wrong with my knee. The swelling and the colour had almost disappeared but then

I got into that fight with Louise on the floor of her hotel room and my knee blew up big and blue all over again. I told Bibi that it was a skateboard accident.

'Rad. Pity, though. What about our skiing?'

'I can strap it up. It's not a problem.' I have always wanted to learn to ski.

While I clean my teeth, Bibi fills the bathroom with steam. She whacks my bum whenever she catches me bent over the basin. It's a school locker thing. Bibi's excuse is that she is still at school, she graduates in the spring. It's strange how different she is in the mountains, closer to her own age. She does that model hauteur really well but she shines without it.

I soon find out the truth about skiing: if it was difficult, how many people would do it? I'm not Olympic material immediately: I have a bad leg. But within five days I can do all the runs around the town. When I get competitive about it, Bibi points out that Courmeyer is hardly the toughest Alpine skiing. Its unique selling point is its restaurants, and the fact that it is only a two-hour drive from Milan.

On the mornings that Vincente, the driver, is not required in Milan with Osano, he drives us to the ski lift. He drops us on the main road and Bibi and I clump down a short hill to the cable car. Bibi is always complaining about her rent-a-skis and telling me that she would whup me if she had her own equipment. I was doing a red run before I learned to turn properly, and when she asked me how I did it, I said I just screamed all the way down. If you fall over, you fall on snow. When we go for cocktails at night, I hear people in the bar saying that snow can be as hard as concrete. I haven't found any snow like that. When I fall, it is always light and fluffy and perfect for making snow angels.

My ski clothes are also rented. For the evenings, in the bar of the Grand Hotel, I've got some T-shirts and the suit that Fred gave me. I keep it pressed, so I don't look too bad. But with my rent-clothes on, I am the piste tramp. The reason that I don't try snowboarding is that I will stand out too much in my Alpine accountant wear. Not the finest excuse: to plead vanity. And some of the boarders look terrible anyway, like they were dressed by a Hollywood wardrobe department to be the crowd at a Limp Bizkit concert.

A better reason not to go snowboarding is that Bibi prefers to work on her skiing and she only has eight days in the mountains before she returns to America to prepare for the New York shows. They begin with Puff Daddy's collection, broadcast live on television on 10 February, and continue until the seventeenth. Louise is staring at the calendar on the wall of Osano's kitchen. I can tell that she too is counting the days until she goes.

Louise is entirely dependent on Osano now. She has no bookings for any other shows in New York because she no longer has an agency. She doesn't even have any work arranged for London Fashion Week. I know that she has left the number of the villa with a few designers, but no one has called. I hear her asking Maria the maid for messages, twice or three times a day.

Louise wakes last, appearing at breakfast with a flourish as though we should applaud her for not sleeping all day. We eat in the conservatory; just the three of us now that everyone else has decamped to Milan to work in Osano's atelier. The conservatory looks out across the snow-covered lawn to the line of pine trees where the forest begins. In the mornings, Louise seems fine, happy to read the papers and wince over her grapefruit juice. Bibi sits beside me, drinking her way through a large pot of espresso. The arm that she drapes over my shoulder always has a cigarette burning between her fingertips. As she whispers at me to pass the sugar, I wonder why her breath never smells like a smoker's.

In the evenings, Louise's mood shifts, just around the time she has her fifth Negroni. She will suddenly turn around and tell me that I only stayed because of Bibi. I tell her that isn't true. It's not – Bibi is only here because of me. But I am also watching the calendar. I am not looking forward to going to New York, definitely not as part of the Osano travelling circus. When I stare at the calendar, I am trying to calculate how many weeks I have left before my application to St Martin's is due. I devise timetables in my head, like the exam timetable I made for my A-levels. If I return to college before the end of the second week of February I will probably be okay if I work hard. The seventeenth is too late.

The bar in the hotel lounge is made of local stone: a wall of granite chunks topped with a thick slab of weathered pine. It juts out into a room of low-slung sofas and oriental rugs. When I order our drinks, I feel guilty charging them to Osano's account, but neither Bibi nor Louise asks whether he can cover the bills we run up.

I try to warn them once, saying: 'You aren't worried? Like, this whole thing is running on a shoestring. Osano seems close to being bankrupt and he's always drunk.'

Louise doesn't think he's different to any other designer: 'Except that he drinks so much. Westwood almost went bankrupt a few times, even Donna Karan. It's just a rollercoaster. You get bought out by a big corporation or you win a sponsorship deal, then you're in the money again.'

There's news that the English designer Luella Bartley has done a deal with the Italian accessories company Bottega Veneta, and fresh rumours that Louis Vuitton Moet Hennessy are about to buy Lanvin, who have just lost their designer. But it is a different situation to Osano's. It's not as though there is still a Monsieur Lanvin around, staggering into meetings or trying to call the shots. I can't see anyone bidding for Osano, or Osano welcoming anyone who did.

Osano spends most of his nights in Milan. But every two or three days Vincente brings him back and drops him off at the Grand Hotel. He arrives late, always after ten. By then, Louise has usually managed to ingratiate herself with a group of wealthy young skiers and left Bibi and me on our own. Osano drops down into one of the settees and sends me to the bar for his drinks. He refuses to use the waiters, who circulate slowly around the lounge. He seems to have got more homophobic over the past week and will do anything to avoid the lone gay steward who teasingly flirts with him. Perhaps not homophobic, because he never causes a scene or insults anyone. The steward's attention just seems to depress him, sending him into a dark mood as he twists his glass of Cutty Sark around and around on the paper coaster.

I ask Bibi whether she thinks Osano is going crazy. She tells me, 'For definite. But what makes you think so?'

'He barely talks. He just mutters, and when I try to listen I realise he is speaking Italian and I can't understand him.'

'He's just tense. He's working so hard on the New York show.'

Louise speaks excellent Italian; she uses it as she moves around the lounge, her antennae twitching for drugs. She can always find the group that has cocaine and soon she is sliding off to the bathrooms. I don't think about trying to stop her, I wouldn't be able to do it. I did ask her, would she eat chocolate or truffles off a piece of toilet? Why is cocaine the only delicacy consumed in the same place you piss? She looked at me like I was retarded and told me to change the record. I can't remember her ever talking to Osano; I doubt she has any insight into his state of mind.

I have to help Osano walk across the slippery stone path from the hotel to the Range Rover. One day he pauses and I assume that he is trying to catch his breath. Even when he starts speaking I barely listen because I don't expect to understand. But he keeps on talking until I realise he has a question: he wants to know whether Louise has got final confirmation that Amanda Van Hemstra will model at his show. I nod, telling him that Amanda is playing hard to get, but there is nothing to worry about. It is a complete lie. The truth is I have no idea whether Louise has spoken to Amanda since Paris. She never mentions her name when she asks Maria about telephone calls. But she has not mentioned Etienne's name either, and for some reason, an intuition, I believe that she is still in contact with him. I am not sure their break-up in Paris was as irrevocable as she claimed.

After I reassure Osano about Amanda, he stands and nods for about half a minute. Then he says, 'It may not matter anyway. New York might not happen.'

'Oh.' For a moment I am relieved, because now there is nothing to prevent me returning to college. I am not even thinking about Osano or his business. But then it hits me: Louise will be devastated. I could end up missing even more of college, because she will certainly refuse to return to Cornwall to rest.

'Does my sister know?'

Osano shakes his head. 'It's not definite. But we lost the site in Bryant Park. And it's late to be looking for a new venue.'

It turns out that everything now depends on Fred: whether he can raise enough money in the next few days.

Fred is around even less than Osano. He makes his first lightning visit on his way back from Geneva. Instead of spending a couple of hours there, he was gone almost two days, arriving in Courmeyer long after Osano and his assistants returned to Milan. No matter what time Fred arrives, he always knows where we are. He either has Maria spying for him, or he just tours the cafés and restaurants until he finds us. Courmeyer is a very small town. There is no sign that Fred shares Osano's money worries. When we eat together, he suggests dishes and picks up the bill, after persuading us to sample at least two different grappas per meal. I know that regional differences count for a lot in Italy and assume that Fred is a Northerner because he knows so much about the local food and wine. But when I ask, he shakes his head. He isn't from these parts and, anyway, he spent the last ten years in the States. He is just glad to be back among Italians.

Fred likes me. I don't know what I've done to be treated as a friend. He has a dry sense of humour, but so do Bibi and Louise, and the fact that I appreciate it does not necessarily give me and Fred a special bond. When Fred joins in a conversation with a group of snowboarders on the next table, he nods solemnly as he asks them about 'rodeo flips', 'method grabs' and 'stiffies', using the words so easily that the boarders never realise he has no idea what he is saying. After he is done talking, he turns back to the three of us with a shrug. We are biting our napkins, trying not to laugh. In the end, I take Fred's friendship for what it is: he likes easy-going company.

I tell him that he would like my friend, Stan.

We are walking the two miles back to the villa; the girls have gone ahead in the Range Rover. Fred is sauntering along, wide legged, keeping his balance on the under-salted country lane. I was happy to walk with him, but now I wish that he would hurry. I am beginning to get cold and he is much better dressed than me, with his overcoat and gloves.

'How is your buddy?' he asks. 'Out of prison?'

He must know that he is. Fred is following the story because of the insurance claim. I tell Fred that Stan is now back at college in London. I have spoken to him a couple of times in the past week. Though now I have let the battery on his mobile run flat so he can no longer call me and berate me. He doesn't need to try hard to make me feel guilty about his arrest. I should have waited at the Institut until he arrived. But if I had, I still might not have seen him. He seems to have entered through the back way, before getting lost in the corridors. His excuse was that he didn't know what floor the roof terrace would be on. I asked him, what floor is a roof terrace usually on? I also wondered about the time of the incident. Because I had a feeling it was at least two hours after the show ended, even though we were running so late.

The one thing that Stan has promised, he won't let either of our mothers discover what happened in Paris. My mother is worried enough that I am missing college. That's despite the fact that she can blame Louise for corrupting me. Each time I have spoken to her, she has refused to let me call Louise to the telephone.

Fred listens to the story. There is only one thing he doesn't understand. 'Why was your friend wearing a dress on his head when he was arrested?'

'You don't think that's funny?'

Fred twists his face as he thinks, lit orange by the headlights of passing cars.

'It could be funny. He would have to be singing, though.'

He starts singing, not in words but in tones – *bom bom bom* – a crazy folk tune with a melody that speeds up at every cycle. As he sings, he dances between the ruts of snow left by the vehicles, his shoulder bag slapping rhythmically against his thigh.

I tell him, 'I don't think Stan was singing that.'

'You never know. It's a real favourite.'

'If you're at a Mafia wedding.'

'That's where I heard it.' Fred taps his head. 'The beginning of *The Godfather*, right?'

We take a short cut through the forest, guided by the lights of the villa through the trees. Fred has found himself a big stick and beats the fir trees as he passes to send showers of snow down on my head. I manage to avoid a drenching by pausing and then running, counting the beats when it is safe.

I stop when I am safely ahead of him and ask, 'What did you do with that pistol?'

'What do you think I did? Turn it over to the authorities?' He throws his stick away and beats his gloves together to clear the snow off them. 'I think the cops would have loved that, immediately after the collection was hijacked.'

They would certainly have had more questions for Fred. I say, 'So you kept it?'

'I've still got it.' He undoes his shoulder bag and pulls out the padded envelope from the Institut du Monde Arabe. 'You want it?'

I shake my head, but I walk towards him and peer inside the envelope. The lights from Osano's conservatory are just bright enough for me to see the shape of the gun.

'How did you bring it through airport security?'

'It was in the luggage. I'd forgotten about it and no one found it.'

I remember how careful Fred had been at the Swiss customs, insisting on handling everything himself. I don't believe he could have forgotten about the gun. I put my hand inside the envelope and touch it, remembering how heavy it felt. It got heavier and heavier the longer I carried it around.

'You ever fired a gun?' Fred asks.

I shake my head.

'Hey, now's your chance.'

I don't think I can do it. But Fred says, 'Why not? We're out in the country, it's safe.'

I take out the gun. The handle part is empty. I reach back into the envelope and find the magazine. It slots into place, just like it should do, like it does in films.

I look through the trees. I can see figures moving about inside the conservatory, and although I cannot make them out I know it must be Osano, Bibi and Louise.

I rack the top of the pistol.

'Where should I fire?'

'Not towards me, and not towards the house. That gives you the whole rest of the forest.'

I aim at the nearest tree. But then I worry that it could be too close, the bullet might ricochet back towards us. If a bullet can ricochet off wood. I aim a little farther away, bending my knees slightly. The gun feels too heavy. I change stance and use a two-handed grip.

I fire. My arms feel the recoil even before I hear the explosion. Snow cascades from the trees around me, shaken by the noise rather than anything I have hit. I turn back towards Fred, the gun still kind of up in the air rather than down at my side.

'Careful.'

As he warns me, I slip on the snow. Even as I fall, I see Fred dive to one side, scared that I will accidentally fire off another round.

'Are you okay, Jamie?' His voice comes from behind a tree.

I nod and then say, *Yes*. My ears seem to be ringing a little. 'Maybe you'd better take it back.'

I hold the gun out, by the barrel. Fred is now above me. He takes the gun and drops it back into the envelope. As he folds the envelope over, I hear the popping of the bubble wrap. That must prove that my ears are not damaged.

'How was it?' asks Fred.

'I don't know. An anticlimax?' I have imagined firing

a gun for as long as I can remember, but it doesn't mean that it is a life-changing experience.

Fred looks across at Osano's villa. 'You probably scared them.'

I climb to my feet and follow his gaze. Through the trees, I can see faces at the glass of the conservatory, looking in our direction. But it is the countryside; I imagine there are occasional gunshots in the night.

Fred says, 'When does Bibi leave for the States?'

'Tomorrow.'

'You going to miss her?'

'Yes.'

'You know, it's definite, we're not doing New York,' he says. 'I wish the cops had charged your buddy. The fucking insurance still hasn't paid on the robbery.'

8

Fred has come to Courmeyer to break the bad news about New York in person. As we walk across the lawn to the villa, I ask if he can wait until after my sister has gone to bed. I will find a way of telling her in the morning. Even if I cannot do it delicately, it would be better that she didn't hear it late at night when she is drunk and coked up. But I still haven't told her by the time that Bibi has to leave. Louise stands in the front doorway, waving goodbye. I watch her over my shoulder and then shrinking away inside the wing mirror.

Vincente is driving. Osano sits in the back as usual, wrapped in his fur coat despite the air-conditioning being turned to warm. Ten miles down the road, he asks Vincente to stop and climbs out of the car to remove the coat. He throws it into the boot and we continue. I had thought he was going to offer to swap seats with me so I could sit with Bibi. It will be the last time I see her, perhaps for a very long time. Bibi does know that New York has been cancelled, and although she seems upset all she has said is: 'There's always Milan at the end of the month.'

I walk Bibi to the check-in desk. She twists her hand in mine while her passport is checked, stroking the inside of my palm as she answers the questions about who packed her bag. She has her own airport ritual – she has to stay until the moment the bag disappears along the conveyor belt and down the hatch. As though that is proof that it will end up on the same flight as her. Once she is satisfied that the luggage is safe, we shuffle towards her gate.

I don't think either of us knows what to say. I have one of those urges to say that I am serious, without being able to spell out what makes me serious. As soon as I can safely leave Louise, I will return to Cornwall. Because I still live with my mother, I have close to an hour's drive to Falmouth every day. I often get back at midnight and then I wake again at seven. The only time that I have to think is when I am alone in the car, but I don't know how I will think about Bibi. I know that I will daydream. I will imagine the choreography of my final degree show at St Martin's, with Bibi up on the runway. She'll be a top model, doing a favour for an old friend and making my designs look beautiful, just by being on the inside of them. By then, Louise will either have climbed her way back to the top or become a booker or a fashion editor; Amanda Van Hemstra will be pleased to do any show Louise asks, even a degree show for her younger brother. I could make the three of them a part of my fantasy grand finale. A fantasy that will always turn to panic, because I don't have much hope of being accepted at St Martin's. Falmouth is a good college, but its strengths are pottery and sculpture. I am kind of on my own.

Bibi and I kiss. Warm and shallow kisses that slide from upper lip to lower lip. She has her long fingers against my head, I have mine in the small of her back, a magic place like the centre of a propeller, the pivot of her whole body. It is exhilarating, to have someone move for you like that, to know someone well enough to find their secrets. And she has found my secret, too.

Her fingers are poised on the trigger spots beneath my scalp, and as she presses I feel the tension uncurl and slip away.

Until a hand falls on my back and Osano is standing there, breathing heavily and sweating last evening's alcohol. He moves me to the side and embraces Bibi, kissing her three times, right and left and right again, as he tells her that she is beautiful, she is wonderful. *Ciao.* He pushes her through the gate with a wave. I am left standing slightly behind him, leaning to one side so that Bibi can also see me wave.

'Come on,' Osano says, moving off.

I watch as Bibi gives me a last over-the-shoulder look. Then she disappears.

Osano shouts, 'Come on, kid. Vincente has the motor running. We're late.'

'For what?'

'What do you think? For work. Who needs New York when there's Milan and Paris.'

I follow him.

Milan Linate airport is close to the city centre. There is none of the usual stretch of blank freeway. We travel on ordinary city roads that grow denser, the buildings becoming taller and older. But then Vincente peels off, away from the city. It turns out to be another forty minutes to Osano's atelier. We arrive at a small industrial estate, finally stopping outside a glass-fronted two-storey building. I see a skeleton of steel tubes behind the windows, supporting stairways and corridors. It could be a zipper factory or a computer plant. The only sign that it is Osano's headquarters is a brass plate on the door, engraved with Osano's name. Osano has been quiet for most of the journey. He still doesn't say anything when he climbs out of the car and crosses the carpark. I run to catch up.

Osano stops me on a staircase and asks me for the time. I am not wearing a watch but remember that the dashboard clock of the Range Rover read twelve o'clock.

'Okay, I've got a meeting in half an hour. Come and see the workshop.'

We enter a brightly lit studio, with overhead fluorescent tubes and anglepoises screwed to the various desktops. There are five people sitting at drawing boards; another ten people are cutting or sewing cloth. The cutters are closest to the door, leaning over a large, rubber-topped table, working on patterns. In the centre of the room, a couple of women are using sewing machines. And at the far end, another pair hand-sew outfits that look to be all but finished. These are the only two women I recognise; they were in Paris and travelled on the plane to Geneva.

Each area has its own mannequins, clothed either in paper or in roughly finished gowns of cheap canvas. Those at the end are wearing completed outfits. Standing inside a real design studio, I wonder what I am supposed to be doing here.

Osano nods in the direction of one of the women at a drawing board. She is a few years older than me, her hair roughly cut in an expensive style. Her high stool is on wheels like a desk chair, and as we approach she pushes back and rolls around to greet us. Osano double-kisses, calling her *darling* in English but introducing me in Italian. I think he has told her that I will be working on the show. While he stares at her drawing, a design for a woman's suit, she stares at me. I hold out a hand.

'It's good to meet you.'

'Katie. Hello.'

I don't know why I am surprised that she is English; she is a Geordie. I feel myself squirm inside as she continues to look me up and down.

'Are we supposed to be doing a menswear show now?'

'I'm not a model,' I say. Then, helplessly: 'My sister is.'

Osano turns, saying, 'He's going to be working with me. This . . .' He taps at her drawing. '. . . this is a piece of shit. Where's the original?'

Katie stiffens, but she keeps her voice firm. 'Let me see.'

Reaching under her drawing board, she pulls out a pen sketch, scrawled across the back of a used envelope.

'Here's your sketch.'

Osano stares down at his own indecipherable doodle. There is no trace of embarrassment when he turns back to her drawing and tells her that she has messed up. He jabs at the picture with a felt-tip pen in his hand, leaving an angry rash across the paper.

'The way you've done it, it looks like a drape jacket. How long is this?'

'It will come to the end of her palms. It's not a drape.'

'It looks like a sack.' Osano puffs for a moment. 'This isn't going to work. Forget it, Katie. We need to rethink. New York isn't going to happen. We're working towards Milan now.'

A mobile phone begins singing before Katie can ask him any questions. She ends up tilting on her stool, her mouth open, Osano glaring down at her. Everyone has realised that it is Osano's mobile, except for Osano himself. He eventually fishes in his pocket, turning to one side as he looks at the screen.

'Look after Jamie,' he says. 'I've got to take a call.'

He is halfway across the room before he flips down the mouthpiece. He was practically shouting at Katie over the sketch of the jacket. Now his voice is a low murmur. After another few more strides, he disappears through a doorway at the back of the room.

Katie stares at me. 'What exactly are you helping Osano with?'

I have no idea: it is all news to me. I have never even had a job before, except for summer work in a local sailing school. I did a paper round for six months when I was fourteen years old, about the only job where a skateboard is an asset. I was qualified for that. When it comes to the fashion industry, I don't even know the names of most of the jobs. Katie has cold blue eyes and a hard stare, but I don't know whether I should feel as intimidated as I do. I definitely cannot answer her question.

'Osano was short staffed in Paris. I helped as a dresser, that's about it.'

'You know why he was short staffed? He managed to piss Gina off. She was the only one around here who could organise anything. What's your experience?'

I shrug.

Katie isn't the only person from the UK in Osano's studio. One of the cutters is from Cardiff. Both of them went to good colleges, Katie to St Martin's and Rhonda to Nottingham. The two tailors are both French and everyone else is Italian. Katie tells me that she has worked with Osano for a year, although she was hired by the missing Gina. During the past two months, she has spent part of each day answering telephone calls from fashion editors and denying that the Osano brand is close to collapse. The reason that so few of his staff were in Paris is that they were so far behind with the fashion week cycle they had to remain in Italy.

The fall-out with Gina happened in New York. Katie was actually there at the time. She tells me that Osano tried to raise money using his lease on the New York shop as collateral. Apparently the lease was so short it would raise very little, and if he failed to make the repayments it would swiftly threaten his whole retail operation. His only source of cash.

'Osano was in talks all the time. Gina was left to run the shop in New York and supervise the work in Milan. And even when it looks like Osano has actually found some backers, he takes them to a party and gets so drunk they start to freak out. Then Louise fucking Greenhalgh decides to take an overdose, and we never hear from them again.'

I didn't know that. I remain silent, but so do Katie and Rhonda. They are both staring at me now.

'You know . . . you look a lot like Louise.'

I nod. 'Yeah?' I have to put up my hands to this. 'I'm, like, her brother. You know.'

'Oh, fuck. What are you going to do? Drop acid in the water coolers?'

Rather than say anything, I let my eyes fall down to the table. The rubber top is covered with paper patterns, pinned to a piece of gold fabric. The original bolt lies at the end of the table with another of more sparkly gold material and a third one in a very eighties Thierry

Mugler crimson. The patterns are similar to Osano's Paris collection, although the material is different.

'More togas?'

Katie looks at the table. I think she is surprised for a moment, but remembers that I have seen the Paris show. 'It's his signature this year.'

Rhonda says, 'To be fair, Gina designed it. But when she's doing four collections in one season how many good ideas is she going to have?'

I look back at the table. The pattern is not quite the same as the designs I had seen in Paris. The trouser suits apart, there were two basic styles: an asymmetric design that fell off one shoulder and the other with the complicated, string-drawn halter necks. Both styles worked only because the models were laced in tight.

'No, this is better,' I say. 'More like Empire line.' There was a design similar to this at the Paris show. I remember, when it was shown, how the mood lifted. There was more applause and the flash of the cameras was brighter. Perhaps it was only Amanda, her star quality, that drew the applause, but when she returned from the catwalk she seemed to be walking above the floor. I tell Katie, 'A design like this went down really well in Paris.'

'I guessed as much. Osano's been revising the collection so that we have more like this. Gina must have had a last-minute burst of inspiration.'

'Who chose the material?'

'Oh, yeah. That's Osano's infallible touch.'

Rhonda looks uncomfortable. She touches Katie's arm, trying to steer her away from any outright criticism of Osano. 'Maybe it makes sense to do so many collections, that way you can cater to different markets.'

'Yes. If you're Armani, you can think global. But we don't have enough people to do one show properly.'

'Maybe it's good news that Fred couldn't raise the money for a New York show.' The moment I say it, Katie and Rhonda look at me as though I have alien information. They are still suspicious but there is an undercurrent to it; even I can pick up on it.

'What's Fred like?'

'You've never met him?' I look from Katie to Rhonda. They both shake their heads.

'He's only been working with Osano since Gina left and he's never visited us.'

I tell them what I can about Fred. I would sing like a canary but I don't know enough to spin it out into a narrative. I am shocked that his relationship with Osano is only a month old but I try not to show it. After the conversation with Katie and Rhonda breaks down, there is nothing to do except mooch around the studio. I am mostly interested in the two French seamstresses but they are doing appliqué and it's like the joke about watching animators work with plasticine: the process is so slow it is unbearable to watch. What I would really like to do is take the clothes apart and find out how they are built, the way that I do with the suits I find in jumble sales and charity shops. But I can see that wouldn't be helpful, with the Milan show only twenty days away.

Osano has been gone for almost an hour when I decide to go down to the warehouse on the ground floor. It is the lost clothes graveyard, samples from past collections stored on rails and forgotten. I drag my hand across the fabrics, imagining I'm the first person to disturb them since they were hung here. I try and play a game of 'Guess the year, name the designer'. The clothes have paper

labels attached but they are coded rather than dated
so I have no way of telling when I am right or wrong.
A lot of designers will sell their samples. Osano either
prefers to keep his experiments out of circulation or he
hasn't developed the outlets to sell them successfully.
The more that I learn about Osano's organisation, the
more I realise that he has long-term problems. Perhaps
Fred is not the best choice, but Osano needs someone
prepared to take action.

The first racks I come across are designed by Gina, I
am sure. They might date back over two or three years,
or four to six seasons. I pull out a chocolate-brown jersey
dress with a low waist and a floppy, outsize polo neck.
Then, a few racks down, a two-piece suit that is kind of
ironically grannyish, almost something that you could
imagine Nancy Reagan wearing. The designs relate to
ideas and styles that were of their time a few years ago.
I assume they are by Gina because I cannot imagine
Osano either noticing or caring about the latest ideas. I
do. I read fashion magazines with the same enthusiasm
that everyone else reads the music papers. But looking at
these samples, I see the downside of knowing too much.
The designs are so disparate, there is no single dramatic
signature. Again, it is similar to music. If I hear a voice
that sounds authentic, and is different to anything I have
heard before, I can already feel that the singer is going
to be huge, even if I don't particularly like the music.
It is the same with big designers – there is always one
idea so bright no one ever forgets it. Dolce and Gabbana
have that ultimate Homo feel. Helmut Lang might be
Austrian, but he designs uniforms like a Prussian, even
going so far as to put special bits of kit into them like
knee-pads or straps that will keep a coat-tail from

flapping in a tornado. Gaultier loves English Goths, and though his designs have moved upscale recently, it is that image that stays with me. Armani designed for *American Gigolo* and *The Untouchables* and he has that high Hollywood cachet. Prada has it too, but it is version 2.0: the new, digital Hollywood. Versace claimed to have invented the whole idea of Celebrity, and had the chutzpah to get away with it. Dries van Noten is Belgian, but he manages to be both gentle and austere.

Perhaps the problem is that Gina was working for someone else; she couldn't express herself through the Osano name. And these clothes are only samples, after all. Ideas that were ultimately rejected. But confronted by this eclecticism, the range of ideas drawn from retro looks and delivered with ironic twists, I am reminded of English character traits. The idea of restraint: the old stereotype about maintaining a distance from your feelings. Being English is also about the way that one expresses oneself, using words in a self-conscious and ironic way. The best English designers are not necessarily models of restraint, but they have a tendency to design from the head, rather than with real sensuality. Vivienne Westwood, for instance, is an iconoclast; whether she is using tartans or creating bustles or printing classical paintings on to bustiers, her real enthusiasm seems to be for their impact, not their beauty. Paul Smith manages to sell the romance of English menswear by conjuring up a vision of a Playboy Lad, someone like Michael Caine, as he was in the sixties. In both cases, their designs can almost be expressed better in language than in fabric.

Perhaps this version of Englishness is not so deeply rooted. The ironic picking-and-mixing of styles may have been a passing phase, it might be coming to an end. I can easily find other younger role models, like Alexander McQueen. Or I could describe myself as British, if being English becomes a handicap. Couture was invented by an Englishman, Frederick Charles Worth of Lincoln, but he had to move to Paris to open a salon.

As I move deeper into the warehouse, I begin to come across some of Osano's own samples. Having seen his designs before, if only in photographs, I am not going to forget his style. There are the lurid colours, the flimsy materials that can only be filled by a steamy imagination – a real-life body could never do it. Osano's problem as a designer is unusual, almost the opposite of the English problem. He doesn't design from the head, he designs purely from sensual feelings. And I am sure that his sensual feelings burned out a long time ago. He barely notices other people, and it is not because he is in love with himself. He keeps looking at himself in mirrors, but it is only because he is ashamed.

If Osano can no longer get interested in women, maybe he should think about menswear. I keep on rummaging through the racks, hoping to find something for myself. At least another suit, so that I can get the one that I am wearing laundered. But I don't expect there to be anything. If it's possible, Osano is even worse with men than with women. Both Fred and Etienne make him sullen and uncomfortable. As we were driving to the atelier, I could feel a hum of tension running beneath the warm-air blower. Even his driver, Vincente, makes Osano nervous. The night after his show in Paris, when he was stretched out on Louise's bed with his champagne bottle, he could talk to me. But I am thirty years younger and obviously impressed by him. And he was drunk.

I keep on through the rails, hoping that I will find a suit that I can alter myself. The warehouse ends in a roll-down steel door, large enough for a wagon to pass through. There is a further set of clothes racks here, the clothes piled on them haphazardly, unlabelled and uncoded. I only have to glance at them to know what they are.

It is the Paris collection, all safe and accounted for in Osano's own warehouse. It's not as though I am surprised that the theft was an inside job.

9

Osano doesn't want to return to the villa tonight. He emerges from his office in a fury as I am making espresso for the seamstresses and Lipton's Yellow Label for the British girls trying to decide whether any of them know about the stolen collection in the warehouse below. Osano shouts at me to put everything down, we are going to Milan. It is too far to travel to Courmeyer.

'I don't have time to waste my time like that.'

He says something similar in Italian to Vincente, staring across the man's head as he speaks.

Osano doesn't explain either why he is angry or why we cannot go back to the villa. He isn't interested in talking; he says maybe two words to me on the journey from the industrial estate to the city. I am worried about leaving Louise on her own in the mountains. If she gets bored, she might invite Etienne to stay with her, so that he can feed her worse drugs than cocaine.

I try to talk to Osano but he shakes his head and puts on his sunglasses. The overcast sky is already turning to dusk, but I like the glasses. It is the first time that Osano has worn anything that I wished I owned. The glasses are a vintage Italian design: minimal, with elliptical lenses suspended from gold wire frames, the kind of wraparounds that *nouvelle vague* heroes would wear. I think of Jean-Paul Belmondo and the way that his eyes would flit behind his glasses as he spoke longingly of America and Italy, as though his dream home were somewhere between the two. Without realising that he was already there, it was the space that he lived in, his own version of Paris. Osano's eyes also flit around, but I cannot imagine what he is thinking about.

I have been to Milan once before, and although I barely know it, I recognise the junction to the Via Alessandro Manzoni as we sail across the top of it. A little farther on, Vincente edges left into the courtyard of an old palazzo, pausing while a dark-suited man opens the iron gates. The courtyard is a column-lined cloister with a fountain at its centre. It could be a beautiful garden; instead it is a residents' carpark. There are three other cars sitting on the yellow cobblestones, a Ferrari, a small Fiat and a Lexus. It's a reminder that people really live and work in these buildings. The palazzo is divided into offices and apartments and Osano has a penthouse on the top floor. He nods to the gateman as we step into the elevator. Finally, he turns to me and says, 'So are you going to work for me?'

'What?'

'You've seen what it's like. I can't trust anyone.'

'You want me to spy on your staff?'

Osano jabs the air with his house key. 'Don't forget Fred. I especially want you to spy on him.'

He unlocks the door to his apartment and wanders down the corridor ahead of me. He has already disappeared round a corner before I think to move on. I drift in the same direction, then detour through an arch into a sitting room cum study. The apartment is not what I would have imagined. His country villa had a holiday home feel, bright with a mix of contemporary and oriental. I thought his Milan apartment would be modern; perhaps seventies, reflecting the years when he was at his most successful. But the feel is English, almost academic. The living room has a set of those oxblood leather chairs with the deeply embossed buttons that appear in television dramas about gentlemen's clubs and university common rooms. After sitting in one for forty-five minutes, I begin to think that they are not so horrible after all. They are more comfortable than I had expected.

Osano's walls are lined with bookcases. I am not surprised to see books, but I imagined he would use them as soft furnishings: a few photograph books and art monograms, some classics in leather, and all of them carefully arranged. Osano's shelves are a jumble of paperbacks and hardbacks in haphazard piles, a reader's order rather than an interior designer's. I think of myself as well read: it is all relative, and my best friend is a dyslexic. Osano is in a different league, and even when I recognise a particular name he has many more books than I had ever known the author had written. Osano seems to have a completist streak.

I am thinking about his job offer, and how to turn it down, so it is a long while before I realise what is strange about his collection. Every book is in the original language: French, Italian, Spanish, German and English. Although the Chekhovs are in Italian and his complete works of Freud are in the English Pelican series. Maybe that is a deliberate design touch, the out-turned spines a splash of colour among the disorder around them.

Osano eventually returns with a whisky decanter. The decanter is square and cut into deep patterns, a sign that he takes the academic look too seriously. He walks around me to a sideboard while I continue to sit, staring at the united colours of Freud.

'Call your sister.' He throws a roving phone at me. I catch it.

'Why?' I need to call Louise anyway, to tell her that I am not going to return tonight. But I sense that isn't the reason why Osano wants me to make the call.

'Amanda is definitely doing Ralph Lauren in New York. I've just heard that she'll sign a contract for the Berardi shows when she's over here.'

I shake my head as if I don't understand, but I am just buying time to think. Osano is not a naturally devious man; if he were, it would not be so easy to tell when he is being duplicitous. There is definitely something strange about him at the moment.

'There are other models.'

'Not many that can guarantee my collection is in every magazine and half the world's newspapers, and will still agree to work for scale.' Osano is fingering the side of his face. I have read that liars play with their faces.

'What about a celebrity instead?'

'An Italian weather girl? How about one of those girls that wave their hands over the prizes in a quiz show? I can get one of those, easy. But the American magazines will never run her picture.' He dips a finger in his whisky and brushes the liquid over a back tooth. I realise that he may actually have a dental problem, perhaps an abscess. Maybe that is why he seems so sly. 'It's got to be a celebrity that Americans recognise. Or at least the daughter of an American celebrity. And what the fuck is a celebrity anyway? A friend of Donatella. Why doesn't America have real stars any more?'

'Who's a real American star?'

'Chaka Khan. I met her once. She's so beautiful. Beautiful and barely a metre and a half tall. That's why we use models.' Osano is nodding earnestly. But he ends by shaking his head. 'They're like white mice – they are all cute, they all look identical, and they all sleep with each other. But I'm stuck with them. Call your sister.'

'Let's talk about my job first.'

'Oh, right. This is it, then? Now we start bargaining. You want to shake me down?'

I tell him: 'I don't want a job, Osano. I want to go back home.'

'Really?' He sits himself down on a chair. 'I've got such a fucking toothache.' So I was right.

'I want to go to college, Gianni. I have to apply this month.'

'I thought you wanted to be a designer.'

'I do. I'm applying to St Martin's.'

'Forget that. Work for me.'

I get defensive: 'St Martin's is the best.'

'It's okay. But getting experience is the best. How old are you? Twenty-one, two?' I don't correct him. 'If you get a place, you'll be twenty-five when you graduate. But no one will see your degree show, so no one is going to sponsor you. You'll end up looking for a job: the same job that I'm offering. Pretty soon you'll be thirty with all the experience in the world except that you will have never done a collection. Which is the only experience that counts.'

'If I work for you now, I still won't have that experience.'

'Listen. Work for me for two years. I'll speak directly to St Martin's, and you'll get on the masters programme.

You leave college at the same time, except that you've got a masters degree, you've got connections and people notice your final show.'

'How can I do a masters without a first degree?'

'How did Alexander McQueen do a masters without doing high school?' Osano has all the answers. 'You really want a degree, enrol in college in Milan. The work you do for me will count as course modules – in two years you will have all you need for a degree.'

He has won the argument. I feel like I should be thanking him just for the offer. He senses it too.

'If you really want a degree, take mine: anthropology, University of Roma, class of '72. I'm serious. I hope it does you all the good it did me.' He takes another gulp of whisky, swilling it around his tooth. He knows I am hooked. 'Call your sister.'

The villa is number two on the speed dial. I am about to press it. But I stop. 'Louise has to come to Milan.'

'Why?'

'Because I'm here. How am I supposed to keep an eye on her if she's in the mountains?'

'Leave her there. Keep her out of trouble and concentrate her mind.'

I get it now. It wasn't just the toothache that was making him seem so odd, he really was trying to be devious. He wants me to be his spy in Milan. He keeps Louise bored and lonely in Courmeyer until she does what he wants. We'll be two prisoners, both working on his project.

'You think Louise can't get into trouble in Courmeyer?' I am angry now. 'It's a holiday resort for rich people, she can do anything she wants there. I want her in Milan.'

Osano doesn't say anything, he just waves the decanter

in my direction as he fills his glass. I shake my head. I don't want to drink. He must have been playing for time while he thought because eventually he says: 'Vincente can bring her here in the morning.'

Osano decides that we will all live together in his apartment, at least until after the shows are over. Each morning I wake and do what I can to acclimatise to the day. I have my own ritual that has nothing to do with the strange bedroom; it is the same mostly every morning, even when I am back home. I lie face down in the bed and imagine someone firing a rifle into my back. Part of the ritual is to imagine the exact place the gunman would choose, just to the left of centre beneath my shoulder blade. Now that I have fired a pistol, I can even imagine the sound. I lie completely still, feeling the weight of my body on the bed, imagining my flesh being torn to pieces. It sounds horrible, I know. But I often wake feeling so low that it is the easiest way to both shake and comfort myself. I can barely remember the days when I woke and wanted to swing out of bed.

I always shower quickly, unless it is one of my shaving days. Then I trot along the corridor to eat breakfast with Osano. He is either reading the Italian papers or scrolling through *Women's Wear Daily* on-line, using a palmtop on the breakfast table. Once the New York shows start, he talks me through the press coverage. I listen and wonder how our collection will be received. I am already thinking of the show as 'ours', something that I am deeply involved in. The truth is the pressure is getting to me. But work is not the reason that I keep retreating to a pretty grim place. I guess I am the type to internalise things, and then when I reach a certain point, and I am filled with all the things that I have never said, I turn all the frustration around. And turn it into a blow-myself-to-pieces game.

It doesn't mean that I can't function, or that anyone else can tell I am unhappy. When Osano starts translating the Italian reviews to me, or turns the papers around to show me the photographs, he really does have all my concentration. He reads Suzy Menkes and skims over photographs of the models: Kimberley Stewart, daughter of Rod Stewart, or Elizabeth Jagger, daughter of Mick and Jerry.

He takes a sidelong look at an interview with Paris Hilton, the hotel heiress, in my copy of the *Guardian*, and grunts: 'What's her sister called? Bangkok?'

I find a picture of Bibi in a bronze evening dress taken at the Caroline Herrera show. She looks good, her body running diagonally across the photograph, relaxed but looking as though it only needs to tighten to swing out of the frame. I remember how much easier I found the mornings when she was around. But there is a far more prominent photograph of Amanda Van Hemstra, modelling at Ralph Lauren's show. It is carried in all the newspapers, both the Italian and the English. Osano stares at her for a long time before he throws the paper down. He says, 'A collection like that is so professional, but the profession is marketing: make a collection you can describe in a word or two. This year it's pony club.'

Amanda is wearing a tailored hacking jacket and trousers with soft leather patches sewn into the inside thigh. Riding trousers.

'How do you describe Yves Saint Laurent? When he's at his best, there aren't words. Even at his worst, all you can say is that it's Saint Laurent.'

Osano always manages to work himself into a temper by the end of breakfast. Vincente picks us up at nine o'clock, too early for me ever to see Louise. I never even hear her feet or the sound of a toilet or shower. But each lunch hour, I borrow a car from someone at the atelier and drive back to Milan to meet her. Any of the women at work will lend me their car when I ask. They have such an easy way with cars. It is strange at first when you're used to a more careful English attitude, but they are only cars after all.

Parking is such a problem, I always park back at the palazzo and meet Louise either in the Four Seasons Hotel on the Via Gesù or at Armani's new department store on the Via Alessandro Manzoni. The store is co-owned by Sony and has a Japanese noodle bar. That tends to be our preferred venue. We can almost afford to eat there. Not that I have much time – the journey to the city leaves only twenty minutes for lunch.

Louise spends her day arranging her evenings. I spend mine listening to Osano. It is a week before I realise that he is trying to read my *hmm*s and *err*s and head movements to discover what I really think about his designs. I don't trust his abilities to read body language so I start telling him the truth. I also work; not on the real collection but on rough versions, made from stiff plain cotton and pinned to mannequins. I am very fast, mostly because I have no skills to slow me down. One thing I am good at, though, is getting Osano to explain himself. He is not particularly good at sketching and he needs to be questioned closely before his intentions become clear. Perhaps his sketches are so bad because his ideas are not even clear to himself; they become a lot sharper as he stands there waving his arms to convey his enthusiasms. Soon I am following him around the atelier so that when he needs to talk to anyone I can prod him with the questions that they won't ask. His relationship with all his workers is so dysfunctional. I hope that I am good humoured enough to be tolerated by everyone, rather than just being seen as Osano's office boy. But to make sure, I spread as many Osano stories as I can.

I tell everyone about Osano's inability to remember faces, or even distinguish them. He is always losing his temper with waiters, because he cannot remember who took the order or who brought the wine. And there are his superstitions: Osano will loudly describe himself as an atheist but has an African carving in his bedroom that he treats the same way any Catholic would treat a Madonna. He makes a vague wave, a kind of economical version of the sign of the Cross, before he kisses his finger and touches the carving's round, fertile belly. And he looks painfully guilty as he does it.

Or his fear of dentists, which I discover because I have to accompany him to the surgery as an independent observer. As though I would recognise dental malpractice if I saw it.

In the evenings, Osano takes me to his restaurants. He doesn't cook and only keeps a maid in the villa, which he rarely visits. Over one of the meals, I learn that he once owned the whole of his palazzo. The atelier used to be on the first three floors; he lived above the shop. He was forced to make economies, which is how he ended up on an industrial estate. In the streets around his apartment are the headquarters of Prada, Armani, Gianfranco Ferré, Ferragamo and others.

Osano is on the fourth course of what will be a five-course meal for him, a two-course for me. He is already calling for the third bottle of wine. I have had two glasses. His lips are stained red from the Valpolicella and swollen into a sloppy grin, the remains of the dentist's novocaine. He is no one's idea of an elegant couturier, although I know that he still has a few private clients; he conducts the fittings in his apartment, the location of his new atelier remaining a dark secret.

Osano pauses, his knife flattening a dark piece of pigeon. He is about to ask me a question. I expect it to be the usual: his consternation at my thinking my meal is over before I even get to the meat course. Instead, he asks: 'Have you heard from Fred?'

We both saw Fred the previous day. He called by the apartment before Vincente took us to work. So I shake my head.

'He hasn't called you?'

'He called the studio. I passed him over to you.'

Osano nods his head. 'You know that he has the insurance money?'

I haven't heard. 'That's great news.'

'Yes, it is.'

We sit and nod at each other. We aren't putting all this work into the collection for no reason.

Osano says, 'Do you know how I met Fred?'

'In New York, after Gina resigned?'

'I'd gone to meet some moneymen. It didn't work out, they couldn't understand the nature of the business. Then I got a call from Fred who tells me he heard about my problem. He offers to raise the money for me.'

'How had he heard about your problem?'

'It took me a while to discover. He was the bodyguard to one of the men: he was actually at the original meetings but I didn't notice him. He came to me later with a deal – he would fund my shows all year, spring-summer and autumn-winter. With each successful show, I would give him an interest in the company.'

'Funding them how? Through insurance scams?' I stop. I have never told Osano that I discovered his stolen collection at the studio. I do not know how much Osano knows about Fred's methods.

Osano nods. 'I heard the collection was recovered. But the insurance has paid out, so why get into technical complications? Fred did a good job, considering he has no resources. But it can't go on like this.'

Osano is looking crafty again, his anaesthetised lip sliding down to help form a rivulet of wine. I don't like the way his mind is working: he is already wondering how he can double-cross Fred. Suddenly, working in Milan for two years no longer seems like a good idea. I remember that Osano's original plan was to keep Louise prisoner in Courmeyer while I lived under his nose in Milan.

I decide that I had better get my passport back as soon as possible. If we need to escape, I don't want to have to rely on an Italian fake.

After a meal with Osano, I either run or catch a tram across town to meet Louise. The bars where she meets her friends are either in the south-west of the city, around the canals, or in a quadrant either side of the *Giardini Publici*, not far from the infamous Hollywood nightclub. Both are quite a way from the *quadrilatero d'oro* of the fashion district. Louise has a large number of Milanese acquaintances, among them stylists and photographers but also students and shop assistants and some other sleazy characters who have no real jobs. She knows fewer people who actually work for designers, I don't know why since her Italian is so good. I try my best to learn as we move from bar to bar. Some of the places are smart, others are bare enough to be youth clubs and, even though the weather is cold, we will stand outside in the street with the scooters and the constant beeping of cellphones. In a dark bar that could be an old Goth club, Louise asks me to buy the drinks while she slips off to the toilet with a man who claims to work in PR, using the English term but not, I am sure, accurately. I stand by a fibreglass pillar, made to resemble a stalagmite, and try to follow the conversations around me, my eyes on the toilet door, waiting for Louise to come sniffling back.

Most nights, I break off before she moves on to one or another of the nightclubs. I walk back to Osano's if I have missed the last tram. The Italians think that Milan is ugly but they are probably spoiled by their other cities: it can be beautiful walking through Milan at night, even when it's raining. Coming from the Porta Ticinese, I run through a triumphal arch and up a street lined with Corinthian pillars, the only remains of a Roman temple. Spotlights throw the shadows of the pillars across the road. I count my strides between them as I jog up to the Duomo. One morning it was almost light and the sound of my feet on the coloured stones of the piazza sent clouds of pigeons up into the air. They wheeled across the face of the cathedral and settled on the far side of the square.

From the Duomo, I continue along a pedestrianised shopping street, through San Babila, and now every step is carrying me past stores whose names I could see anywhere in the world, but which actually belong here in Milan.

Osano is usually in his bedroom by the time I let myself into the apartment. Sometimes I sit for a while, hoping that my body will stop buzzing and begin to unwind for sleep. I nearly always read. I began by choosing French novels but each day I would read a paragraph of a different book and then forget what I was doing. Now I read case studies from Freud which work as little fairy stories, one short tale a night. Then I go to my room, clean my teeth, undress and get into bed.

I use different fantasies at night. With my head face down in the pillow, I imagine suffocating. Or I think about a machine that will put me to sleep. There are a dizzying number of them, the ones invented by the Dutch and American doctors who campaign for voluntary euthanasia, the ones illustrated on the Internet taken from a book by a Japanese man, and the ones used for executions in the States. I find the last ones the creepiest, because they are used on people who might not necessarily want to die. The electric chair fails so often and takes so long, it seems to me to be a torture machine that kills only as a side effect. I remember reports from Amnesty International about the uses of electrocution by Israeli security services during interrogations, and the story of the electrified iron bedstead used by General Pinochet's regime in Chile. The gas chamber is better, like the easy death of running a car motor in a sealed garage. Lethal injection seems the worst. I imagine a reluctant man strapped to a bed, forced to watch as a needle is pushed into veins that years of alcohol, drug abuse and bad diets have turned into thickened ropes.

The perfect machine must be the guillotine, and I don't understand why it is never used in those countries like China, Saudi Arabia or the United States that perform hundreds of executions a year. I guess the Americans prefer to leave a complete body behind for burial, either for religious reasons or to spare the dead man's family the sight of a dismembered corpse. But then I don't understand why they use the electric chair, which leaves serious burns and explodes the victim's eyeballs. Gas and poison leave their marks on the skin, too. I imagine the Americans want the illusion of a hygienic death more than they want to be humane. It's a way of marketing death.

I have to prepare every aspect of my execution in detail. Sometimes I realise that I have a small technical aspect out of place and have to start again from the beginning, making sure that I get it exactly right. If I didn't, it would lose all of its power.

These fantasies sound more disturbing than they are. They aren't much different to the lyrics of nu-metal bands. But the music that brings me the most comfort is on the RZA's CD for the film *Ghost Dog: The Way of the Samurai*. Between tracks, the voice of Forest Whitaker reads extracts from the Hagakure: *The Way of the Samurai is found in death. Meditation on inevitable death should be performed daily. Every day when one's body and mind are at peace, one should meditate upon being ripped apart by arrows, rifles, spears and swords. Being carried away by surging waves. Being thrown into the midst of a great fire. Being struck by lightning. Being shaken to death by a great earthquake. Falling from thousand-foot cliffs. Dying of disease. Committing seppuku on the death of one's master. And every day without fail one should consider himself as dead.*

When I first heard these words, I felt a wave of exhilaration, even though I never believed that the passage was genuine. I assumed it had been written by Jim Jarmusch for the script of his film. I know now that it is: it really is the code of the Samurai. The reading appears on voice-over in the film and the sleeve notes credit the original source and the translator. But lying in my bedroom, I assumed that Jarmusch had at least embellished the passage; the list seems too long. But even the length helps, because it is also funny. As a mantra, it works in the same way that the phrase *Bonjour tristesse* does, when I say it to my face in the bathroom mirror each morning.

I often play the CD. The spoken passages help to create a sense of distance. If my feelings can be put into words, then they stop being an inner craziness that I cannot shake. The words are about meditation; it is just something I do that helps me to relax. If I wanted to die, I could easily do it. When I want to sleep, I empty my mind.

10

The weekend of the end of New York Fashion Week and the start of London is a difficult time for Louise. The newspapers carry pictures of three of the best known British models, Stella Tennant, Erin O'Connor and Karen Elson, modelling at the only New York show to fly in the face of the Manhattan-goes-to-the-Hamptons collections seen everywhere else. The alternative New Yorker, as modelled by the British, has a neurotic and urban sexiness and wears tight mini-dresses with slashes and zips. She has tough-girl cap sleeves or wasted-girl overlong sleeves. Louise should have done a show like that, being more neurotic, sexier, tougher and probably more wasted than Stella or Erin or Karen.

I only work a half-day that Saturday, and instead of meeting Louise in a store or hotel I return to the apartment where she is eating breakfast and crying angrily over the fashion reports. I don't need a brother's intuition to guess the problem.

'It's not too late to go to London, Louise.'

'Yes it is.'

'But after New York, the signs look really good for London. The newspapers think the shows are going to be more interesting. I'm sure you could get work.'

'I told you. It's too late.' She sounds adamant. But then she asks, 'What would we do for money?'

I don't know. I don't have any and I am not exactly

being paid for the work I do for Osano. But perhaps Fred would lend me some, if I think of something to offer him in return.

'I might be able to get some.'

'Not off Osano. He is going to hold us to ransom until I make sure Amanda does his crappy show.'

She is right. 'Has Amanda said anything yet?'

She shrugs. 'I'm supposed to hear tomorrow.'

She is hiding something, but I know I won't be able to dig it out of her. When I ask whether she wants to come into the city with me she refuses. I am sure she will go anyway, if only to avoid Osano. But I don't say anything. I have to run, anyway, to catch the General Post Office on Piazza Edison before it closes. As I reach the locked doors, I wonder why I even tried. There is a special system in Italy: anything official is closed any time you need it. I was hoping to pick up my passport, which Stan was sending care of the post office rather than direct to Osano's apartment. I am worried that Stan might have wrongly addressed the envelope. When I telephoned him in his studio at college, I told him to get someone else to write down the address. He said, 'Like who?' I told him, 'Like someone who isn't dyslexic.' As he dropped the phone, I heard a scuffling in the background and raised voices until Stan came back on the line to tell me that there might be a non-dyslexic student doing an MA in sculpture. I had to wait while he found her.

Milan is beginning to gear up for Fashion Week. A lot of the shows will be held in the Fiera, the giant expo centre to the west of the city. But some public buildings and museums are closed for redecoration ahead of parties. The designers with their own palazzos have vans parked on the roadside, delivering pot plants or lighting rigs for their shows. Even the models are beginning to arrive, so many of them pale young girls from eastern Europe. There are some terrible rumours: that a fifteen-year-old Slovakian model was raped by three men in a nightclub during last October's shows. The city prosecutors are said to be about to bring charges against her agency: the agencies are supposed to provide chaperones for the youngest models. From what I've seen and heard on my nights out with Louise, these chaperones can be the same people who provide Louise with cocaine.

Apart from all this, the city is quiet. There are no tourists in mid-February. When I notice that some of the museums are closing, I telephone ahead to book for Leonardo da Vinci's *The Last Supper* and manage to get a viewing slot two hours later. I walk to the church slowly, stopping for espressos or cigarettes that I don't really want and thinking all the while about mutant turtles. When I arrive, the fifteen people sharing my tour are Americans; just ordinary everyday people rather than the wealthy Americans that I usually see in Europe. They get into an argument with the women on the bookings desk as they discover that the tickets are non-refundable. They have two spare. I realise that everyone in the group is of Italian descent; they scream and shout a lot, which I have never seen the Milanese do. Apart from Osano.

There is a long strained moment as we wait at the doors to the old refectory of the Santa Maria della Grazie, and not just because the doors are sliding air-locks, like those on spaceships. The Americans are suddenly very quiet. I don't think any of us know how we are going to react, and there is a definite mood of anxiety. We are stranded, paused before a possible life-changing event. And there's the self-doubt: are we good enough or sensitive enough to actually recognise a transcendental experience? It's not quiet, it is disquiet. Then we step through the airlock and it's there, in front of us. *The Last Supper* fills an entire wall.

The painting has an immediate cinematic power; it even has the same dimensions as Cinemascope. And it is so full of ideas and narrative that it is impossible to take in. My eyes have to travel backwards and forwards simply in order to read it and, as I do, the drama of Christ's betrayal seeps through. I don't actually speak to the others, but by the time I step back to ask myself what I really think, I know that the painting has got under their skin, just as it has got under mine. But not in the way that I originally thought it would.

Stan would never understand how I could value fashion over painting or sculpture. As far as he is concerned, fashion is somehow less than a real art. But that is because he has a dogmatic streak; he thinks in terms of great art and total crap. I know that I am more insecure than Stan. That is the reason why fashion is so important to me. I am not dogmatic, and so taste is something I worry about. In real life, we bury our insecurities, otherwise we would be destroyed. But in the fashion world, we have to risk displaying them. That's how it felt, looking at *The Last Supper* in a group of people that I had nothing in common with. The anxiety was there, but rather than bottle it up we left it crackling and sparkling until it turned into something else. Beauty out of anxiety: is that a transcendental experience?

I return to the apartment in both an edgy and an exhilarated state: buzzing with ideas. Louise is out and hasn't left any message about where I can find her. I wouldn't care, but Osano is angry. He wants to have a final showdown with her: will Amanda Van Hemstra appear at his show or not? I try to reassure him, telling him that we will certainly know tomorrow. But he still wants to see Louise.

She doesn't return at all that night and I have to watch over Osano until he stumbles through his bedroom door, dead drunk.

Louise telephones after lunch on the Sunday. When Osano realises who I am speaking to, he says, 'Ask her. I am serious this time.'

'He wants to know about Amanda.'

'Is he standing there?'

'Yes.'

'Okay. Well, wait a minute and listen. It looks like we might be able to swing it but only if Osano goes personally to speak to Etienne.'

'Etienne!'

I wish I hadn't said anything. Osano explodes behind me.

'That fuck.'

Louise says, 'You have to make him do it. Etienne will be at Hollywood around midnight, so make sure Osano is there.'

I know that Osano will hate going to Hollywood. I ask her, 'Is this really going to work?'

'You'd better hope so. I've heard Amanda will sign a contract for the Berardi shows tomorrow, so it has to be sorted tonight.'

I click off the phone and tell Osano what I know.

'Hollywood? How are we going to talk in there?' Osano takes a gulp of his post-lunch wine. 'The bastard knows how to make me look bad. He is going to turn up three hours late. Meanwhile everyone is staring at me wondering why Osano is waiting for a deadbeat photographer.'

He drops into one of his leather chairs and begins thinking; I can practically see a think bubble above his head.

'I've got to meet a financier. You go to the disco and when Etienne shows, you call me.'

'Okay,' I say. And then: 'What financier?'

Osano looks at me, evidently weighing things. I still feel that he basically trusts me.

'Financiers with money. They are venture capitalists though they also own Internet things.'

'Is this something that Fred has set up?'

'This is something that Fred doesn't know about.' Osano's stare seems to flatten. 'And I don't want him to know about. He's keeping my show on the road. But it can't go on like this.'

We eat at Bagutta's, a 1920s restaurant close to Osano's apartment. So close that we walk a long way around. All the shops are closed, but inside the lights are blazing. And it feels busy walking on the streets. There are plenty of people strolling along the pavements, talking in pairs or threesomes, some walking their dogs. It seems that there is no one in the whole town capable of walking by a shop window. Again, Osano is the exception. He mostly ignores everything, but he is such a slow walker that I have all the time I need to absorb the things I see in the windows. He stops once, in front of the window for the brand-new Paul Smith shop in the Palazzo Gallarati Scotti. Smith has filled his first window display with screwed-up copies of the *Financial Times*. Osano doesn't think it is much of a joke.

In the restaurant, Osano orders rapidly without reading the menu. When I try to catch the waiter's eye to ask a few questions and make a choice, Osano tells me that he has already ordered for me.

'You don't think I made a better choice than you would have done? I've only been eating here for twenty-five years.'

As we eat, I think about the coming rift with Fred, and whether Fred is as dangerous as I feel he is. I don't know whether Osano has a clearer idea than me as to what happened at customs in Geneva airport. I assume that Fred brought the stolen collection back aboard our plane and chose Geneva so there would be no Italian record of the contents of our luggage.

I ask, 'How is Fred supporting himself while he raises the money for your shows?'

'Smuggling,' Osano says. 'It's his day job.'

I feel my mouth drop open. I lose control of my fork and it splatters down on to the white tablecloth. Osano laughs.

'You think he's smuggling drugs? No way. He's smuggling money.'

'Oh.' I didn't know there was any law about bringing cash in and out of Paris. Or Switzerland, for that matter. 'Who is he smuggling money for?'

'Americans. I didn't ask for the details.' Osano wipes a piece of bread through the mix of oil and herbs – all that is left of a sea bass. 'But don't worry. Fred may be a crook, but he's crooked like the guys you see working market stalls. He isn't a gangster.'

I realise then that Osano has no idea. He is in his

own world where people like Osano triumph, no matter how drunk and clueless they are. He is an intelligent man, probably as intelligent as any other contemporary designer. He never seems to have lost that art school thing of wanting to stay up late talking about what he's read and what he's learned. When he found out that I was reading his Freud collection each night, before I went to bed, he started trying to test me. He began to ask questions about the conscious and the unconscious and then argue with my interpretations. I do like him. But he's the kind of friend you try to avoid, and I know that he is fast losing any sympathy he had within the industry. He is only getting more isolated as he gets more out of touch. He shouldn't be careless about Fred.

I wish Osano good luck with his potential backers. His appointment is scheduled for 10.30, which seems late. I would have assumed that businessmen keep to business hours, especially on Sundays. I guess I am not looking at things in the right way. Milan is like Cannes during the film festival, a huge trade fair, and it seems people make appointments when they can, right around the clock. Even though Fashion Week doesn't start for a week.

Before he gets in a taxi, Osano hands me his mobile and gives me a number where I can reach him.

It is barely past ten, and I do not need to be at Hollywood for almost two hours. There aren't many experiences as lonely as going to a nightclub on your own. So I walk. I turn left, heading for the glow of shop windows and a suitable café. But immediately a kind of dissatisfaction comes over me and I cannot choose anywhere. The perfect place would have to be the newest thing Milan has to offer, but also a totally

Milanese experience. I keep on walking, rejecting every bar I see until I decide I am in the wrong area. I hop on a tram for the Porta Ticinese, close to some of the bars that Louise has taken me to. Then I choose one at random, the bar of a canteen-like restaurant with a huge pillar in the middle shaped like a hand, holding up the roof.

Bibi will arrive in Milan soon. She has rung only twice during the past week, and because she is not going to London she has promised to arrive in Milan a few days before the start of the shows. She is not completely sure of her schedule. As I wait for the waiter to pour my orange juice, I scroll through the memories I have of Bibi and me skiing. I am drifting, staring out of the window at the people passing by.

I see Louise.

I run to the door and look down the street. She was with another woman, I am fairly certain it was Amanda Van Hemstra. I want to run after them but the bartender is standing at the centre of the bar and staring at me. My orange juice stands in front of him, on its paper coaster. I wonder whether to run back, hand him some money and then take off. But as I look back at the street, Louise is gone. I may never find her, no matter how long I run around. I return to my stool at the bar.

It is exactly midnight when I reach the nightclub. It is still fairly empty. I am feeling uncomfortable, mostly because I do not like the clothes I am wearing. And beneath the suit, I am still wearing yesterday's underwear and socks. Osano had a couple of T-shirts in my size at his home, still in their plastic wrappers. I am wearing one of those, but I didn't ask him for anything else. I go over to the bar and buy a rum and Coke and move into the shadows to drink it. I think Osano is probably right, Etienne will wait until about three in the morning before he shows up. I have so long on my own.

When the mobile goes off, I assume that it is Osano. I press the button and hear a short burst of Italian. I have no idea what it means, but I know it is Fred.

'Osano's not here. It's Jamie.'

'Jamie? So where's Osano?'

'I'm meeting him later.' I don't tell Fred what Osano is doing. I don't need to. I tell him the story of Etienne, what the deal is and why Osano sent me, explaining that he did not want to lose face by waiting alone.

'That prick Etienne. It's not going to help if Osano just crawls to him. This needs rethinking.'

Fred hums a tune on the line, then breaks into the full song. I am surprised: it is 'Ride On Time' by Blackbox. He laughs and asks me, 'You enjoyed that?'

After another moment he says, 'Okay. I can be there in a couple of hours. If Etienne shows first, keep him there until I turn up.'

'What about Osano?'

'Ring him, tell him there's a change of plan.'

Fred clicks off.

I call Osano immediately and tell him the new plan. He is disturbed when I say I've spoken to Fred, but when he grasps the situation he is actually relieved.

'Okay. Let Fred sort it out, it's more his thing. Just don't tell him who I am talking to. Or you're fucked.' My skin tightens when he tells me that. I really don't need to be threatened. I *could* walk on him.

The nightclub fills slowly, but only with men. I am the youngest person in the place by maybe a decade; I would say the average age is closer to thirty-five. When the women arrive, they arrive together as though a bus has landed at the door and emptied them all out. They are all models. No matter how many times I see packs of models together, I doubt that I will ever stop being surprised. A group of twenty or more tall and slim women, aged between fifteen and twenty-five years old, is so striking. It can leave you breathless. It doesn't matter if you think that your taste in women is different, that you relate particularly to the Lil Kim type or to Christina Ricci, or to Catherine Keener or Debbie Harry; if you ever see a group of models together, they will mess and confuse you. And when it's night-time, when they are beautifully dressed, the effect is so much more intense.

It is clear that the men were waiting for them to arrive. They begin to bristle, they emerge from the shadows at the corner of the room and move into position. They do it so slowly it could almost be a sequence from a film, played in slow motion. But they all do it. I am maybe slow myself. I realise that the men around me are trying to attract the attention of the few guys who arrived with the models. One man, a handsome business type of about forty standing close to me, simultaneously manages to point to a leather corner banquette and to signal to the bar. The two gestures are timed; he is indicating where he is sitting to one of the model's male chaperones and also ordering champagne from the waiter. The models are shooed towards his seat; he saunters over and is introduced around the circle. The introductions are still in swing as the bottles of champagne begin to arrive. I imagine that the businessman intends to take a model home later. He is both suave and rich and handsome: it would take a long while to appreciate that he is basically a sleaze.

I realise what is happening. The nightclub employs male hosts whose job is to bring in the models. These hosts are all similar looking, aged somewhere past their mid-twenties, with only their signature coiffure mistakes to distinguish them. There are all kinds of goatees, from the full muff to wispy musketeers. The eighties revival is echoed by the men's elaborate sideburns, some like the pointed dagger 'burns worn by the singer from Ultravox in his old videos. There are also ponytails and plaits, as well as waxed-down angel cuts. With so many interchangeable men around, it is a while before I notice Etienne. He is seated in an alcove with two teenage models, his camera on the table in front of him and his fingers drumming on the lens in case the girls have failed to notice it.

I slip into the booth and smile at the two girls.

'Hello, I'm Jamie.'

Etienne turns a heavy-lidded gaze my way. It is supposed to be nonchalant but I catch the heat behind it; he isn't heavy lidded enough.

The girls introduce themselves as Jenny and Sophie. Both speak in perfect, Danish-accented English.

Etienne says, 'Why are you here?'

'Osano told me to wait for you.' I have decided to say nothing about Fred. 'He's at a meeting and it's running late.'

'He'd better get here before I find something more interesting to do.' He nods slightly to one of the Danish girls.

I say, 'Should I buy everyone a drink?'

'Yeah. Do that.'

The girls are drinking vodka tonics. Etienne is drinking Jim Beam. I go to the bar with Osano's money and return in a few minutes. Already Etienne is leaning over to whisper in one girl's ear. Her friend is on edge because she is suddenly excluded. They are so young, I wonder whether this could be their first big Fashion Week. I assume they are not close friends – it would be too much of a coincidence for them to have known each other before they got on to a model agency's books. I guess Etienne is calculating on this, casing them for insecurities.

Etienne swivels out of the booth and the girl slides along to follow him. As she moves, her friend asks where she is going.

Etienne answers for her. 'Dance.'

I know that he is lying. There is no one on the dance-floor and Etienne isn't here to get the party going. They head towards the toilets, so it must be a drug call.

The girl looks at me and smiles in a brave kind of way. She asks whether I am a photographer.

'No. I'm . . .' It is going to be the first time I give myself a job description and I am suddenly embarrassed by the sound of it. '. . . I'm working as Gianni Osano's assistant. I'm pretty new.'

'How old are you?'

'Twenty. I was twenty about two weeks ago.'

'How old is Etienne?'

'I don't know.'

'Jenny is fourteen.'

It's a moment before I think to close my mouth. I don't know why I am surprised; it doesn't seem so long ago that I was in the fourth form. I probably did worse things at fourteen than Jenny will do in the toilet with Etienne. But I don't think I can sit here while it happens.

'I'll go,' I say.

The girl is right beside me as I push through the toilet doors. It's pretty easy to guess where they are – there is only one locked cubicle. But I don't have a plan.

I stop. Sophie looks at me. In the quiet we hear Etienne say, 'Move over. I need to take a piss while I'm here.'

It is one way to introduce your penis into a situation. I wouldn't say it is the classiest way. I move softly to the door and use the edge of a coin to twist the bolt back.

The cubicle door swings open.

My main regret, when I look, is that I catch sight of Etienne's penis. Granted, he is waving it around, but I could have avoided looking down.

Etienne's sleazy expression just fades; it is a moment before he looks shocked. Jenny started off looking shocked. Her expression turns to relief as she takes her chance to slip out of the cubicle and join Sophie. The girls head for the exit, glancing back over their shoulders as they push through the door. I don't know why, but they both look apologetic. That doesn't make sense.

I don't even try to pretend the cubicle was unlocked. I just lean back against a washbasin and let it take my weight. Etienne zips up and finishes the remains of Jenny's line from the cistern top.

He wipes his nose with the back of his hand as he steps towards me. 'Mr White fucking Knight.'

Etienne is not a heavy man and he is no taller than me. But I still think he could lift me into the air if he took a swing at me. I am pretty sure that he won't, though.

I say, 'You're supposed to be the man who delivers Amanda. If you're fucking schoolgirls, she might get annoyed.'

'Why should that slut get annoyed?' He pinches his nose and sniffles. There are tears in his eyes. If the quality of the cocaine is so poor, he must be pretty low on the drug chain: a bottom-snorter.

'I'm just saying she must be keen on you to pass up a Berardi contract and work for Osano.'

'She isn't doing it for me. Your sister fixed it up. Amanda is only doing the show because Louise asked her.'

This is going over my head. 'How do you fit in?'

'I get Osano to write a cheque. So long as he pushes some cash my way, Louise will make sure Amanda does his tired-ass show.' Etienne is now checking his eyes in the mirror, pulling down the skin to check the pink on the inside. 'I am broke. You believe that?'

Maybe I am too slow. 'All Louise has to do is ask and Amanda will do the show, but she's fixed it so that you get paid.' Saying it out loud, it makes sense. 'You and Louise split the money.'

Louise is trying to make extra money from Osano without him knowing. With him actually being grateful to her. It is definitely Louise's style.

Etienne nods. 'All her idea.'

'Why are you broke?'

'Work's slow since New York. Someone spread a rumour I was trying to fuck the daughter of the editor of *Vogue*, so I got to stay in the cold for a while.' He shrugs. 'It sucks.'

'How much are you going to ask for?'

'You don't need to know that.'

'Okay.' I rub my wrist. I am not wearing a watch. 'What time is it?'

'Maybe two o'clock. I don't know.'

I say, 'Osano isn't coming. Fred is on his way over instead.'

Etienne quits messing with his face. He looks straight at me. 'What?'

At least he realises it is serious. I say, 'You can't try this scam with Fred. He'll see through it.'

'I don't like Fred.' He is shaking his head.

'Just tell him that Osano misunderstood the situation. Tell him that you only came by to confirm that Amanda will do the show.'

'So where does my fucking money come from?'

'Forget the money?'

I phrase it like a question. I know that I'm going to sound pretty weak if I try and threaten him. But he has to see sense. I figure that it will take Fred maybe five minutes to get the whole story out of Etienne.

'I'm not going to forget the money,' he says. 'And if that fuck Fred touches me, I'll make sure that Amanda never works for Osano again.'

This is really out of control. 'Come on, Etienne. Louise will still persuade Amanda to do the show. Fred will make her.'

He glares at me. 'Not if I tell her not to. Fred can do what he likes. Louise is still on my dick.'

I have never heard a Frenchman say *on my dick*. It sounds so ridiculous in a French accent that it is a moment before I realise what he is saying. That Louise likes him enough to jeopardise whatever is left of her career.

Etienne continues, 'Louise does what I tell her.'

I walk out of the bathroom.

I almost brush past the Danish girls without noticing. Sophie stops me and asks if I am all right. She says, 'Are you crying?'

I shake my head and then realise that I am. The

movement dislodges a tear which slides along my nose. But I know that I have to find Fred. He may already be inside the club.

He isn't in the bar area, or anywhere near the dance-floor. I take up a position on the stairs near the cloak-room, hoping that I will catch him as he enters.

About three minutes later, Etienne comes rushing past me. He doesn't see me and I don't speak.

He is almost on the street when I see Fred approaching the club doors. I have a reflex instinct to shout a warning, but even as my mouth opens I forget how to breathe. Etienne is turning left on the street when Fred puts out his hand and yanks him away. It happens so fast that Etienne seems to be snatched out of the air.

I run for the street. Fred is holding Etienne face down on the bonnet of a Jeep.

11

Etienne's mouth smudges into the rain droplets on the bonnet of a big silver Jeep. Fred holds his head down so that it slides across the paintwork in tight circles. In English, he says, 'Slow down, slow down. You're in such a hurry.'

I am panting as I run up.

'Shoot him.'

Fred looks at me with a *come again?* expression; he is sure that he has misheard. I can't catch my breath fast enough to tell him that he heard right. There are tremors running through my whole body, my eyes are flicking left and right in dry sockets. I need to find a plank of wood or a metal bar: while Fred holds him, I have my best chance to hit Etienne with something heavy. But there is nothing in the neat Corso Como except expensive cars and passers-by. So I lunge forward and punch Etienne on the side of his head. As his teeth scrape against my knuckles, Fred rears back in surprise. Etienne's head lifts up, I punch him again. This time I hurt my hand.

Fred throws up a hand and grabs my wrist. 'Jamie. Hey. Calm down.'

Fred has hold of me with his right hand, his left still on Etienne's neck. I am not even looking at Fred. I am staring at Etienne's mouth. I have split his lip. I let my arm relax so that Fred can feel the tension slip away. And then I kick out at Etienne, trying to get him in the crotch. I miss, kicking Fred in the knee instead. Now he lets go of Etienne.

'Ow. Jesus, Jamie.'

Etienne staggers, then, realising that he is free, starts running up the street. I am straight after him, not even surprised that I am so much faster. Within ten yards, I get a foot hooked under his and send him sprawling to the pavement. As he goes down, I kick him in the chest. I have never done that before. I feel my toes making contact through the soft leather of my shoes. The same shoes that Fred gave me, with the football-boot-like studs on the sole. As Etienne curls up to protect himself, I stamp on him twice, studs down.

Fred hauls me back. 'Christ, Jamie. When did you turn psycho?'

There is a blaze of noise through my head, telling me that no one has even seen psycho yet: *You think this is psycho? You want to stay around for psycho.* Fred is holding me by the back of my jacket. My feet lash out uselessly, missing Etienne's body.

'Let go of me.'

'Jamie. Jamie. Jamie.' Fred's voice becomes progressively calmer. 'Are you going to let me handle this? Yes? Yes or no?'

I need to give it some thought.

He continues to hold me.

'Okay,' I say. His hand wavers then drops.

I retreat to the roadside. Fred steps closer to Etienne and looks down. He says, 'Here's a surprise twist: I'm the good guy. So you listen, or I'll set my friend loose on you.'

He hauls Etienne up by an arm and lets him sit on the

edge of a pavement bin. On the far side of the street, a couple look over and walk on.

'So, Etienne, what's the problem with Amanda?'

I say, 'He wants money.'

'Shut up, Jamie.' Fred turns back to Etienne. 'You want money?'

Etienne doesn't know what to say. He shakes his head.

I won't leave it. 'Ask him where Amanda's staying.'

'Is this true, Etienne? Amanda's already in town?'

Etienne looks over at me. His mouth is filled with blood. He looks like he wants to rip me apart. Fred puts a finger on his chin and gently turns his head around.

'Is she already here, Etienne?'

Etienne says, 'No.'

'He's lying. He's a lying creep. I've seen her.' I cannot help shouting; my voice won't go any quieter.

Etienne is trying to plead with Fred, using his eyes, as though they could ever look innocent. 'I swear, she's not here.'

'Shoot him. Shoot him. Fucking, fucking . . .' I can't think of a word. 'Wet the motherfucker.'

Fred looks at me '*Wet him?* What does *wet* mean?'

It's a word Snoop uses; I heard it on one of his old CDs.

Fred says, 'This is getting stupid.' He turns from me to Etienne and back again. 'Okay, Jamie, I'm not going to shoot him. Etienne, yeah? I'm not going to shoot you. It's illegal. There are witnesses. And I don't have a gun. Are we clear?' Now his voice becomes harsher. 'But you, Etienne, are a lying scumbag. And I want the address where Amanda is staying.'

Etienne is silent. Fred moves closer to him, bending almost theatrically.

'Come on.'

Etienne shakes his head. Then says, 'Okay. Yes, she's in Milan.' He mentions an address I don't recognise. But then says, 'Close to the Porta Venezia,' and I realise that it is just around the corner from Osano's apartment.

Fred says, 'What's your connection? Amanda will do the show if you tell her, she won't if you don't?'

Etienne nods his head.

Fred stares at him. It is a long, slow beat; I can even hear him sucking the side of his cheek. Then he says, 'I don't think so.'

He turns to me.

'Come on, Jamie. We'll call around. Try and charm her.'

He walks back to the big Jeep that he had earlier pinned Etienne to. I hadn't realised it was his car. Behind us, Etienne pushes himself off the bin. I hear his feet, a tired limp down the street with the click of his high-heeled boots.

I say, 'He'll telephone ahead. She'll know we're coming.'

'It doesn't matter. I don't think he has any sway either way with Amanda.'

This is what I think, too. Even Etienne admitted that it would be Louise who persuaded Amanda to do the show. The interrelations between the three of them are so complex, though, I can't work it out. Why Amanda would trust Louise, when no one in their senses does. And why Louise could be smitten by a sad creep like Etienne.

Fred examines the front of his car, I guess for scratches

or bite marks. When he's happy, he beeps the doors and we climb inside.

'You went insane with that French guy,' he says. 'What's the problem?'

'He said something about my sister.'

Fred seems to accept that.

As we drive, I realise that we have made a mistake. We should have got the telephone number of the apartment where Amanda is staying. Fred sucks in his breath, then shrugs. There is nothing we can do now. He seems to be thinking the problem over, but when he next speaks, all he says is: 'That was where Maurizio Gucci was shot.' I turn my head quickly, but I doubt there was anything still to see.

We wind up sitting in Fred's Shogun Pinin – for Pininfarina, an Italian design company – staring at two blank steel doors. This is Amanda's apartment, but the doors are like the doors to a prison, with a smaller door cut into the right-hand side, large enough for a ten-year-old to walk through standing but too small for anyone else. There is no intercom.

'What shall we do, Fred?' I ask.

'I don't know. I might as well have shot Etienne, the good he's been.'

I am embarrassed by my earlier behaviour. I say, 'No. That wasn't a good idea.'

He shakes his head. 'No. I should have held him, let you beat him to death.'

I take out my packet of Marlboro Lights. Fred says, 'Not in the car.' So I step out on to the road and, after I have lit my cigarette, I go and look at the doors. They are solid, old, immovable. I step back into the street and look at the outside of the building. There are no ground-level windows and the ones higher up are barred and dimly lit. They appear to open on to a stairwell rather than an apartment.

Fred leans across the passenger seat and shouts at me through the open window. 'Hammer on them.'

It is approaching two in the morning. I am not beating on a pair of steel doors in the middle of the night, not in one of the wealthiest areas of a strange city.

I move off down the street, saying: 'I'll look around the side.'

There are more windows and some of them are lit. But they are all above head height and there are four storeys. I have no idea where Amanda might be and I cannot hear Louise's bark.

Fred pulls his car around the corner. I can feel him looking at me. I scuff my shoes a little and walk back to him.

'Fred?'

'Yes?'

'Where are you from?'

He laughs. I don't know why I asked, and so I shrug. There is enough light from the streetlamps for him to read the gesture.

'I'll tell you,' he says. 'My grandparents were Italian.'

'But you're not?'

This time he shrugs. 'My parents were Austrian.'

'You moved around a lot?'

'No. They all came from the same place: a little way outside Pula on the Dalmatian coast. When I was born, we were Yugoslavian. But my children are Croatian.' He breaks into a smile. 'Nice place. The best grappa and the best tartuffe in the world.'

'I didn't know you had children.'

'Of course.' As though I should have guessed. He looks back at the building. 'Let's forget this. Do you want a lift?'

I tell him that I'll walk. I am so close to Osano's place.

After he has gone, I return to the front of the building and perch on the stone block that forms the base of the portico around the steel doors. Etienne told us that Amanda was staying in apartment D, and I wonder if there is any way to deduce which is her window from this information. Supposing A and B were on the ground floor? I give up; there is no way that I can work it out.

Every so often, someone passes on the street. Each time, I stand and look interested in the door. After twenty minutes, a pair of feet slow down and stop beside me. I turn and look at a man of about sixty years old, with a toy dog on a leash.

He asks me whether there is a problem as he fumbles with his keys and opens the smaller door. I tell him that I don't speak Italian. And in English I say that my sister is staying there. He squints, and then his face breaks into recognition.

'Ah, the model?'

'Yes.' It stills surprises me that we look enough alike for people to see it immediately, even when we're not together.

'*Bene*. Louise's brother. Welcome.' Louise has only been here for one night, but the neighbours already know her. The man stoops through the door and holds it open for me. The dog leaps around my feet, as though I have been away for a long time and he expected to see me sooner. We pass through a second set of doors and enter the courtyard. The man points up to a row of large and brightly lit windows on the second floor. 'Apartment D. Say hello to your sister.'

He peels off to the left and his ground-floor apartment; the dog thinks for a moment before choosing to follow him rather than me. I head for the stairs.

There is music playing inside; I have to whack on the door several times with the flat of my hand. I wonder whether anyone can even hear me, but then Louise is standing in front of me in a punk T-shirt, saying, 'You took your time.'

'I couldn't get through the door.' I don't know why I am apologising. 'What are you playing at with Etienne?'

'Please, Jamie. Not now.'

She sounds so tired. Even the way she walks down the corridor, she seems to wisp along, like there is no weight left in her. I follow the floating T-shirt, reading the dates of an old Ramones tour: Europe, 1980. The T-shirt is older than me, faded to grey and scarred with what looks like buckshot. I don't know where she got it or how much she paid. She looks seventeen years old.

Being in the apartment is like being in someone's private space. Of course it is: it isn't ours. But I feel even more like a trespasser than I did in the Hôtel Costes in Paris or in the bar of the Four Seasons here. Stepping through the doors into the living room, I walk through squirls of wood, forest trees and flowers. The doors are genuine art nouveau, something that I have only seen in photographs before. I could be walking into someone else's fantasy. The fireplace is also wooden, also squirly and organic and throbbing in the flames of the fire.

'Where's Amanda?'

'Throwing a tantrum.' Louise is standing in the centre

of the room. Her arms are crossed against the Ramones eagle logo with its motto – *Hey Ho, Let's Go!* Her bare legs shudder, her knees are ticcing. She looks cold. The apartment is breathlessly warm.

I realise that Louise is on her own. I ask, 'Whose apartment is this?'

'Amanda's,' she says, then qualifies. 'Her dad's company's. He's in textiles.'

'She's rich *and* beautiful. You've fallen on your feet.' I am being spiteful. I still don't know the real relationship between Amanda and Louise.

'Don't.' She must be upset. Any place else in the world, any other time, she would counter-attack and I could be in tears. Now she is the one who is crying.

There is a strange smell, a heavy floral scent. It was always there, and in my mind I linked it to the carved wooden reliefs, as though the flowers around the fireplace were fanning the room with their fragrance. But it grows stronger as I follow it through to the bedroom. The bed is unmade and the bedspread lies over the floor. The smell comes from the bathroom. As I push open the door, I am hit by a wave of rich perfume. There is broken glass in the bath: this time, a spray bottle. I do not recognise the brand, but the fragrance is steeped in base notes, the kind of old-fashioned classic that seems to fill the air of black-and-white films. I have to sit on the edge of the bath and reach in to piece together the shards before I can read the name: Number One, not an old perfume, but a rare one. I have never smelled it or seen a bottle before. The alcohol in the perfume leaves a caustic burning in the shape of the tooth marks that Etienne left on my knuckles.

Louise is in the doorway. I hold up a piece of glass. 'Is this yours?'

'Amanda's: the perfume and the damage. I told you, she's in tantrum mode.'

I am not sure whether Louise is telling the truth; smashing glass in bathrooms is one of her tricks.

She is holding a bottle of grappa, 'Drink?'

'Yes.'

I expected her to hand me the bottle but she walks out of the bathroom. I follow her. She picks two weighted shot glasses off a table in the living room and pours a measure for each of us.

'Cheers.'

'Cheers, Louise.' I snap it back. After a deep breath that seems to reignite the alcohol, I say, 'I don't know what's going on. Who are you going out with, Amanda or Etienne?'

'Etienne? Not Etienne.'

As though he is only a joke. I would be reassured, but I know that she could be lying. 'Really?'

'Since my agents canned me, he's been useful to have around. That's all. He sometimes gets invites to places I can't, or he hears things that I don't.'

'He helps you shake down Osano.'

'Don't. I'm embarrassed I even tried.'

She fills another glass for herself and passes the bottle over. I pour another and drink it just as quickly. Through the scorch of the grappa on my throat, I hear her say, 'But Osano's being so manipulative.'

Which is true.

'And Amanda will really do the show if you ask her?'

'For sure. She wants to help me. And the twist is, if

she does Osano's show, it will get noticed. But if she does do it, then no one will notice I'm in the show too. I don't even know if I want to ask her.'

I don't know what to say. My sister looks so fragile and young, sniffling tears and rubbing her nose. 'Oh, Louise.'

'I'll ask her for you, baby,' she says. 'It'll be good for you, won't it? If Amanda does the show.'

'I guess.' She really is so sad. I step forward with my arms open and she slips into them. As we stand, she sobs into my shoulder, louder and louder until she reaches a peak and starts to fade. And then, through her sobs, she say, 'Osano's designs are so lame. Can't you get him to change them?'

I laugh. She does too. I say, 'I wish.'

'I need to go to bed.'

I nod. I know that I am close to collapsing. 'It's not far to Osano's.'

'No. Here,' she says. 'Stay too.'

She walks into the bedroom, leaving me perplexed. I have to ask, 'Is there only one bedroom?'

'Sleep with me tonight, Jamie. We can bunk up.'

She is on the bed already in her T-shirt, hauling at the corner of the bedspread to draw it up from the floor and around her. I guess I can stay. I hover and then close the door to the living room against the light of the fire and the glow of the table lamps. The grappa has burned off the moss of the cigarettes on my teeth. I don't need my toothbrush; I don't need anything, there is nothing I need to do. I let my jacket and trousers fall in the darkness and slip in beside her. She is shaking under the cover and pushes up to me for warmth. The pillows have a faint taste of the perfume from the bathroom, maybe Amanda's own smell unless the same fragrance has seeped into everything.

After a long while, when the pattern of her breath has let me think she is asleep, Louise says, 'It's a boat.'

'Not a boat.'

'It's a boat and the covers are the sails.'

'It's not funny, Louise.'

'Little pearls inside oyster shells.'

'I'm not, Louise.'

'You are. I can feel you. Put it inside me.'

She can feel me: the eye pushing through the fly of my underpants. She even presses against it, the softness of her bottom dissolving as she keeps up a slow, slow pressure. The cotton of my underpants first gives and then tightens, sliding to become a tourniquet around a bare neck, the artery gulping in fear beneath the skin.

'We can't do this, Louise.'

'Shush, baby. You're already inside.'

Only by a millimetre, less than a millimetre. But a soft muscle seems to pop out of place inside her and before it readjusts I am all the way through. It's just like we are back on our boat bed again, and we are making waves. As she rocks, the waves pass from her skin across mine. And soon the waves have their own momentum. We aren't doing anything, only letting them slip through us in warm trembles. The water smells of perfume and tastes of salt; it slips between my sister's back and coats my chest, rock-pool water that makes my arms slippery as they cling to her. Her little belly shimmies under my touch, more waves that push my hands up to the sealskin tips of her breasts and down to the spiral of her navel. The movement breaks us apart and, before we lose ourselves, brings us back together.

Louise is riding on top of me. The hard thing between us isn't really a penis any more, it is something that holds us together: something that she needs to push against the swell. With my hands on her bottom, I can feel the muscles straining backward, filling under my grip as they gather the energy to push forward again.

It shouldn't be as easy to play pretend afterwards, once I am in the bathroom. The jet that I aim at the toilet leaves oily sperm trails in the water, floating sea-strings. The apartment is raging hot, the bathroom filled with the scent of Number One; a thought that becomes hysterically funny, considering what I am doing. My penis shakes itself, shakes with laughter. But I have to pop it back through its guilty fly hole. I am laughing, but I cannot hear myself. All I can hear are feet on the corridor and the sound of Amanda's voice.

Amanda starts speaking long before she arrives in the bedroom. A wailing litany of apologies.

'I am sorry, darling. I am so sorry . . .'

She has reached Louise.

She must be on the bed. 'The sheets, they are soaking wet.'

As I flush the toilet, the room seems to explode into a Niagara of sound effects.

'Who is here?' She is wary now, her voice rising more than a pitch.

'My brother.'

I step out of the bathroom. Amanda stares at me, her face softening as she sees that it is true.

'I had a night sweat. But Jamie was here.'

Amanda switches from smiles to concern. 'Oh, darling. I'm sorry it wasn't me.'

12

Amanda wants me to stay.

She loves my sister, I am sure. She may be capricious,
even theatrical, preferring to storm out of arguments
rather than finding other ways to express her feelings.
She may even have broken the perfume bottle in the
bathroom. I doubt that it was her, but it may have been.
What I do know is that she wants the best for Louise and
believes that they have a future together. She actually
begs me to stay because I am a good brother who was
there when Louise was ill, not driving around Milan in
a dark sulk. Amanda tries to make me a bed up on the
sofa, pulling pillows and blankets out of the wardrobe
even as I refuse. When I leave, she follows me down the
corridor with a glass in her hand, asking if I will have
one last drink. I apologise; I can't.

The night seems much colder than a few hours earlier.
Over the next four days, the temperature just keeps
falling, pulling blizzards into the city. The change helps
me to remake Milan as a more dangerous city. I imagine
being watched as I slip through the crowds at the
curve in the Via Torino; a sniper at an upper window
takes me out with a shot to the head. I cross the
street safely but have a stand-off with a man on the
other side: will he go left, or will I go left? He is
smiling, it is funny to him. As we apologise and I brush
past him, I anticipate feeling a knife push through my

ribcage. I tense my stomach, I so expect to feel the blade point.

Running across the Piazza Edison to the doors of the post office, I imagine stumbling blind into a bank raid and being gunned down by the robbers as they make for their waiting cars. It doesn't happen. I want to wear a T-shirt that says *Please Kill Me*.

My passport has finally arrived, addressed to the Central Post Office in Mali, Italy. Stan has included a note, telling me that he never meant to give me mushrooms, girl. Instead of signing it, he writes, *Ha ha ha*.

I pick up the newspapers on the way to Linate airport. The British Fashion Awards were held on Tuesday night and the papers there have photographs of Alexander McQueen, winner of Designer of the Year. I might have applied for permanent refugee status if McQueen had not won. I would have killed myself. I'll use any reason to kill myself, I don't want to even think about the real reason.

Bibi emerges from the customs door. I open my face into the insanely positive smile that I have been practising for the entire forty minutes I have waited for her. She swings her arms around my shoulders, saying *babe babe babe* with a series of kisses that ends with a long, slow one on my lips.

'Yum. Missed you,' she says, clawing a pack of Marlboro out of her bag. Once the cigarette is lit and her lungs are filled, she asks, 'Are you okay?'

I don't know how I must look to her. I say, 'It's getting pretty intense working for Osano.'

'Oh, God. I can believe it. And you're even living with him. Fuck. Now you can move in with me. Four Seasons, baby. Ground-floor suite.'

The Milan Four Seasons must be the only hotel in the world where people want to be on the lower floors. The hotel is built on the excavated remains of a Renaissance convent, and only the ground floor has the vaulted ceilings of the original building. All the way to the carpark, pushing Bibi's luggage ahead of me, I wonder whether I can wake each morning in a space that reminds me of a church or a lavish tomb. I am afraid it will drive me mad. I am feeling mad, anyway.

On the drive into the city, Bibi scoops up the newspapers from the back seat, saying, 'Oh, wow, London Fashion Week, how's it going?' And after flicking through the pictures of the models, saying, 'Your sister should have been there.'

'She should.'

'How's it going with her?'

'She's staying with Amanda Van Hemstra. I haven't seen too much of her.'

I take a detour and park outside the Stazione Centrale. When Bibi asks where I am going, I tell her that I need to check train times and ask whether she will stay in the car so that we don't need to find a parking spot. Running across the tram tracks, I imagine myself slipping and falling, the tram unable to stop.

I want to put my passport in a locker because I don't believe it will be safe in a drawer at Osano's. If I feel I need to disappear, I don't want anyone to be able to stop me. After locking the locker and pocketing the key, I have another thought. I take out the passport in the name of Carlo Tiatto, my Italian passport with its blue Euro-cover, and put it in the diagonally adjacent locker. I assume that there is a real Carlo Tiatto out there; someone who has lost his passport or never had one. But if this one is fake, perhaps Fred also travels on a fake. All Italian names seem unreal to me: Gucci, Pucci, Prada, Ferrari. Do any of these strike anyone as real? Weren't they always already logos, even before the founding fathers opened their first shops or factories. What about Federico Sossa? I think Federico *Fellini*. Fredo *Corleone*. *Kaiser* Frederick. And make up the name *Kaiser Sossa*. The name of the villain who emerges from the smoke of the Balkans in the film *The Usual Suspects* – Kaiser Soze.

Bibi sees me weaving back across the tram tracks. 'Jesus, Jamie. You're all over the place. Do you want me to drive?'

I wonder. There is a weird traffic system in Milan; I have to take a ring road all the way around to the hotel. 'I'm okay. I've kind of stopped sleeping, there's too much to think about. But I'm fine.'

'You know what I'm going to do? Facial. Post-airflight facial repair. You want to have one too?'

'I have to get back to the studio, Bibi. Sorry.'

If Bibi keeps asking me what's wrong, I am scared that I might tell her. When work is over, I return to the hotel to meet her as I promised, creeping slowly into the church-quiet corner the concierge directs me to. I am worried that Bibi might have arranged to meet Louise at the same time. I cannot breathe until I am certain that there is only Bibi and a waitress in the room. Bibi is sitting at a desk with a pack of cards. The waitress isn't interested in having her fortune read so Bibi turns to me. I tell her that I thought only tarot cards could tell fortunes. Bibi corrects me; any old cards will do. I really am not sure.

'Not now, hey?'

'Sure. Any time you're ready.' She riffles the pack and then drops it back on to the table. 'They're always waiting.'

I want no further contact with anything taboo. I even jump as Bibi says, 'I made contact with your sister.'

'What?'

'We're going out tonight.'

I put my hands on the table and look down.

She says, 'You're going to tell me you have to work?'

'That's right.' I hadn't actually thought of an excuse yet, but that's perfect.

'No shit, Jamie. You look terrible.'

'It's not for much longer. Another ten days.'

I even make the spur-of-the-moment decision that, when I go to eat with Bibi, I will arrange it so that Osano is also there. As though eating with Osano is a routine I cannot break. It is getting so that my hands are shaking when I am alone with Bibi. We have kissed but only in a kind of chaste way: I didn't try and sweep her into bed the moment that she checked into her room. I don't do it before we meet Osano in a restaurant at the bottom of a courtyard, opposite the Versace shop.

I have led a mostly crime-free life. My mother once picked me up from a police station after I had been caught vandalising a boat. I was ashamed of that. It was an old rowing boat, wrecked almost beyond repair, and I had burned it on a beach one summer night with a few friends because we were drinking and listening to music and we were too lazy to build a fire. I can justify it, and know that my justification is weak because I cannot imagine how the owner felt, or what plans he may have had for his boat. What I had done was the thin end of the wedge of a world that has gone wrong. I was fifteen then, and Louise and I had already done our own bad thing, more than once. After we stopped, I blocked it out. It wasn't repressed in the psychological sense, but I had managed to lay it down and leave it. I felt more ashamed of the boat burning, because what Louise and I had done wasn't the thin end of the wedge of anything. It had no reference point and no meaning, it was dead centre in a world that no longer made any sense at all. So I treated it as a part of my past, a dim aborted experiment, and left it behind. It won't stay there any longer. It's squeezing either side of my head, coming at me through the frontal lobe and pressing down through my scalp. And I really have to push and push back hard over the meal to begin to talk about anything at all.

It helps that Osano wants to know everything about New York. I ask Bibi about one of the shows I had seen in the newspaper, a collection by a Spanish-born designer called Miguel Adrover. The pictures showed djellabahs, Islamic-style shirt robes and kaftans. I want to know what Bibi had thought. She hadn't modelled the collection but I knew from one of our telephone calls that she had seen it.

Osano often seems to be lost in his food. He grunts as he works at it, as though grilled goat's cheese takes effort to chew. But as Louise describes the clothes, he looks up. 'Djellabahs? You think my clients are going to cover themselves from head to foot? Even the ones who are Muslims aren't going to do that.'

'The clothes were beautiful, the robes were just a part of it, like a mood-vibe. There was also knitwear, really skinny suits. But the materials those robes came in: but beautiful.'

'It's not going to mean anything.'

I sometimes think Osano really has killed each one of his brain cells with his drinking. I say, 'Come on, Gianni. Doesn't this sound like some of your designs from the 1970s?'

'You think I'm an influence on him?'

I almost choke: the first time that I have come close to laughing in four days. But I manage to suggest that Osano may be an influence simply by shrugging. I say, 'We've got all these flowing Empire-line dresses, and they're looking pretty good.' I am smiling at him, trying to encourage him to think at least. And it is mostly true, the dresses in our collection are looking good, we have weeded out the worst ones and concentrated on the best. I say, 'Suppose we mixed these Greek styles with other flowing robes from your seventies collections?'

Osano shakes his head. He is so sluggish. Even having Bibi on hand, smiling vigorously and Americanly at him, is not helping him to spark.

'It's too late.'

The show is in ten days' time. I know that, better than him. 'It's too late for Milan, Gianni, but not for Paris. It would be perfect. No one reported the couture show, but people know it was in the Institut du Monde Arabe. If you show Arabic-style robes now, it will suggest you're developing a serious new look.'

At last, he is nodding. 'This is good.'

'We're going to do it?'

'I don't know. But it's good. I'm meeting the finance guys again tonight and at least I'll have something new to tell them. Maybe they'll get excited.' He chews his food. 'But Arabs. Are they fashionable at the moment?'

'They're controversial. Maybe now is just the right

time to go Arabic.' I'm not actually sure about this. Britain and America bombed Iraq last week: given that I buy three or four papers every day, regular news cannot help but filter through to me.

Now we are all smiling. I look at Bibi, the catlike smile, the big blue eyes and her fantastic thick hair. I don't want to begin to start making out that she is a saint. Just because I am in Italy and can see a Madonna every time I turn around, I don't need to put Bibi on a pedestal. She has faults: she smoked throughout the meal and even upended a stub in the remains of her ravioli. But the one thing about her: she always wants things to go well, she tries to carry things along with her enthusiasm. And she is not sister-fucking scum.

'Are you all right, Jamie?'

I had forgotten to breathe. And my mouth is hanging open.

'Does he have to work tonight, Osano?' she asks. 'He's going to burn out.'

'No, he doesn't have to work. Who's working? Just me. I got to ass-kiss these financial geniuses.'

I am caught in a lie. I do not have to work. As we finish the meal, it's in my mind to try that lowest trick, manufacturing an argument to get out of an evening with Bibi. But by this time I don't need to. She is so worried by my erratic behaviour, she suggests we make it an early night.

The room in the Four Seasons isn't so much like a crypt; it's too obviously expensive, too luxurious, the sheets too thick and too creamy, the lamps on the walls too soft and glowing as they warm the flesh tones in Bibi's skin. I stay there. I could hang out the *Do Not Disturb* sign, add a strip of police ribbon and stay there for ever. But each morning I am out on the pavement, waiting for Vincente and Osano to pick me up and take me to the studio.

I stay with Bibi almost every night but avoid going to any of the receptions or parties with her. She has brought me a charging lead for Stan's mobile phone and I promise to carry it with me. I use it to warn her when I am about to return to the hotel, always after two in the morning. I find ways of asking her whether she is with Louise and Amanda, without actually seeming concerned. But I still tremble as I peer into the bars or restaurants in case Bibi is drinking with them. One time she is, and I push myself back into the wall before anyone sees me. A couple, giggling together, pass in front. The taller man's body pauses directly in Louise's line of sight. I am grateful for the camouflage, so it is a moment before I realise that he and his boyfriend are staring at me. Then they both nod, *Ciao*, and move off. A strange moment and entirely non-sexual; I never really understand what passed between us. But they are soon lost in the crowd and I have to find another group to cower behind, spying across the back of their necks. Louise stands with Bibi and Amanda as a photographer takes their picture. I wonder how long I can postpone meeting the girls, knowing that I cannot delay it for long. But that night I creep back to the street, telephone a message through that I am going to be much later than usual and will go back to Osano's. It is horrendously cold outside, the snow deep on the ground. The blizzards have closed down Linate airport, bringing a sense of anticlimax to the beginning of Fashion Week. The city is muted when no one expected it to be. There are fewer people on the ground, but also the strange sight of women in light frocks, bare legs and strappy heels struggling across the snow on the via Monte Napoleone. The only sign that the international contingent, the buyers and the journalists from around the world, is beginning to arrive, diverted from Switzerland and travelling into the snowbound city by train.

The oddly quiet start continues over the weekend because the first major show, the D&G diffusion range from Domenico Dolce and Stefano Gabbana, isn't until the Tuesday. I miss it. I can't get out of the studio in the afternoon and it would take me three hours to go and see the show and return. I need to apologise to Bibi, because she was on the runway, but this is the same night that I avoid her in the hotel bar. I sleep at Osano's and look for her photograph in the papers over breakfast. Osano passes the papers to me with tight lips; he has seen Amanda's picture. The journalists describe the D&G look as 'rock chick', picking up on the references to Debbie Harry printed across the T-shirts and speculating that Madonna has been superseded in Dolce and Gabbana's affections by Blondie. None of the journalists comment on the T-shirts that carry references to Whitesnake: maybe fashion editors don't know enough about heavy metal.

I do make the Versace show on Wednesday, because it is in the evening. I am close to the back, trying to catch sight of Bibi while avoiding Louise. I can usually always see her in a crowd, she seems to rise above it. Not this time, among the hundreds of people in the room. And there is the dazzle of the celebrities on the front row. I see Suzy Menkes, her trademark quiff rising above a round, bravely cheerful face. And I see Sting sitting with Trudi Styler and wonder what Osano will think and whether he will try to get them to stay another five days to see his show. Donatella's collection is less wild than I expected; the dresses do sex by being slinky rather than by revealing. They are mostly long, like our own. But at the end of the show, I finally get to see Donatella Versace as she takes her bow. She is even more extraordinary in the flesh than in photographs. If she were fifty foot tall she could not make more of an impact. There is a song by the Texan band Slobberbone entitled 'Everything You Thought Was Right Is Wrong Today'. Donatella is the exact opposite: everything you thought was wrong is now made right, she is the walking permit. When the show is over, I run out into a hail-storm. I have a fail-safe plan with Bibi to meet back at the hotel if I don't see her at the show. And even though I do see her, I use that excuse. She was sitting with Amanda and Louise at the edge of the catwalk closest to the wings.

The Versace show seems to change Milan. Suddenly, it is like walking into a high-pressure quiz show where I am shown flash cards from every corner and am supposed to remember them. The feeling continues at the Four Seasons when I see Giorgio Armani walk into the restaurant, a tougher-looking man than I expected, dominating the group around him. I stand in the foyer, picking up a text message from Bibi, and in two minutes I see the fashion editor of *The Times*, the DJ Goldie and two English models, and my mind goes blank, I can't remember their names. The quiz beeper seems to go off in my head: that sense of panic because I cannot remember anything, I do not know anything. It is made worse because the two models behave as though they know me, turning and smiling, and mouthing *hi*. I fumble the cellphone as I read that Bibi has changed our plans. We are meeting at another hotel, the Principe di Savoia.

I look back at the fire-storm of hail, lit by the street-lamps, knowing that I cannot walk. I am trying to remember the metro map in my head when Fred appears at my arm. He is wearing old-style evening wear, a double-breasted suit with wide lapels and silk-covered buttons. He is clearly on his way somewhere, but I don't know where the black-tie code has come from. I hope it is nothing that involves me. For the first time in a week, I feel comfortable with what I am wearing: a lounge suit that Bibi scrounged for me from Prada. She laid it over the back of a chair in her room, so that she could casually ask *What's this?*, when she returned to her room the night before last.

Fred says, 'Good work with Louise.'

'What?'

'Amanda's doing the show. It's definite. All three of them.' He looks across the room and I have a moment of panic fearing that he has seen Louise; the feeling that she is around is so constant. But when I follow his eyes, he is looking at a group of men and women in evening wear: his party.

As he goes, he says, 'The agency was crazy to lose your sister. Me, I think she's the one with real presence.' Fred speaks like a gourmet, as though he has only just woken to a new flavour.

There is nothing I want to say. But I want to pick a fight. 'You've seen the models, so you think the show is going to be fine? Have you even seen the clothes we've been working on?'

Fred angles his head towards me. 'It'll be an Osano show,' he says, simply.

'And that's supposed to be a mark of quality?'

He lifts a finger. 'I don't want to hear that tone ever, not in public. We work for the same team, so act like it.' His arm comes across my shoulder so he can whisper into my ear. 'I know how hard you're working, Jamie. We all appreciate it. But we can't rebuild Osano in a week. All we can do is our best and keep the brand alive in the public's mind while we plot long term.'

'You think you'll be around for the long haul?' I am still on edge.

'Why not? I'm committed. Unless you know something I don't?'

And with a twist of the bile in my empty stomach, I realise I have said too much. Fred has no idea that Osano has been holding meetings with his potential backers almost every evening.

'All I know,' I say, 'is . . . I'm tired and hungry.'

He grins. 'You're out of luck – no eating or sleeping until April.'

The Principe is even more crowded than the Four Seasons. The over-plush lounge has a glass roof throwing back the sparkling lights from the chandeliers. The space is a bubble of noise, filled with the chatter of voices as people drape themselves over the chairs or mill between groups. As my ear becomes attuned, I realise I am hearing more English than I have heard for weeks. And then across the lounge I see Alexander McQueen, who I have seen once in real life but who seems somehow to have made himself handsome in the intervening two years. Not just handsome but kind of brooding with power. He is wearing wraparound shades, similar to the ones that Osano wears, but McQueen's are darker with a panda-eyed slant that gives him a sombre look. I realise that he is talking to Tom Ford of Gucci.

I stay close to the neoclassical pillars at the entrance to the room, until my eyes adjust and the flash of celebrity becomes an ordinary sea of people, clutching cigarettes and glasses of white wine. Louise is the first person to leap out. She hasn't seen me and neither has Amanda or Bibi, who are standing beside her.

I don't feel like drinking. I was at work for twelve straight hours without a break before the Versace show, and I am so hyper that I wouldn't even feel the first glass. I would fool myself into throwing back wine and later I would fall over. But I wonder whether I will find trays of *tramezzini* or canapés at the bar. I want something to awaken my hunger and remind my body that I have barely eaten today. As I move, I occasionally catch inquisitive looks thrown my way, almost as though I am a Furby or Teletubby or some other cute thing that everyone has heard about but never bothered to go out of their way to see. I brush off the looks by lowering my eyes.

Bibi catches sight of me as I re-emerge from the foyer, waving from within a circle. I shuffle over to her group, showing reluctance because I want to hide the way that I am really feeling. I can tell that she is hurt, but it's something that passes so quickly across her face that the next waft of cigarette smoke carries it away. I try to make it up to her by stroking her arm, remembering again the graininess of her skin. A sunburst shoreline of fine sand, rather than the dense milky liquid of Louise's skin.

'How long have you been here?'

'Not that long – Fred grabbed me at the Four Seasons,' I say.

Bibi has learnt to treat anything to do with work as a trigger that will upset me. I have encouraged her, scattering the buzz words like poisoned thorns everywhere we step: Osano, suppliers, fabric, the names of the people I work with in the studio, the name of any other designer in the world. I have been sly, and busy, creating hundreds of catalysts that obviously have nothing to do with her, but have become a part of our landscape. So I can mention Fred and she will not pry; her smile barely shivers before she turns to the women around her and introduces me.

A woman in Chanel 19 and matching sweater dress asks, 'Louise's brother? Of course. I could recognise you without knowing you. And Louise is a special talent.'

I hide my surprise. 'She is?'

'She will model for Prada, my friend just told me.'

'She is modelling for Osano.'

'Yes? Too?'

I look to Bibi for help. Bibi just says, 'I'll tell you later.'

The flow-lines through the room bring us closer and closer to Louise and Amanda. Louise has seen us. I know she has. But her eyes have never rested on us. And then we are in a group together and Amanda is throwing back her head as she laughs.

Louise shoots me a filthy look. As though I really am scum. I try to sink into Bibi's embracing arm, but she really does not have the size or body mass to shelter me.

Something nudges at my back, like a circus horse nudging a ball along with its nose. I look back and see that there is a photographer, manoeuvring people for another model group shot. He says, 'You two.'

It is Louise who puts us in position: just me and her. As the flash goes, she says, 'How are you doing, brother?'

Her voice is gruff; she can sound lewd without meaning to.

I shake my head. She can tell how I am doing. I don't need to lift up my eyes so she can see.

Amanda is still laughing. She says, 'Brother and sister together.'

'What's that?' I sound defensive. Louise just waves a hand at me, dismissing it.

I look at Bibi, knowing that she will tell me. She guides us into the slipstream of a waiter and, as we are carried along, she says, 'Amanda's stupid joke. She is telling people that she caught you and Louise in bed together.'

'What?'

'Forget it. Amanda's so insecure and dating Louise only makes her worse.'

'She can't say things like that. Didn't you stop her?'

'It's just a joke.' She is looking so guilty. Scared, too. She can tell how angry I am becoming. 'Come on, Jamie. Louise is laughing about it. And now that people are talking about her again, she is getting a lot more work. She was fabulous at the Dolce and Gabbana show yesterday.'

13

Bibi follows me out of the hotel and into Piazza della Repubblica but I keep moving. Even when she calls me, I don't look around. This is the moment that will destroy our relationship but I cannot say for sure whether I have manufactured it, or whether I have found real grounds. It doesn't matter to me. I could not go back to her room each night, lie on the bed and stare up at the roof, too slow to respond to her laughter, my fingers too clumsy for our petting games. So I stop seeing her. Or she stops seeing me, because I am in the audience for her runway shows on four separate occasions. On the Thursday I get into Milan for Prada and Byblos, then on the Sunday, as everyone at the studio moves to the Fiera expo centre ready for our own show, I see her at Roberto Cavalli and at Antonio Berardi. Louise is also at three of these, twice on the runway. At the Cavalli show, she is in the audience and we meet on the moving walkway that takes the audiences around the giant exhibition building.

She stares at the long line of people moving ahead of us, speaking without looking at me. 'Why won't you answer Bibi's telephone calls?'

'You know why.'

She doesn't say anything for a long time. We are shoulder to shoulder. There is nowhere for us to go, we just have to wait as the walkway carries us along. Finally she says, 'It happened, Jamie.'

'It doesn't happen to other people. Why are we different?'

'Products of a fucked-up childhood.'

'Our childhood wasn't fucked up. It wasn't even close.' I don't see how this can become an excuse; if I describe our childhood to anyone, it sounds idyllic. But she just shrugs.

'I didn't like it.'

'That's not the same thing.' I have turned on her, at last, my voice hissing with anger. But we are at the end of the walkway and have to take the four strides to the beginning of the next. Somehow, walking in a crowd isn't conducive to arguing. I don't pick up my thread until we begin to be carried along again. 'It wasn't Cornwall. You just didn't like being a child.'

'Okay. There's no explanation. Just tell yourself: DCOL.'

'What?'

'Doesn't Count On Location.'

As we reach the next set of security barriers and our invites are checked, I let myself be squeezed to the side before the final escalators and lose Louise. I end up sitting on my own.

I know all of Louise's locations, from the chat inside the studio and from the newspapers. Besides the Prada and Byblos shows, she modelled at the main Dolce and Gabbana show and for Emporio Armani. When I saw her at Cavalli, she was supposed to be on her way to Fendi to have a fitting with Karl Lagerfeld. We are working so hard on our collection and our studio is so far outside the city I miss most of them. But we share out the invites as they arrive and we devise a schedule between ourselves that allows everyone to see something. There is already a consensus, and not only in the British press, that New York was dull and London was better. We are so much in the midst of Milan that it is impossible to say whether anything exciting is happening, or whether it is just so much smoke. Rumours spread across the shows and the parties, about what might be good, what is worth tipping and what should be avoided. The weather has improved and the Milan Carnival has started: moving through the streets, I see stilt-walkers, their huge colourful headdresses hovering above the pedestrians. It seems to lift the whole city. The women in Osano's studio bring the mood into work with them and, although I avoid all the parties, the gossip is fed back to me. The press has begun to argue that the common theme is a Lolita fixation. It is the best angle that they can find, although it is hardly evident everywhere, and then only in patches: schoolgirl coats, a few A-line dresses that end at thigh level in that baby-doll way. One designer showed an apron dress and there was a sailor outfit somewhere else. I am not at all sure that this is the real story of Milan: I think it is a froth of showmanship at the edges of a few collections. The Lolita fixation has become so much a part of our times, from the teenage girl pop stars to the image of gangly prepubescent legs on the cover of every other book. The Lolita-look is probably *the* image of the early twenty-first century, an image that signals either abuse or protection, nostalgia or emotional honesty, depending upon the way that the person writing the lyrics or the copy wants to swing it.

The news that really interests everyone at the studio is how many other designers are also trying to sell the Empire line. The style is definitely in the air, and we cannot decide whether this is good or bad. It means that Osano will seem at least as contemporary as anyone else. But then, if our designs don't stand out, if our tweaks don't work, then we are going to look even more second rate. Alberta Ferretti's high waists are quite classical. Prada's version, cut to the length of mini-dresses, is actually pretty baby doll, to be honest.

I notice another trend. The number of English voices I heard in the Principe turns out be a true reflection of the number of British designers at work in Milan. Antonio Berardi is British, as is the designer at Byblos. Bottega Veneta emerges as a largely English-run house. Armani, especially Emporio Armani, is full of Brits. The London-based designers Sofia Kokosalaki and Luella Bartley are both showing here, on the final day. At the same time, Alexander McQueen is here *en masse*, all his organisation getting to know their new business partners at Gucci. It seems that I was mistaken about the impossibility of being both English and a designer. Perhaps a new generation is emerging.

A certain kind of Englishness even seems to be becoming influential. I keep hearing people talk about Jean Muir, about her style, and even the possibility that her house will be bought by one of the big companies. And other British influences are becoming apparent. The YSL collection in Paris from Tom Ford was said to be inspired by the tailor Tommy Nutter, the man responsible for John Lennon's white suit and Bianca Jagger's wedding suit. I also hear suggestions that Biba provided the underpinning for Dolce & Gabbana's new hippie. Prada are said to be referring to both Biba and Ossie Clark, another English designer of the sixties and seventies. I don't know whether it really is a time for the British to be optimistic. But everyone in Osano's studios tells me that I should get out more, speak to the British designers working at the other houses. I don't follow their advice. Even if I wanted to do all the shows, I wouldn't have the time. As the week goes on, I am putting more and more hours into the collection. By Friday, I am even sleeping at the studio. If I finish at three in the morning, there is no reason to return to the city. On Sunday, although most of the collection has already been sent to the Fiera, there are still two of us working in the studio, our work delayed because we each saw two shows on the Sunday. I end up asleep on the floor of Osano's office while Rhonda, the Welsh girl, sleeps on the sofa.

The van arrives at nine to pick up Rhonda, me and the last of the clothes. We arrive at the Fiera at eleven. The show is at three, so there is already a feeling that we are late, that time was lost as we loaded the van. The models were told to arrive by eleven, though only one has shown up so far. Osano went straight to the Fiera from his apartment and has spent so long waiting, virtually alone, that he is pretty strung out. He continues to supervise the carpenters and technicians, as he did yesterday. Unlike in Paris, they all seem super-efficient. The runway was repainted the night before and the paint is dry and pristine, and any extras that Osano wants, like a triumphal arch, are already built and ready to be set up.

Backstage, midday. Two hairdressers, a make-up artist and a manicurist are working on our lone model. She is a nervous fifteen-year-old Lithuanian who speaks no Italian and very little English. She looks terrified when she sees her picture pinned to a corkboard on the wall, until she realises that the photographs of fifteen other models are also there, their names written below. I spend some time marking up the clothes intended for each of them, but we really need to begin the fittings. When I notice that I am assigned Bibi and Louise, I move the tags around. If I have to do a fitting with anyone, let it be Amanda Van Hemstra. She has probably been told that I am angry with her for spreading silly rumours. If that is what she believes then she is not going to find my behaviour too strange.

At one o'clock, with only two hours to go, a group of six models arrive together, all with stories about delays and overruns. Monday is the busiest day of the whole of Milan, the final flurry before the twelve days of Fashion Week end tomorrow. Now that we finally have some models to work with, the noise increases, and there is even more backstage gossip. We are still waiting for another eight girls but we are probably at capacity in terms of what we can handle. As long as the rest arrive before 2.30 we will be fine. The one model who arrived on time is sat rigid on a chair; too scared to move her head in case the towering back-comb she has been given falls, and barely able to breathe because her Empire-line dress has been spiced up with a mini-corset. The corset is worn over her dress and she could take it off if she wanted, but no one has thought to tell her. I would tell her but she is talking gingerly into her cellphone in Lithuanian, and I decide not to disturb her.

One or two of the newly arrived models are mildly drunk and I wonder what condition Louise will be in when she arrives. At least this is an afternoon show and everyone is so busy there is no time for them to get completely trashed. Amanda arrives before Bibi and Louise. For some reason I had expected the three to arrive together. I move towards her at the same time as Rhonda, who greets her familiarly with a double kiss. It had never crossed my mind that these two would know each other and be friendly. When I suggest that I look after Amanda, Rhonda tells me, 'No, you're all right, love. Me and Mandy can have a natter.'

As she goes to wheel a rack over, I ask Amanda whether everything is fine with her.

'Absolutely. But I hear you're mad with me.'

'Forget it.'

'So are you going to be sweet to Bibi?'

I nod and go to rearrange the tags again. I am now going to do Bibi but definitely not Louise.

My way of dealing with any problem that is going to bring me anywhere close to tears or a breakdown is to operate within as narrow an emotional bandwidth as possible. I sabotaged my affair with Bibi because that would cut out a whole register of possible emotions. I don't want to swing backwards and forwards, I want to stay right here, in the narrow dark valley of sister-fucking. But as I pin the hem of Bibi's gown, she feels so stiff and cold above me that I begin to think how I can warm her and make her happy again.

'Bibi . . .'

'What?' She is blank and stern.

'The length of this gown, I'm not sure about it.'

'Whatever.'

'Suppose I bring Osano over and ask him whether we could shorten it.' I am thinking about the baby-doll versions at Prada; perhaps not so short, but Bibi is tall and slender enough to carry off something like that. I ask her what she thinks.

'I'm just the clothes-horse.'

'I want your opinion.'

'You're not getting it.'

I am kneeling at the hem, my head lower than her knee-cap. How more abject could I look? So I tell her, 'It will be different after the show.'

'Congratulations.'

I look up. 'I came to nearly all your shows. I wanted to see you. I've just been so wound up.'

She looks down at me. Not warm yet, but she is softening. I brush the back of her calf with my fingers. But she is not speaking. It's up to me to expand and it is too late for me to blame everything on work and the shows. She has heard that too many times already. There is a long pause. I can't fill it with lies, not even half-truths. But I cannot say anything else either.

My mouth starts moving. 'We could take the sleeper to Paris tomorrow night. Just the two of us.'

She shakes her head. I know that this is my last chance: I don't need to push any farther, I could just finish the hem and move on to the next fitting.

Then she says, 'The last night of Milan? The sleeper's booked up.'

I know that. I already have a ticket booked through Osano. And now I am babbling: 'I can arrange it. I'm supposed to be sharing with Fred but he won't mind taking the plane.'

I try to think of books or films where the lovers ride the sleeper train. There are the last few seconds of *North by North West* and more than one James Bond film. I also remember *Some Like It Hot* and Jim Carrey in *Me, Myself and Irene*. Patricia Highsmith's *The Boy Who Followed Ripley*. None of them sounds auspicious.

'Please, Bibi. I could bare my soul on the way.'

She is nodding now, but slowly. 'Let me think about it.'

My promise to tell Bibi never quite leaves me through the rest of my fittings. I didn't mean it, of course. As I work, my mind blurs with the intensity around me, my fingers move on their own. I find ways to alter seams to the models' figures and I don't even have to think about it. And because it is all so fluid, I begin to backtrack over the idea of talking to Bibi. Maybe I actually could tell her. On a moving train we couldn't suspend the conversation, I would have to say something, to take our relationship through to somewhere better. I still don't believe that I will really tell her, but the possibility is there. I *could* do it. People are supposed to talk things through, it says so everywhere you look.

Osano circuits the room, keeping on top of everyone's work. I feel we are all in the same rhythm, and Osano is efficient and unselfconscious with us. He is warm and generous to the models. Better, he is wearing his spectacles and will even get down on to the floor to examine every part of the stitching. And once he is satisfied, the models help haul him back to his feet. Osano stresses that it is not just the way the dresses look on the runway that is important. When the fashion editors come backstage, they will examine the clothes in detail. I suggest we leave them in the street, make sure they get stolen before the critics have a chance to tear them apart.

Osano says, 'I've got more good news. It looks like the deal's in place.'

'You've got backing?'

Nodding. 'I've got serious backing.'

He looks back over his shoulder: either at the clothes and the models, or to reassure himself that no one is within earshot. 'This show, it is going to be mediocre, but that's okay. Mediocre only means average. And Paris will be better. The future has never been brighter, not for twenty years.'

I follow his eyes around the room. Louise is being pinned into evening wear by Katie, who I know hates her. It looks to me as if Louise is fuelling the froideur. As Katie skittles around the floor, Louise stands stalk upright, sipping a glass of champagne and smoking a cigarette. The cigarette is even in a holder. I don't believe this, a tortoiseshell holder about ten centimetres long: Louise could not look more distant. But then she takes the holder from her lips and says something, there is a pause and then Katie collapses laughing. So maybe I misread the signals. Maybe now Louise is going to take her second chance at being a successful model with something like grace.

There is no doubt that Louise's career is back on the tracks. I even heard her joke earlier that she is making more money than ever because she no longer has to kick back a percentage to her agency. And there are agencies interested in signing her up again: the Fendi show absolutely clinched it. It was Amanda's stupid rumours that put her back on top. I don't know what that says about the fashion industry.

I could blend those rumours into a version of the truth when I talk to Bibi. A soft version of the truth, which sketches in something of the story between Louise and me, giving the mood but not the facts. That would explain to Bibi why I became so upset when the rumours about Louise and me were started. I could tell Bibi that Louise felt she had lost something, from our pre-Cornwall life, something that I never missed because I was too young. How she began to use me as a combination comfort blanket and fashion accessory, to make up for the thing that she had lost. I could definitely tell Bibi all that. But I don't know why I should tell her, because a confessional is supposed to be therapeutic and I don't know how talking about this would help me. I am not even sure it is true: I believe it is true, of course, but that's my own perception, and saying it out loud isn't going to produce a sudden re-evaluation of our childhood. And it wouldn't begin to get to the actual fact, because I would never confess that far.

There is a better narrative there, that I began life as a fashion accessory and I used that as the basis for my own life story. That would explain how I arrived here, in the Fiera, with a pocketful of pins and cotton reels. There has to be a reason why I can sew darts, tailor the backs of jackets to give a woman a waist, why I developed the skills to find or to lose a bum. It's not an everyday talent. But I don't like this story either, because although it is smooth it doesn't explain why I actually care about these things: there is a difference between having a talent at your fingertips and having it in your heart. Who's to say I couldn't have sailed yachts or become a French teacher or turned pro as a skater? Well, I couldn't have done that.

I continue rehearsing the conversation that I may have with Bibi, *en route* to Paris, as the models rehearse their walk. We are using church music now, not the ideal soundtrack but better than using rock or dance stuff that Osano doesn't understand and cannot relate to. The idea is that, once the audience recognises classical music, they are going to accept his collection as classic in style. But we have fresher ideas for the Paris shows, music from North and East Africa; something that no one has ever used before. Still, Bibi delivers a stately march to the choral chant coming through the speakers and I begin to feel that today's show won't be bad at all. It will be good mediocre. And buoyed between the success of Milan and the anticipation of Paris, I will tell her that I am . . .

Possibilities are still meandering through my mind as the lights in the hall shade down. I take a look out of the wings and see Suzy Menkes' quiff, notebook clutched on her lap. There are no international celebrities in the audience. But maybe there are plenty of home-grown Italian ones. And the music starts again. Bibi is ready, she will be the first model. I whisper *good luck*. And she steps out.

The photographers are on a raised scaffold platform. As Bibi approaches them, their lights flare and she is in silhouette, like a statue, just as she had practised. The gown flows around her. And then the next model is taking off and Bibi turns, walking back towards me. Her face is expressionless, but not in arrogance. The word Osano had used in his pre-show talk was beatification, and that's how she looks. The mask slips as she steps into the wings.

'Okay. I'll come to Paris on the train with you.'

I smile, my mouthing forming *thank you* as my mind sets off again: *What will I actually say, when we are alone together?*

And Amanda is off down the runway, swinging her arms, a more militant style of saint than Bibi, her dress a bright red.

I move back out of the wings, catching a smile from Louise: a sweet one. The show is going well, we are so much better prepared than we were at the Paris couture shows. Louise is wearing one of the most dramatic of the dresses: a sheer material that is loose only around her breasts, everywhere else clinging to her body in a bias cut. As she begins to gather pace on the runway, the body and dress merge like an Indian rope trick, relaxing between the strides and pulling taut with every footfall of her dagger heels. She doesn't even stand still at the end, when the cameras flash, but continues to shimmer; the nap of the silk appears like the fibres in the rope, catching the light in their twists.

Fred is beside me. I catch his shadow and turn. He is smiling, saying *This is good*. If he knows about Osano's future plans, he is hiding it.

'Can Bibi have your rail ticket, Fred?'

'What will I do?'

'Fly?'

He nods, smiling again. 'No problem. You deserve it.'

Four more girls pass by and then Bibi is on the catwalk again, followed by Louise again, half a length behind her. I am back at the rails, checking the final dresses. Osano is beside me, wearing a clean suit this time. Each model who walks past he wishes *good luck* and tells her she is beautiful. I have never seen him so on form, or so connected with anything.

Then the final walk down the runway comes, all fifteen models parading in line. There is clapping from the audience that, to me at least, sounds enthusiastic. The column of girls turns at the end and marches back, in perfect step. Osano is ready to go and take his bow. He rolls out, doing a strange wave with his hands. Maybe it is his trademark wave; I have never seen him take a bow before. And then he is beckoning up the runway. I don't see his problem, but Louise is slipping her arm under mine and I realise that I am supposed to go out front.

As I move towards the applause and the flash of lights, part of me is thinking that I don't deserve this and another part is thinking I don't deserve it any more than Katie or Rhonda or the other women but I will take it anyway. And I am halfway along the runway with Louise on my arm, and as I turn to her, to share the moment, she winks and moves in for a kiss. The camera flashes are like strobes that slow time down and Louise's lips are there to milk every long second. I realise that I have somehow become a part of the show, the show-business part of the show, and as I peel away from Louise's lips I wonder what the cameras are registering: panic or surrender?

14

The end of the Milan show should give us time to breathe. Instead it shocks us into realising how close we are to the Paris show. There is no post-show party; Osano hosts a reception in the Fiera for press and buyers but soon everyone leaves for Armani's evening show and the lure of a grander party. I return to the studio, knowing that I will be working until the train leaves for Paris tomorrow evening. The timescale, finishing at the Fiera on Monday and preparing to show at Les Invalides only a week later, was forced upon us by the director of the museum in Paris. Osano prefers to blame Fred. At any other time, his behaviour would infect everything, making work even more tense. But he is only bad tempered towards Fred, and it is clear that he is simply trying to disinvest from their partnership. In fact, Osano's mood is upbeat from the end of his show and continues at work the next morning, with the news coverage of his collection. The fashion editors may have received the show with mild interest, but at least they all reviewed it, and some even praised the romantic longings behind the collection: meaning that there were so many billowing frocks it often looked like a costume drama, perhaps *Gladiator* meets *Sense and Sensibility*. One editor even praised the standard of tailoring, which is incredible. Our tailoring was not good, we didn't have the time. At least some of the work was mine and I know that I am useless. Better, though, the papers picked up on the spin we were selling through our PR people, that this collection had to be seen in the context of our Paris show, where the ready-to-wear and diffusion lines would be shown together. They didn't even ask, if we were showing those lines later, what the hell had we shown in Milan?

Osano was particularly pleased by the photographic coverage. It mostly made me feel uncomfortable, the pictures of Louise and me kissing, a naked arm draped across my shoulder and my body crossed through by the lean, fluid silhouette of her torso. She had been careful to change back into the most beautiful dress before the finale. It was a stunning image, because Louise exuded both old-fashioned romance and high vamp, a combination to draw in the eye. But then came the double-take: we look so much alike. I had been exploited, and it worked. But don't ask me how I feel about it.

The press coverage gives everyone a lift, and if I have difficulties with it, then a single look at the new collection refreshes me. Some years ago, Osano had paid someone to catalogue and file all his patterns from the seventies. This helped immeasurably. So far, the work of duplicating them has presented few problems. But we have been trying to do more than that, and Osano has been right out there encouraging us. Katie has been working on the closest thing to a djellabah we found in his archives, and she has also taken inspiration from the robes in Miguel Adrover's show in New York. Suzy Menkes described his collection as over-literal. The same could not be said of our version, which has elements of a European hooded cloak: and everyone talks about cloaks being in this season. The finished outfit is reminiscent of the picture on the video box of *The French Lieutenant's Woman*. I am a little too familiar with this image, thanks to my storm-tossed mother. But Katie has done great work getting a viable rough version together, and she and Osano have begun to select possible materials for the finished gown.

I had volunteered to work on a series of long shirts, inspired by the clothes of the Gulf Arabs. I can make shirts: not just approximations, I can actually do a lot of the tailoring, and what I can't I quickly learn. We already know that these will be made in chiffons, in a lightweight silk and also, possibly, in a cotton that Osano bought in huge quantities from Egypt. These are the three materials used in his – or Gina's – Empire-line dresses. The idea is to send the girls down in pairs: one in the more masculine, Islamic wear, and one in the feminine Greek or French revolutionary-style frocks. The intention is a version of high classicism that crosses East and West: quite puritan but with a faintly transgressive edge. If anyone is likely to find a lesbian undercurrent remotely transgressive.

Osano suggests that I should also model, paired up with my sister. I am not surprised. Even secluded in his studio this past week, I knew that interest was brewing in Louise and me as a pair. As an item. It was constantly around me, carried in by the women in the studio, as they returned from the shows and parties. I ignored it but, since our photographed kiss, I have no longer known what to do. I am helpless, and being helpless I start to listen to what they are actually saying. I begin to realise that the interest isn't even prurient, it is just something that is buzzing around. There is no reason for it to drive me crazy. No one finds it titillating, it is just a style motif. So when Osano makes his suggestions, I don't argue. I try to deflect it with a joke, asking who will wear the dress.

I wonder why Osano has waited so long to ask: until we are in the car on the way to the Stazione Centrale. He laughs when I answer, telling me to choose; if I want to wear a dress, go for it. Katie is in the back of the car. She tells me that she can make the alterations, we can have a fitting on the train.

It is past 9 p.m. when we walk into the grand main hall. Bibi and I have been text-messaging each other all day, without managing to speak. I assume that she will meet as we arranged, by the barriers to the platform. But the only person I can see is Fred, waiting with our tickets even though he has surrendered his own place. He waves as we arrive. He tells us that the collection is ahead of us, it is already being loaded on to the train.

Osano turns brusque: 'Why aren't you there? You want thieves to take this collection, too?'

It is nonsense. We both know the collection is safer the farther away Fred is from it. But Osano clearly wants to provoke an argument, no matter what the grounds.

'I want you supervising them.'

Fred says, 'Okay. I've got people on it, but if you're nervous, fine. There's just one thing, if I could have a brief word with you.'

There is nothing in Fred's manner to suggest danger. Osano certainly doesn't see it; he saunters after Fred to the edge of the station hall. Maybe I am super-sensitive, but I feel that Osano is in trouble. I caught the artificial edge in Fred's voice: the synthetic fibres. I would follow them, but I have very little time to retrieve my passport from the station locker. And what would I actually do if Fred turned nasty?

The cellphone rings before I am halfway across the floor. I flip it open as I continue towards the lockers, putting a finger in my ear to dim the noise of the station and the jabber of the station announcer.

It is Bibi, frantically repeating my name.

'I'm here, Bibi. Where are you?'

'The hotel.'

'But the train is about to go.'

'I know that.' She had sounded anxious; now she sounds indignant. 'Fred told me to wait here.'

'Why would he do that?'

'You tell me.'

'Stay where you are, Bibi. I'll find out what's gone wrong.'

'How will that help?'

I shake my head. I don't know. Then I turn around and start running back towards the platform barriers. I cannot understand what has gone wrong. I wonder whether Bibi has simply misunderstood Fred's instructions.

'Just wait. I'll be there soon.'

My only plan is to ask Fred to put everything right. What else can I do? There is no other train today, but perhaps we could fly. I close the connection and, as I run, I keep scanning the station. Soon, I am circling at the centre of the grand hall, trying to see into the corridors and the stairwells that lead off it. There is no one waiting at the entrance to the platform. Perhaps they are already on the Paris train.

Then I see Fred and Osano, arguing by a magazine kiosk. As I run towards them, I first register Fred's smile and then the sweat on Osano's face.

When I am close enough, I hear Fred snarl. 'When did you think you'd tell me about your backers?'

'It wasn't like that. It was an informal approach.' Osano is trying to jolly things along but the strain is showing. It is difficult to believe that he was niggling and bullying Fred only a few moments ago.

'Informal enough to keep your finance chief out of the talks?' Fred almost looks to be enjoying himself. He has conjured up so much menace, though he has not yet laid a finger on Osano. 'And did you have any ideas about my ten per cent of the shares?'

'Of course. There's a generous offer to buy them. I mean, I don't know the details, but it's ahead of the market.'

'There is no fucking market, Osano. You're just about surviving, thanks to me. The only asset you've got is the brand name. And the major deficit is that you are still around.'

'Come on.' Osano is scared. And Fred has gone too far. Either he backtracks now, or he escalates. 'Let's calm down, Fred.'

Osano counts the seconds almost audibly while he stares at Fred. I am only feet away, waiting for Fred to slap Osano's stupid face.

Then Fred stares across Osano's face and he is looking directly at me. 'Did you know about this?'

'I knew.' No way am I going to lie. But I can feel how lame I sound as I add, 'I mean, it's not about being in or out, it's just about trying to raise the value of the brand and then everyone wins.'

'If I didn't have to get you on that train . . .' Fred pauses. Maybe this is the death threat. A high-pitched Italian voice cuts through on the station Tannoy. Fred uses the interruption for effect, before saying, 'Then we'd have time to talk this through. I expect to do that tomorrow: dates, figures, everything.'

'Absolutely.' Osano's feet slip on the tiles as he tries to get the traction he needs to turn and run back to the platform barrier.

Fred says, 'Where are you going, Jamie? They're calling you.'

I have enough Italian now to know that the announcer is talking about the Paris train.

'I'm not going. Bibi's still at the hotel.'

Fred shakes his head. 'She's not coming. Louise wanted her ticket. You two are sharing.'

He puts a hand on my arm and starts leading me towards the platform. I feel I am hovering across the marble. In a moment, I am at the barrier, looking at Louise a few yards ahead of me. She turns in a Max Mara pea jacket that she didn't own before this evening. The train platform has its own peculiar smell of tar and diesel fumes. Even against this backdrop, Louise's perfume leaves a trail for me. She is wearing one of those powerful eighties brands, maybe Poison. If it is, she has only recently put it on: I smell cinnamon and coriander and honeyed-flower blossoms swimming in heavy musk.

She waves. 'Hurry up, Jamie.'

Louise sits beside me, her hands resting on the white linen tablecloth, her fingers covered in rings. Osano sits opposite. We are in the dining car, the table lamp bringing us together in a charmed red-orange glow. Beyond the window, we could be skirting the Alps. There is a dark wall chasing us, somewhere in the distance, but

I cannot make out the shapes. The window throws the reflection of the three of us back at me. Osano is happy and squinting, I am skinny and poised between dazed and intense, Louise is hypnotic and unreadable. She leans back slightly as a waiter refills her champagne glass. Her blouse is unbuttoned to show a deep cleavage, white skin with a smattering of sun freckles. I don't know where the freckles came from; there hasn't been any sun.

'We already have orders from the Milan show.' Osano is telling us how his clothes will soon be everywhere: at least in the Far East but also in a few European stores. He expects the Paris show to produce even more orders, raising the equity of the company. When his new backers see the order book, that will only make them hungrier for Osano: for a bite of the Osano cherry. He is actually rubbing his hands together.

The three of us at the table. Katie and Rhonda should be here to expand Osano's audience, but they have already returned to their cabin. None of us has slept in days. By the end of the meal they were almost falling on to the table. I knew how they felt, but I am still determined to hold on here, in the restaurant car. I definitely don't need to return to the cabin that I am sharing with Louise. The beat of the wheels on the track sounds as though it has an in-built delay, a soft ticking followed by a heavier beat that needs to skip to keep the rhythm. I concentrate on that delayed moment.

Osano has moved on from the wonders of his collection to the wonders of the woman who modelled it. Louise is now hot, the kind of hot that knows how to look cool, in a sheer blouse, unbuttoned, smoking a cigarette in a tortoiseshell holder. Her hand is no longer on the linen tablecloth. I have to stare to assure myself that it is not on the table, that it really is in my lap, her ringed fingers interwoven with my own hand.

Osano says, 'You have so much style. I won't dismiss my clothes, you understand, but they came alive when you wore them. You bring the ideas to life.'

'Only Louise?' I ask.

'But Louise is special. I always knew that. Maybe I didn't realise enough. Everyone was telling me that I needed Amanda Van Hemstra, making me crazy, and I ended up putting my anxieties on to you.' He is talking to Louise, not to me. And now he taps the side of his head. 'But I knew in here I needed you around, that you would end up being magnificent.'

Is this bullshit? I have never heard Osano speak quite like this before. He has praised models before but this is not praise, it is becoming liturgy.

Louise is saying, 'And I want to work with you, Gianni. I love the way your work is heading, there's a whole new vision. I want to be there, with you and with Jamie.'

And her hand flexes slightly in mine, finding a pulse that lights a chain of sparkling reactions through my body. Keeping me permanently dazed, but also keeping me intense. One side of the equation – the wine, of course, the rich food, certainly, and Louise's perfume, her touch, her long lean body and the soft sneer of her lips as she exhales cigarette smoke: all that has me definitely dazed. And the other side of the equation – the bullshit, the bullshit, the bullshit, keeping me tense.

I excuse myself. In the bathroom, I check my eyes in the mirror. No reason to do that, I am just checking. I pull the cellular out of my pocket: there are six missed calls. I let all of them ring, too scared to answer but too guilty to turn the phone off.

As I step out of the bathroom, Osano is right in front of me.

'What's happening?'

He grins. 'You're what's happening, kid. We're what's happening.'

I push him. 'This kissy arse-kissy stuff with Louise.'

He shrugs. 'Okay. You've got me. She's what's happening.'

He shouldn't have done that shrug. As his arms move they leave his body clear. I punch him in the stomach, sending him staggering backward to the bathroom door.

Before he can catch his breath, I have punched him again. The steward passes, his hands filled with cloche-covered plates. He cannot stop the fight. He is too bewildered to try anyway. He calls out in French, first at me then over his shoulder, summoning help from somewhere down the corridor, towards the kitchen car.

Osano is wheezing harder, trying to drag oxygen from somewhere deeper inside his stomach. His face, wine blushed, is beginning to turn almost purple now.

'Stop it, Jamie.' His hands come up, trying to push me away. I have my own fists up, wondering what I will do. Try to weave inside like a boxer, try to bring a fist up into his face.

There are arms on me now. Someone drags me back. I cannot see and I cannot turn around. Then I feel Osano's hand fall on to my shoulder, not a slap or a punch but just a heavy hand, lying on me.

'Jamie.'

His eyes are big. They are probably less bloodshot and wandering than my own.

'Jamie, are you going to hit me again?'

I don't say anything. He continues looking at me and then nods over my head. The arms holding me drop. I look to my side to see a white-uniformed steward hover then shrug, disappearing back to where he had come from.

'I'm not playing with Louise. I'm serious.'

I am suddenly exhausted. All I can say, again, is: 'Arse-kissing.' I don't sound so sure of myself any more.

'Listen, Jamie, I've seen these things before. A model's been around for a while, no one quite clicked with her. But then it all turns around and suddenly she's the woman of the season. Everyone wants to work with Louise. Everyone. And if she wants to work with me, I am pleased. More than pleased, I want to grab it, feed off that energy.'

'Use her.'

'No, Jamie. I mean it. You know what my clothes lacked?'

I can think of lots of things: a designer, for instance. But Osano is expanding, wedged in the bathroom door for support as he drags up the exact words he needs.

'What they lacked was desire. I'm serious. I was getting so far down in myself, I lost that. Depression does that. But Louise brings it back.'

'Sex with me.'

Osano laughs. 'Yes, an idea like that. A great taboo. A great fantasy. It's sex but better than sex. It's romance, romance with passion, romance and the forbidden. What is fashion? Just the concrete expression of a fantasy. That's all.'

*   *   *

I am naked in our cabin, leaning against my reflection in the window while Louise lies fully dressed on the couch bed, watching me. She is smiling.

'How do you feel?' she asks.

'A little drunk. A lot tired. Not bad.'

'Do you want me to tell you the story?'

'One moment.' I alter the lights in the room so that only the tube over the washbasin remains on. Then I lie next to her on the bed. 'Shoot.'

'There was a crazy woman . . .'

'I thought we'd sorted this out. She's not crazy.'

'Okay, there was a raven-haired woman with large sad brown eyes and a tendency towards melancholia. And one day, she is walking along the beach and finds an oyster shell. It's almost as big as her, because she's so short, but she has her wheelbarrow with her.'

I am giggling. The wheelbarrow is a new touch.

'She wheels the oyster shell back to her four-bedroom detached house and tips it gently into the swimming pool with the all-weather cover. Then she makes herself a cocktail and goes to bed.'

Louise strokes my stomach with one hand; the other supports her head.

'When she comes down to her pool the next day, the sun is shining and the pool is full of a shimmery light. The dark-haired, mildly depressive woman looks deep into the water and sees the oyster shell is beginning to open; slowly, slowly as she continues to watch. And inside there is a beautiful oyster-shell princess with big blue fish eyes and long golden sea-spray hair. The woman is amazed. She forgets to take her Valium pill, and it almost seems that she doesn't need it, she is so full of happiness. She calls through the water, "Who are you?"

And from the bottom of the pool, a voice like a little sea puppy calls back, "I'm lost, and until I work out where I should be, I guess I have to be your little daughter."

'Three and a half years pass and the oyster-shell princess learns to walk on the land, although she prefers to splash around in her swimming pool. And her hair is still golden, but it has lost some of its special watery fineness, and her eyes are still round and blue, but they have lost a little of their deep-sea shine. And the depressed woman manages to focus on something outside of her own self for about two seconds and asks the oyster princess what's wrong. In her seal-pup bark, the oyster princess tells her that she is lonely. She wants a little oyster boy to play with.'

Louise plays with her little oyster boy, whose shell is beginning to open.

'Back to the beach, to get another shell, yadda yadda yadda. Tip it into the swimming pool. Splash splash splash. And the beautiful oyster princess swims to the bottom of the pool and whispers into the shell: Hello, what's this? A golden-haired oyster prince with his barnacle nipples and his fishy dicky.'

We can kiss now. And it's easier than ever before, easier than when we relied only on the testimony of the mother figure and her story, which carefully and conveniently establishes the absence of a shared father, or any direct family link between the two oyster babies. Easier, maybe, because the train skims across a dark country, far away across the sea, and because our cabin is small enough to be our personal shell. The shell also has an inside lock. But I know that it's also easier because Osano has said that this isn't real, it's fantasy, and better than fantasy.

There is a flip-down table below the cabin window, mounted on hinges on a bracket only ten centimetres wide. It is just large enough for Louise's bottom. She perches there, her back against the steamed-up glass, her arms and legs wrapped around me. I stand, buried deep inside her, my hands on her thighs and my nose in her hair. The cresting and falling of the train does half the work, not all; we keep stroking in together, stroking away, stroking back. When our orgasms come, it's like a naked electric cable dropped into a fish tank.

15

The train slows as it passes a sports stadium, its vivid green walls rippling in the morning sun. The walls appear to be made of grass. I keep on staring, and then I see the wires where the hover-mowers are floated up and down its steep sloping walls. Louise touches my arm. We are ready to go. We sneak along to the next carriage with our bags in our hands, and when the train stops at the Gare de Lyon we leap out and run down the platform. This is our secret plan, to leave Osano and the others to deal with everything, while we take the day off. Our disguises are not perfect but we behave as though they are: flying down the platform in space-white Dolce and Gabbana coats spun from the skins of Afro-haired llamas, the lizard-effect patterns on our skinny-legged trousers blurring as we race across the boulevard Diderot, our Cuban heels rattling off the sidewalk. The single difference between Louise's clothes and mine is that my T-shirt says *French Kisses From Debbie* and hers has the Led Zeppelin *Zozo* symbol. She borrowed the clothes from the D&G workshop, 'borrowed' being a word that no longer means steal, now that she is in demand.

We share breakfast in the Pause Café on the rue de Charonne. Sharing because every time I laugh Louise stuffs a chunk of her croissant into my mouth. Which makes me laugh harder. She tells me to shut up, but I can't. It only makes me worse.

'I'll put jam on your nose.'

'Don't.'

'I haven't seen you laugh like that for years.'

'Like I'm going to stop if you spread jam on my nose.'

'But you're jammy Jamie.'

I didn't think that Louise knew my school nickname, but she knows the whole phrase.

'Jammy Jamie with the fittest sister in Cornwall.' She is grinning.

The name was given to me in all innocence at school. At least, in half-innocence: what did they imagine was lucky about being related to the girl that all the boys fancied? Unless they thought that in my place they would do exactly what we did do, on two separate occasions when I was fourteen years old. And five times since, three of them last night, once this morning.

Louise takes a slurp of milky coffee, deliberately getting a smudge of milk on the tip of her nose. 'Creamy Louisey.'

'Cheesy Louisey.'

'Watch it.' She wags a warning finger. 'Hey. I just thought, we've got the same clothes. But we don't smell the same. Should I spray you?'

She has pulled a big bottle of Poison out of her bag. I bring my hands up. 'Please, no.'

'No? What's the matter with you?'

'I want to salvage a little individuality.'

'How about we go shopping for scent?'

That's fine with me. I already know what I want to buy with the thousands of US dollars Louise now carries in her purse. I want a bottle of Neroli Sauvage from Creed.

I even know the address of the store, and it is close to rue Saint Honoré and both the Hôtel Costes and the stores where Louise intends to continue her borrowing spree. We are going to make our way slowly there, leaving the others to unpack the collection and scout the marquee that Osano has hired in the grounds of Les Invalides.

'Why Les Invalides? Doesn't that make him sound lame?' asks Louise.

I explain the reference. 'It's where Napoleon is buried.'

'What's this thing between designers and Napoleon? Because they're all short megalomaniacs?' She dabs another blob of cappuccino on to her nose. 'You'll never be a designer because you're too tall.'

'Haven't you noticed? Everyone successful is short.' I am thinking of actors, really. I quickly say, 'Except for models, of course.'

'It's the only reason I got into the business, there was nothing else I could do.'

'You're a freak, baby. Look, even your T-shirt doesn't fit, it's for a normal-sized person.'

The T-shirt is riding way above her navel. And so is mine. It's a bright day but with a chill to the air. Both Louise and I are shivering we are so way under-dressed. Even though we are inside, we ought to put our matching coats back on. The café has a terrace, deserted because of the weather and because it's still early morning. Soft-playing North African music blows across it, fanned by the speakers above our heads. When the music changes, the rhythm is recognisable as an old James Brown track, right up until the moment that the melody begins. The voice is light and romantic, singing in a language that I have never heard before. The moment that I hear it, I know it is what we need for the show;

something African, something unfamiliar, but something immediate. I get up to go to the bar and ask the man the title of the CD.

Louise asks, 'Booty call?'

I pause and look back at her: 'What is a booty call, anyway? I always wondered.'

'It's actually a date. But I wondered if you were going to the bar.'

'I am.'

'Then champagne, bro.'

'This early?' I sound shocked. I am never too far from being the straight-edge kid.

She says, 'Welcome to my kingdom. All rules are frozen or suspended.'

I lean over the bar as I read the CD liner notes. The barman disappears to fill the ice bucket. The CD is called *Swinging Addis*, a compilation of Ethiopian music from the early seventies. The James Brown funk riff moves into another, this one a stolen reggae rhythm. I am fairly sure it is from something by the Upsetter All-Stars, but again the melody is new. And again there is that yearning romantic voice sweeping across the room. I decide I am definitely going to learn to speak Ethiopian. I'm thinking of making it the official language of Louise-world. I begin to try to negotiate with the bartender for the CD, telling him that I need to buy it to use in a fashion show.

The barman looks at me, up and down, and a glimmer of self-consciousness runs through me. The word 'fashion' implies consensus. It suggests at least a tacit agreement as to what is and what is not fashion, *la mode*, the way to do things. But I am wearing Dolce & Gabbana drag so new that it was on a catwalk four days ago, and to believe that it could be fashion is pure speculation. I need to be close to Louise to have the confidence to storm through Paris like a superstar: then I know that everyone in the world wants to dress this way. It's only when I lose eye contact that I begin to get queasy. I am about to turn and tell the man to forget it, I don't want the CD, but then I catch sight of my own reflection in the bar mirror and have a rush of confidence. I see myself through Louise's eyes, and share her belief that wearing these kinds of clothes is easy. And I do look good, I can dress and behave like this.

I meet his eyes and up my bid: '*Trois cents francs.*' It's thirty pounds, it must be double what the CD is worth, if it is even his to sell. I pull a wad out of my pocket and spread it on the bar top.

'Okay.' He turns to the player, pings out the CD and hands it over to me. I put it in the case and turn around, still with that feeling: that I've been underwater holding my breath and once I sit back down with Louise it will be like reaching the surface.

Louise is fending off the advance of a Frenchman as I return to the table with our champagne. She can do it with her eyes, she doesn't need to speak. He soon scurries away. As I swing the bucket and the bottle on to the table, she says, 'Gimme a drink.'

Of course, I was drunk last night. In a few minutes I can be drunk again today. But on the other hand I couldn't have been so drunk because I woke without a trace of a hangover or a thought for the ritual suicide that I plan each morning. I woke smiling, because I was imagining Louise. And when I opened my eyes, she was lying right there, smiling back at me. Jammy Jamie.

We must have been woken by the cellphone. I hadn't

registered the noise, and when Louise asked how long it had been ringing I didn't understand what she was talking about. She reached across me, wriggling over my chest until her hand located my bag beneath the couchette. She pulled out Stan's cellphone, switched it off and threw it across the room. I watched it arc across the window. We had never bothered to pull down the blinds, and now bright countryside was flashing past us. When we started kissing again, I felt we were on view, seen through an open window. I asked Louise what I tasted like. She told me, *like my baby*.

I kissed her breasts and around the pale swollen aureoles of her nipples. Her perfume had settled deep into her pores. I knew that smell, it was what she wore those summers, BC, before we moved to Cornwall. She would steal it from the bedroom of the neighbourhood girls' mothers. So when she asked me how she tasted, I could have described it for hours, but instead I said: 'Like last night.'

'I'll show you a trick,' she said as she stepped off the bed. We had left one unopened bottle of champagne lying in the sink. She began shaking it, doing it as a dance, the naughty-girl grin on her face. 'Shake it up, baby, now.'

I put my hands up. 'Don't point that at me.'

'Watch this.' She got a strong, manicured and bonded nail under the tag and twisted it off. The cork exploded into the ceiling with so much force that I was dazed by the sound and fearful that I would be hit by a ricochet. There was a microsecond before I looked back at Louise.

She had the champagne bottle between her legs. 'A champagne douche.' She was shivering and grinning, the blond moustache-tuft of her pubic hair sparkling with champagne drops.

'A champagne douche?' I'd never heard of that. 'Is that a real thing or something you invented?'

'Real, of course.' She ran a finger between the shining lips of her foo-foo, her foo-manchoo. 'It's for field conditions, when you don't know where your next shower is coming from.'

As she walked towards me my eyes were level with the pink blushing folds of skin either side of her finger, all buffy and smooth from a Brazilian waxing.

'Better than a shower, because you're thinking, how does that taste?'

It was exactly what I was thinking.

'You got to chew the foo, baby.'

She was on the bed by then, walking on her knees, one either side of my body. As her thighs brushed my face, I scooted down a little to meet her, breathing through my mouth so that her smell would leave an imprint on my tongue. Drops of champagne spattered my face but there was very little taste, just the slight bitterness of wine warmed on her skin. Then my tongue met a deep musky smell, not the musk of the labdanum in her perfume but her own smell. I licked upward, using the soft fat part of my tongue, only flicking with the tip. She was making a sweet burbling call somewhere above me, shifting slightly so that she seemed to balance on the angle between my lips and the base of my nose.

Walking through the Bastille area, Louise slips her hand into mine. The champagne we drank with our croissants has done something to me. I suspect it has reactivated the traces of last night's champagne, lying dormant in my bloodstream. But it's not a bad feeling. I am tripping along while Louise talks about how she felt when she was sacked by her American agency. Well, she felt betrayed, that is obvious. But she claims that there is a deep suspicion of English models over there, because they tend to be seen as more hardcore than other models. Or, at least, they are less apologetic; failing to appear in the mornings in the gym, refusing to drink the things that are supposed to be good for them, and never showing proper contrition for their behaviour the night before. Though Louise did something worse than simply failing to apologise; her behaviour impinged on business. She scared people.

There is an English-away-from-home syndrome: you can see it in foreign holiday resorts and among travelling football fans. Louise was born with it.

'Your agency want you back, now.'

'Now the rumours have made me fabulous again.'

Again I get a tremor of self-consciousness. But Louise squeezes my hand. 'Fabulous together.'

She wants to walk to the rue Saint Honoré. We walk parallel to the Seine on a long road leading through the Hôtel de Ville. I am always reassured by Louise's touch, it's the only anchor that I have. I could worry about her other lovers, Amanda Van Hemstra, possibly Etienne, but they make such a strange collection; there isn't any sense to Louise's choices except as elements in a crazy constellation. When things make no sense, when the rules that bring order to the world seem to have disappeared, there are two alternatives. I tend towards the first, which is to look at the mess the world has become and then tread carefully because I don't want to disturb or scatter the broken pieces any farther. I either tread carefully or I just sit down and stare around me, wondering how the principles that kept everything in its place could have disappeared so completely. I might tell myself a story: that there has been a war, or a hurricane, or an economic crash, or simply that a big bastard foot has come down and crushed everything. But what I tend to do is internalise the emptiness, not blaming myself or anyone else for the mess, but still trying to close myself down so that I do not make it any worse.

The brighter alternative would be to look at the chaos around and, instead of seeing it as a landscape that has lost all rules and principles, rather see it as a space full of sparkling shards. Not even shards, because that would imply that something was broken. As jewels, then. Or simply atoms, some deadly, of course, but others just neutral, until you react with them. Atoms of civet, for instance, which is supposed to smell like raw sewage, but which combines with the smell of flowers to bring a sexual heat to perfumes. That is how I imagine Louise sees the world, never asking any questions about an underlying order, or its absence, because everything seems to be in its place to her, a world absolutely strewn with possibilities. These two views sound like opposites, but it is more than that – they are genuine alternatives and if you live in one sphere, you cannot even imagine that the other exists.

We buy perfume as we go: not scientifically but with a nose-burning stupidity. After dropping our bags off in the Hôtel Costes, we zigzag haphazardly in and out of the boutiques along rue Saint Honoré. Louise spins me around between the shops so I soon forget which side of the road we began on, and whether we have come from the left or the right. We visit both the Saint Laurent shop and the rival Tom Ford YSL, the Prada shop where I buy myself a fingerboard, a skateboard only three inches long. And we sample the perfume everywhere until we are incapable of distinguishing one from another. It doesn't matter to me because I know the one that I want to buy. But it is a shame that after hours of walking along the one small street we swoop into the Creed shop and I spray Louise with Fleurissimo, the perfume that Grace Kelly was married in, and I can barely smell it at all.

We are laughing as we walk back to the hotel. The concierge passes me a note with my key. I unwrap it, expecting it to be from Osano, demanding to know where I have been all day.

The note says: 'Lok behind yuo Jams.'

It is Stan's handwriting. I spin round and Stan is there, sitting on a warm brown chair with his green dayglo rucksack propped beside him. He is carefully posed, his legs crossed and a quizzical finger placed beneath his chin. Then he breaks into a smile and he is on his feet.

'I've been waiting for you since last night, man. Why didn't you answer the phone?'

I shake my head. I am dazed but smiling. It is only as I walk towards him that my smile begins to waver. Stan and Reality could not be called close acquaintances, but he is a reminder that the other world exists. I realise that I cannot blank it out as easily as I blanked out the ringing phone last night.

A group of men are approaching from my left. I welcome the delay, hovering to let them cross my path. But instead of flowing past, they seem to coalesce, becoming solid in front of me.

One speaks: 'Jaimes Grenage?'

No one French can pronounce my surname. I shrug,

exchanging another look with Stan. I can see his mind working, his eyes and brow pulling together as he grasps a situation that I am too slow to comprehend.

The man is becoming more impatient. 'Jaimes Grenage?'

'*Oui?*'

'*Vous devez nous accompagner, monsieur.*'

'*Pourquoi?*'

'*Police.*'

He is holding a warrant card in his hand.

16

I am led into a room and pushed gently into a chair. With my eyes at waist level, I find myself staring at the short length of telephone flex that secures the inspector's gun to his belt. The flex strikes me as a detail from a 1960s science fiction film; simultaneously modern, cool and dated. The same effect is repeated over and over, throughout the interview room: in the quality of the utility furniture, the smell of the rubber floor tiles underfoot, the shade of the melamine on the desks. I think about Louise, sitting in a similar room, answering the questions they put to her. I have lost the ability to speak French, or claim to. Using a translator slows down the speed of the interrogation, allowing me time to think between responses.

The inspector sits down. 'You were seen arguing with a man in the restaurant carriage.'

'With Gianni Osano. Yeah.'

'Can you tell us what it was about?'

'I don't know. I guess he was making changes and I didn't like it.'

I listen as the translator relays my answer to Inspector Hervé and wonder whether I could have said even less. There was no chance to confer with Louise. The police put us in separate cars outside the Hôtel Costes and I have not seen her since. As we drove away, I heard Stan shouting from the pavement that we should say nothing. He had said the same thing the last time that I was arrested, for burning the boat on the beach. I didn't follow his advice then. I am trying to this time.

Hervé asks what things had been changed around.

'My friend Bibi was supposed to be on the train. Osano had given her ticket to my sister. That was all.' I stop, and then decide I can say a little more. 'It wasn't a big deal.'

'You fought with him?'

'It wasn't a fight.'

There are four of us in the room; myself, the translator and two policemen. My translator is a nondescript man of about thirty, with very thin blond hair that he wears too long. Inspector Hervé is in his early forties. He wears a dark suit, a little tight for him, though he is not particularly overweight. His hair is cut short in an almost military style. His partner is older, with a large moustache that seems to hold his cigarette like a fur clip. All three are quite small, and although the policemen look tough, they still seem too small to actually be policemen.

I no longer feel comfortable in my French Kisses T-shirt and D&G fur coat. I feel pretty stupid. But at least I don't look the type that habitually fights on trains. I wouldn't even say that I had been fighting with Osano and, if I had, I doubt that it would be a criminal offence in the way that fighting on an aeroplane is. I focus instead on the crime that I *have* committed, with no idea how French law regards my and Louise's real offence.

I say again, 'It wasn't a fight. Osano was quite drunk.'

The translator translates 'quite' as 'a little'. I don't correct him, although it gives the wrong picture. Osano was steaming.

'Then what happened?'

'We finished our meal. It was completely, totally peaceful. Then we went to bed. I went to bed.' I could leave it there but I decide to carry on. 'It was a quiet night.'

I remember the state of our cabin as we left it. There were the empty bottles on the floor and upended in the sink, the bench seat turned into a single bed and the single sheet screwed up on the floor, sodden with champagne. The pillowcase stained with lipstick, peppered with mascara and impregnated with sweat and Poison. The windows marked with my handprints and Louise's full body print. We were so anxious to escape at the Gare de Lyon there was no time to straighten the cabin. And even if there had been time, we wouldn't have done it. We were careless superstars, planning our escape.

I wonder how quickly the train would have been turned around, cleaned and sent back to Italy. I hate to think of the police combing our cabin for forensic evidence.

When Inspector Hervé rubs his short hair, it sounds like a man rubbing the stubble on his chin. I realise that Stan had recognised the inspector as he approached us: Hervé was the guy who questioned him after the theft of Osano's collection. Stan did his best to interfere with my arrest, grabbing my arm and telling me to make a run for it. I was too slow and Hervé won the tug-of-war.

'So. You say you didn't see Osano again all night?'

I haven't said that. It is not even true. I left the cabin at some point in the night and walked to the nearest toilet. The corridor seemed quiet and, when I went out, I was wearing only a pair of trousers, pulled on without underwear, and a T-shirt. But then I found the toilet door locked and I wondered whether to go through to the next carriage or remain in the corridor. I stared at my reflection in the dark windows, trying to gauge how decent or how dissolute I looked. The toilet door opened at that moment and Osano appeared, trying to fold himself around the cubicle's flimsy door.

I waited for him. Osano was clumsily drunk, still wearing the same clothes that he wore during the meal. He hadn't yet been to bed.

I asked him if he was all right. He shook his head. 'I don't know why I took the train. I never sleep.'

He probably hadn't tried.

'Okay,' I said. 'I need to use the bathroom.'

'You were fighting with me.'

He looked hurt. I nodded apologetically. 'I'm sorry. It was just this idea you were using Louise.'

'How do you use Louise?' he asked. 'It's not possible, she's always ahead of you.'

My temper flared up again. 'Don't even try it. Two weeks ago you were ready to keep her imprisoned in the mountains. Now you need her, you don't want to let her out of your sight.'

'It's true, I need her. But I didn't make her take the train. It was Louise who insisted on taking Bibi's place.'

Fred had already told me this so I knew that Osano was telling the truth. I should have shrugged and said *whatever*. But he continued by saying, 'She's your sister, you know what she's like.'

There was something in his manner, his confidence that we shared an insight into Louise's character. Osano may read Freud but he cannot pretend to understand my sister. I found myself lashing out again; although not physically. I am not much of a fighter; I got into maybe three fights all the time I was at school.

'You think you can even try not to be rude about Louise for two seconds?'

'I am not being rude. Be rude about me if you want to. I was too slow to see how perfect she is. She's seductive, she's manipulative and that makes her dangerous. You don't even realise until later, when it's too late and she's got you.'

None of this sounded like praise. I was breathing heavily. All I could say was, 'She's my sister. And she's sweet.'

'No one else ever called her sweet, but she has that, too.'

And I pushed him, not hard, but he must have expected me to hit him again because he lurched and slipped. When he fell against a cabin door, there was a boom that echoed all along the corridor.

So I can tell the policemen that we had another argument, some time in the middle of the night. And using the translator, I have all the time I need to choose the right words. But I don't understand why they are interested in this, or what fantasy Osano has spun out of his drunken memories.

'I saw Osano once again, in the corridor. He was coming out of the toilet.'

'And you fought again.'

'No.'

'We have statements from two witnesses. You were shouting at him, and then you pushed him over.'

Louise knows nothing about my second fight with Osano, so the police cannot have got the information from her. It seems that Osano is behind our arrest, but I don't know what he hopes to gain from it. The other witness could be either Katie or Rhonda.

When Osano fell to the ground, I did nothing except look down at him. My temper cooled so quickly I said only, 'Get to bed, Gianni. We want people to take you seriously. You shouldn't even be out in public when you're in this state.'

I tried to slam the toilet door behind me. It made a hollow rattle, which seemed appropriate.

When I emerged, Katie and Rhonda's cabin door was open. Katie was crouching in the space between two beds, examining Osano, who was sitting on the edge of her bed. His eye was cut and bleeding badly. I knew that I hadn't done that, he must have fallen again while I was using the toilet. He was so drunk that any movement of the train could have sent him tumbling.

Katie looked at me.

I glared at her, gave a defensive *what?*, and stomped back down the corridor.

The questions are beginning to disorientate me. I know what I have done wrong but the interview has focused entirely on my arguments with Osano.

'Did Osano say I fought with him?'

'He did not.'

'So what's the problem?'

Hervé looks at his partner, who is lighting a fresh cigarette, if a cigarette can be fresh. The tobacco is the dark, French kind that burns with a near-blue smoke. In French, Hervé mumbles, 'You tell him.'

Although I understand what he's saying, I don't believe it, expecting the translator to alter the words and say something more plausible.

'Osano's body was found at eight a.m. this morning, five kilometres north of Lyon. It seems that he was dragged under the train for some distance. But Monsieur Osano was certainly dead before he left the train. He was shot in the head.'

My mouth is hanging open long before the policeman finishes speaking. I don't even look at the translator as he repeats it.

I ask for an advocate and refuse to say anything more.

I am led to another room, a clinically clean space where a two-man forensic team takes samples from beneath each of my fingernails. A patch of my arm is dry-shaved and the hairs put on to a glass slide. The two scientists even take skin scrapings. I had expected only to be fingerprinted, and the thoroughness of the examination unnerves me. I continually ask questions about my sister: in French, because my translator has been sent away.

Neither of the men says anything.

Inspector Hervé reappears as my arms are being painted with chemicals. I assume that he will know about my sister, even if his forensic team doesn't. But Hervé doesn't answer my questions, he only shrugs and watches as my skin is tested for reactions using different chemicals and also an ultraviolet light sabre that is passed up and down my arms, a centimetre from my skin.

Finally Inspector Hervé looks at his watch and says, 'Your sister has been released on police bail. But your French improved so much in the past hour, we'd like you to stay a little longer. You might be fluent in a few days.'

I have to wait until the following day before anyone

speaks to me again. I have a strong sense that Louise is still in the building, that she is waiting for me. I have no way of knowing, though. I am left in a cell that has a bed, a toilet and little else. When I need to use the toilet, which I do more often than I can believe, I wet the edge of a single square of toilet tissue and stick it over the spyhole in the door. When a policeman comes to look at me, he blows through the hole and the tissue wafts loose and drifts to the floor. At least I wasn't actually on the toilet. I was lying on the bed, my eyes wide open.

I am taken to a new room, the visiting room, and instead of Louise, I see a tall man with a severe side parting. Until now, I have felt either frustration or anger. Now something like despair begins to build inside me. Even when the man explains that he is the advocate Louise hired on my behalf, it is still there. He bends over his notes on the table, nodding at my questions and only looking up to congratulate me on my French. But at least he reassures me that my next visitor will be Louise, it was merely necessary for him to see me first. He doesn't explain why. He leaves me with the impression that his presence benefits the police as much as me. Once it is formally established that I have an advocate, the interrogation can resume. He says that he will return in ten minutes.

He taps on the door and a policeman opens it to let him leave. Together, they fill most of the door frame but, as they separate, a gap opens. Louise is there. In a second, we are in each other's arms, filling each other with warmth and blood. I don't ever want to let her go, but the policeman touches my shoulder and I release my grip. Louise's hands stick like tendrils, only dropping away as I fall to my chair.

She is no longer dressed like me. She wears a dark suit that makes her face seem drawn and pale but her body strong and shapely.

'How bad is it?' I ask.

'Bad? It's not bad.' I had expected Louise to sound brave. But she also sounds fiercely confident. She sits down opposite me and, as she speaks, I begin to realise how stupid the whole situation is.

'You're accused of murdering Osano, for fuck's sake.' Her eyes bulge, bright and true, rolling towards the policeman standing at the door. The whole thing is just incredible.

'We have to make sure Mum doesn't find out about this, Lou.' I hate to think of our mother travelling to Paris. I imagine her in the lobby of the police station, frantic and hysterical, trying to put her hands through the glass in the doors the way she once shattered all the panes in our greenhouse.

Louise shivers. 'She won't know a thing, I promise. What about bail? How soon can you get out?'

This is something that I have talked over with my advocate, at least in part. I try to explain the situation to Louise.

'I can't get bail without a passport.'

I lean forward and whisper that my passport is in a locker in Milan. Louise immediately offers to fly to Italy. Then changes her mind – she will send Stan so that she can stay close to me in Paris.

'Where's the locker key?'

'In my sponge bag at the hotel.'

'Then the police already have it. They've got all the luggage.'

This had never occurred to me, although it should

have done. Louise tells me they have even confiscated her luggage. She touches the lapel of her suit as she explains that she was allowed only a few clean clothes. She changed into the suit in a café toilet across the street, trusting Stan to alert her if there was a chance to see me. Stan has sat with her all night.

'How long will it take for the police to match the key to a railway locker in Milan?'

'Can't you just tell them?'

I shrug. 'I don't know if I should be volunteering stuff. Stan's advice is always to keep quiet.'

'Is that Stan the international legal expert?' She slaps the table. 'Talk to the fucking lawyer, Jamie. It's what he's paid for.'

I nod. I wonder how much the advocate is costing.

'Has Fred offered to help with the legal costs?'

'No. The bastard says he can't because of the publicity. He helped me find a lawyer, but that was it.' Louise pulls a torn piece of newsprint from the pocket of her suit. 'Read this.'

I flatten the paper on the tabletop. It is the front page of *Le Monde*: I am front-page news. The story is illustrated by one of the photographs of Louise and me taken at the Institut du Monde Arabe.

'They don't actually mention your name anywhere,' Louise says.

'That's good.' I try to smile, but the tension is still there. I am mostly worried that the English press will take up the story, and that our mother will find out.

In the middle of the text, in larger print across two columns, I read that the Osano show will go ahead at Les Invalides on Monday.

'Are you going to model?'

'I have to take all the work I can, until this is over,' she says.

I understand: she needs the money for me. I skim the account of the discovery of Osano's body, and its state after being dragged five kilometres under a high-speed train. The police report that a man is helping with their enquiries. There is a box at the bottom of the page, the fashion editor's speculations about the forthcoming Osano show. I learn that Osano's long-time collaborator Gina Manteuffel is expected to take the bow. The show receives warm preview notices. And it ends by noting that Gina Manteuffel has been appointed creative director of Osano Srl. I wonder who has appointed her.

Someone with shares in the company.

I take hold of Louise's hand before turning to the policeman at the door and telling him that I am ready to see my advocate. When he reappears, Inspector Hervé is at his shoulder. Louise and I barely have time to kiss before I am marched away.

I know what I am going to say. As soon as we are back in the interview room, I tell the police where they can find my passport. I warn them that they will find another passport, a fake, in another locker. The fake was given to me by a man calling himself Fred Sossa, but I do not believe that is his real name.

Hervé nods. 'You like station lockers, isn't that true?'

'I use them.'

'And at the Gare de Lyon, did you use a locker?'

'No.'

'I ask because we discovered the weapon used to kill Monsieur Osano in a locker at the Gare de Lyon.'

'I didn't use a locker at the Gare de Lyon.'

'No. You ran from the train the moment it arrived in

Paris, and you were missing the entire day.' He is reading from a transcript in front of him. Another statement.

'I was with my sister.'

'She will confirm that you didn't use a locker?'

'Yes.'

'Of course. Yet the gun has your fingerprints on it.'

I sit absolutely still, my eyes locked on the policeman. I don't know how I can behave with such calm, especially when I am so frightened. But this is it, isn't it? It is the way things are going to work out, and I just have to make sure that we establish the truth, at every moment along the line.

I say, 'The gun is easy to explain. If it has my fingerprints on it, then they are more than a month old.'

Then I remember the forensics tests. Hervé is there ahead of me.

'But we have evidence that you fired a gun recently. Could that be the same gun?'

The police give me a jump suit made out of plastic-treated paper. I would have preferred low-slung prison denims. Better yet, I want my own clothes back, but they are still needed for tests in the forensics laboratory. I have learnt that the chemicals left by the discharge of a pistol cartridge can leave traces on the gunman's arms for up to three months. I have also learnt that a mixture of lager, the cardboard in beer mats and cleaning fluids leaves a similar residue to the explosive Semtex. The police cannot have placed all their faith in science because they have still not formally charged me with the murder. Yet my name has now appeared in the newspapers. As far as I know, our mum still hasn't found out, though. She is unlikely to have done so from the English newspapers because she doesn't usually read them. But I am sure that one of her neighbours will want to keep her updated on her children's careers. The one child who is a model, the other a railway killer.

I have a new advocate.

The next time that the police ask me to attend an interview, they place two passports on the table in front of them, mine and the other in the name of Carlo Tiatto. They wonder why I need two passports and I repeat that the second one was given to me by Federico Sossa, the director of the Osano brand.

'Why would you need it?'

'He wanted to pass through Switzerland on the way to Italy. Why don't you ask him why he wanted to do that?'

I want to tell them the story that Osano told me, that Fred had been smuggling money, but I don't have the proof. My new advocate has promised to investigate Fred but so far he has turned up nothing, not even how Fred travelled from Milan to Paris on the night of the murder.

'But you can prove that you are James Grenarkh and not Carlo Tiatto?'

I ask them how they would like me to do that. The passports are open at the pages with the photographs, and I look nothing like Carlo Tiatto, a scowling man in his mid-twenties. But I don't look much like the startled twelve-year-old boy in my own passport, either.

Inspector Hervé says, 'We can take biographical details. Place and date of birth. The name of your father.'

'I don't have a father.'

'There was no name on your passport application? No name on your birth certificate?'

I really don't know. I didn't make my own passport application. All I can do is repeat that I don't have a father.

'But that is a biological impossibility, no?'

'You haven't met my mother.' I immediately regret saying this. I don't want them to request an interview with my mum.

Hervé sucks his teeth. 'It is not the first virgin birth, but it remains rare.'

After I am charged, I am taken from the police cells to a real prison and issued with real prison clothes. In the police station, I had begun to sleep in two-hour bursts, but even this routine is thrown out by prison. The police station could be noisy. There was a moment in the middle of the night when arrests seemed to increase dramatically. I thought of it as the sound of the underworld. I suppose it was really just the sound of night street life, amplified. Prison doesn't have these regular bursts of sound, it has individual wails and it has a constant moaning hum. I have a cell to myself, probably because I am on remand. There is no fifty-year-old rapist on the bunk above me, eyeing me for his bitch. There are few older men at all: prison is full of the young, men around my age. It is scary but in a cold and blank way.

Stan had to return to England before he could visit. Louise says that the last thing he asked her was whether she thought he could handle prison. I shrug. He probably could, you just adapt.

Louise looks down the bench at the visitors on her

side and across to the inmates on mine. Then she sniffs. 'I should have told him about the smell.'

'Tell him you never get used to it.'

Stan probably has fantasies about ruling a prison. Louise suspects so. She says, 'Should I tell him you're the daddy?'

I shake my head. 'There isn't one. It's like home in that respect.'

There is still no sign that my mother has heard the news. Stan tentatively telephoned his own parents before he left Paris. They were surprised to hear from him, but they never asked about me. Louise has left an emergency number on the answering machine at home but our mother has not called back. My only other visitor is my new advocate and, once, a doctor. His job is to assess whether I was mistreated by the police. I tell them that they arrested me, I don't care for that treatment.

He also asks how I am sleeping. I confess that I don't, but I meditate and that helps. That's when he begins to take a genuine interest in me, asking whether I use any special techniques, whether I use TM and whether I am familiar with different Hindu schools. I realise that, disguised by his short hair and glasses, the doctor is very much a hippie. He is disappointed when I tell him that I know little about Eastern philosophy. I tell him I meditate about committing seppuku on the death of my master.

Shortly after, I am put on suicide watch.

So far I have always refused Bibi's requests to visit but my advocate tells me that I should see her. She is the only witness who can corroborate my story of how I came to have a gun.

Bibi looks actually thin, for the first time since I've

met her. She was always thin, I guess, but it has stopped being natural. Her cheeks are hollowed out and the grey smudges under her eyes are deep and defined.

I tell her not to worry, there is no case against me.

She nods and then asks if I did it.

'Of course not.'

'But if it was the same gun you had in Paris.'

'I returned it to Fred.' I try to explain what happened later, in the mountains. I say, 'We were messing around with it. I fired off a shot.'

'So Fred killed Osano?'

She doesn't look at all convinced. I put my hands on the table and look at her as I ask, 'Did Fred fly back from Milan with you?'

Bibi shakes her head. I don't need her confirmation. I already know that he didn't. My advocate has checked all the flights arriving from Italy and Switzerland that night and the following day. In his interview with the police, Fred claimed to have driven to Paris.

Bibi says, 'If Fred is a killer, why is Louise still working with him?'

Bibi's tone is accusatory. I feel myself getting cranked up by it. I try to soften the edge, but she catches the anger as I say, 'Louise has to work. Who do you think is paying my legal bills?'

'She doesn't have to tell everyone that you spent the night with her. She doesn't have to say that you didn't kill anyone because you were too busy fucking her.'

I keep my head down, my knuckles turning white as they grip the table. I don't want to look at Bibi, not because I am ashamed but because I don't want to see that desperate, stupid look on her face: the bright stare, the tears filling the dark rings around her eyes.

Bibi won't shut up. 'The cunt's using her horrible incest story, and she's getting even more bookings than ever now you've been arrested.'

'Get out, Bibi.'

'It's true.'

'I mean it. Fuck off.'

If anything, I am even angrier with Bibi when my advocate visits. The only reason that he is here is because Louise can afford to pay him, and she can barely do that. She has had to borrow to ensure that he stays on the case. But when he also starts asking me questions about the train journey, I clam up.

The advocate speaks through my silence. The police have worked out a place and time of death. The train's doors were alarmed; if they had been opened while the train was moving, then the alarm would have rung. The only time that Osano's body could have been taken from the train was during a stop in Lyon. It seems that Osano was tied to the undercarriage of the train by his neck. The killer used Osano's own belt, which snapped a few kilometres outside Lyon station.

The advocate says, 'The train stopped at Lyon for thirty minutes. It was ahead of schedule and was held up to ensure that it arrived in Paris at the correct time.'

These thirty minutes become the crucial time, nothing else matters. The advocate waits, but when it is clear that I am not going to say anything, he takes out a newspaper.

'Your case is not improving.'

It is Tuesday, the day after the Osano show. Another front-page picture, another shot of Louise and me kissing. This is the picture taken at the Milan show. I turn to the fashion pages and see a photograph of Louise on the catwalk, flanked by a woman wearing one of the shirts that I designed. Just from the headlines, I can tell that the show has been well received. It is a surprise: I don't think any of us expected to get rave reviews in Paris. But I cannot read the full report, my advocate is too impatient. He takes the paper from me and refolds it, pointing to an inside story, illustrated by my photograph alone.

It says that I have been refused bail because of passport irregularities. And there is a new angle: an account of how I attempted to kill a French photographer outside a nightclub in Milan. There is even an interview with Etienne. He had completely faded out of my memory; I didn't see him at all during Milan fashion week and never once wondered why. But now all my hatred comes back. The photograph shows Etienne mid-sneer, his eyes slitted against his cigarette smoke. He has a graphic tale, which includes me kicking him senseless in the street. He confesses that he was too scared to fight back, he knew that I carried a knife. In the interview, he blames me for carving up his mattress at the Hôtel Costes.

The advocate asks me again: Do I remember the stop at Lyon station?

I nod. I do remember stopping. It must have been about 6 a.m.

'And where were you?'

'In my cabin.'

'Your sister can confirm that?'

I pause. The pause turns into another long silence. The advocate's mood is changing; perhaps he isn't charging enough to represent me.

'Can she confirm it? Was she awake, asleep?'

I say, 'She can't confirm it.'

'Why?'

'She just can't.'

Louise tells me that our mother has arrived. It has taken more than a week for her to discover that I am in prison. I hate to think what state she is in.

I ask Louise whether she has seen her.

Louise shakes her head. 'She's mad that she wasn't told earlier. She spent the day with Monsieur Marty.'

Monsieur Marty is my advocate.

'When are you two getting together?'

'Tomorrow. We're hoping for some good news before we deal with each other.' Louise tries to look upbeat. It is difficult when her eyes are so scared. 'I've been talking to Monsieur Marty, too. About the stop in Lyon.'

'Yeah?'

'Do you remember it?'

I nod.

It was dawn when we arrived and I recognised the city because of the cathedral. Louise was wrapped in the sheet from the bed. I was wearing the same T-shirt that I had on when I went to the bathroom and fought with Osano. The T-shirt had been off and on again since then. This was a moment for dreamy resting, talking as we shared a cigarette. We had erected the flip-down table so we had somewhere to rest our elbows and place the ashtray.

Louise now says, 'We don't need to rely on my alibi. Some railway workers saw us in the window.'

'I don't remember.'

'You do.'

I continue to shake my head. We were sitting at the table, our arms entwined as we played a game, similar to arm wrestling. Our heads were the lovers, moving in for the kiss, while our arms were the enemy, forbidding it by trying to keep us apart. Louise's sheet slipped; she claimed that she needed to rest her breasts on the table for balance and stability.

And it is true, there was a crew of railway workers standing outside the window, cheering us on. They thought they had the joke on us, that when we noticed them we would blush and stop and pull down the blinds.

I told Louise, 'You could show them how to champagne-douche. It could become a railway emergency procedure.'

Louise winked. 'I could teach them a lot of things.' She poked her tongue out at them. The railwaymen stood as though they were watching a film, angling their heads to the side as they assessed the image, framed by the rectangular window, pressed under glass.

'They think we're going to get embarrassed.'

Louise grinned. 'What do we have to be embarrassed about?'

Now that she is asking me to recall every detail, I want her to be embarrassed. She is sitting in front of me at the table in the visitors' room of the prison, shaking with nerves and with anger. She tells me to stop playing games: Monsieur Marty is already in Lyon, it won't take him long to find a whole work crew. He will take affidavits, he may even be back by the evening.

Monsieur Marty has spent this morning with my mother. I am not sure he will be running straight back to Paris.

'How did Marty get on with Mum?'

'He took her to the police station.'

I nod. The police used what they termed 'passport offences' to refuse my application for bail. The advocate wanted my mother to confirm which was the real passport. When I first needed a passport for a school trip, she had me sign the blank form and told me that she would take care of the rest. I never saw the completed application, nor the birth certificate that she had to send with it.

'Have they made her talk?' I ask.

'Monsieur Marty says she's vouched for you. There's no reason to refuse bail.'

'But did she admit we have a father? The same father?'

'Come on, Jamie. We both know who our father is.'

'I don't.'

'It's not exactly a mystery.' Louise mentions a name I have never heard before. She says, 'Three doors down? The house with the yellow clapboard on the dormers?'

I shake my head. It means nothing to me.

She shrugs. 'I guess you were three years younger than me. But he looked so much like us . . . I thought, you know, come on. There's no great secret here.'

There was for me. I say, 'So we're absolutely normal.'

'I wouldn't say one hundred per cent,' she says. 'But we're in the normal range.'

I have my eyes cast down at the melamine surface of the table, the kind with the deep intaglio of fake wood grain. The tabletop is made out of two bonded sheets of melamine, abutted in the middle. I try to work out where the pattern in each sheet begins to repeat itself, the way that I do when I look at wallpaper or curtain fabric.

'Don't do this, Jamie,' Louise says. 'Look at me.'

I do. 'You know why I agreed to see you today?' I

hold up a hand; there is a blue ink stain on it. 'The Biro started leaking while I was writing my confession.'

'What?'

'The police have it now. I told them that I was in Osano's cabin. I said you were in our cabin with someone else, so I made myself scarce.'

'But you can't. It's not true. The workmen saw us.'

'I doubt they were looking at my face.' I smile, I want her to know that this is final. I have made my decision – in the space of seven breaths as the Samurai do. But I do want her to understand before I go. I say, 'I don't want what happened between us to become a fact in this world. I don't want people to talk about it. And I'm not going to use it to save myself.'

Now she flashes. 'Why the fuck not? *I* used it. And I used you, again and again. I used you.' Flashing through her tears. 'I'll prove it. I'll prove it.'

She grabs hold of my hand. A prison officer sees her and starts running towards us.

'That night at the Hôtel Costes when I tore Etienne's bed to pieces. I told you we'd had a fight but he hadn't even been in the room. I'd never even seen him.'

The officer takes her by the wrist. But he can't break her grip.

'He'd been spreading rumours about me, so I wrecked his room to teach him a lesson. That's all. Then you walked in and I decided to mess with you. I made everything up, Jamie.'

The prison officer prises her fingers away. The tears flood down her face so fast her face swims behind a screen of water.

'I wanted you to come to Italy with me. I was using you.'

'You didn't do anything wrong,' I say.

I don't have much time. The officer pulls me across the room, back towards the block with all its cells.

'I love you, Louise.'

ACKNOWLEDGEMENTS

I would like to thank the following for their witting or unwitting inspiration.

Leila Sansour, Robert Blincoe, Carole Welch, Jocasta Brownlee, Emma Garman, Leslie Shaw, Amber Burlinson, Katie Haines, Antony Harwood, Matt Thorne, Alex Garland, Matthew Branton, Candida Clark, Daren King, Rebbecca Ray, Toby Litt, Simon Lewis, Ben Richards, Anna Davis, Tony White, Geoff Dyer, Bo Fowler, Michael Turner, Kristin Kenway, Alexandra Heminsley, Kinda Haddad, Huda Abuzeid, Jean-Luc Godard, Françoise Sagan, Jean-Pierre Melville, Christopher McQuarrie, Eric Ambler, Patricia Highsmith, Immanuel Kant, Gilles Deleuze, Michel Houellebecq, Haruki Murakami, Tsunetomo Yamamoto, Jim Jarmusch, the RZA.

Suzy Menkes, Lisa Armstrong, Lisa Duncan, Anuj Desai, Susan Irvine, Jess Cartner-Morley, Deborah Brett, Charlie Porter, Murray Healey, Hadley Freeman, Hilary Alexander, Joanna Coles, Jodie Kidd, Yves St Laurent, Dries Van Noten, Alexandra McQueen, Scott Henshall, Donatella Versace, Luella Bartley, Miguel Adrover, Martin Margiela, Dolce & Gabbana, Alberta Ferretti, Antonio Berardi, Bottega Venetta, Helmut Lang, Max Mara, Anna Molinari, Trussardi, Daryl K, Olivier Creed, Patricia de Nikolai.

The Dope Priest
NICHOLAS BLINCOE

David Preston is the Dope Priest and he has a
headache. If you've smuggled drugs out of war zones,
you're not going to worry about a spot of illegal
land trading between the Palestinians and Israelis.
But David never planned on amorous nuns, kosher
egg racketeers and the full might of the Israeli secret
housing service. Even now, he feels he could cope. If
only he could win the heart of the local drive-time
DJ, or at least find something decent to smoke.

'One of England's most gifted writers . . . He flips
between entertaining and challenging his readers
with an intelligence that is both embracing and
unforced'
Alex Garland

'Blincoe skilfully manages to address a deadly
serious theme while at the same time offering the
reader a fast-paced, funny, page-turner of a book.'
Lisa Darnell, *Guardian*

'Blincoe's brave decision to set his thriller in one
of the most charged political climates takes his
sharp storytelling to new heights' Matt Thorne,
Literary Review

'Combines intelligence, pace and simple prose to
produce an intriguing yarn of drug-smuggling in
Jerusalem'
James Hopkin, *The Times* Books of the Year

SCEPTRE